Hannah Murray

Jane and the Sneaky DOM

Ellora's Cave
Romantica Publishing

What the critics are saying...

"Where have you been hiding *Ms. Hannah Murray* ... and when is your next book coming out? This being *Ms. Murray's* first foray into the world of Romantica proves, in my opinion, that some people are just born to write hot and sexy Romantica stories for Romantica junkies just like me." ~ *ecataRomance.com*

"Hannah Murphy has set the pace for laughter and romance in this scorching exploration on the light side of BDSM." ~ *Coffee Time Romance*

"If you like erotica at its best with a great plot, you will definitely want to read *Jane and the Sneaky Dom*." ~ *Romance Junkies*

"The writing style is fresh and sassy, funny and surprising moments, situations turning out other than anticipated giving you a glimpse of the author's great imagination, strong and well developed characters you laugh, cry and love with. A new author is in town and you better watch out for *Hannah Murray's* next strike." ~ *Mon Boudior Romance Reviews*

An Ellora's Cave Romantica Publication

www.ellorascave.com

Jane and the Sneaky Dom

ISBN 141995203X, 9781419952036

Edited by Mary Moran
Cover art by Syneca

This book printed in the U.S.A. by Jasmine-Jade Enterprises, LLC.

Electronic book Publication November 2004
Trade paperback Publication July 2005

Content Advisory:

S - ENSUOUS
E - ROTIC
X - TREME

Ellora's Cave Publishing offers three levels of Romantica™ reading entertainment: S (S-ensuous), E (E-rotic), and X (X-treme).

The following material contains graphic sexual content meant for mature readers. This story has been rated E–rotic.

S-*ensuous* love scenes are explicit and leave nothing to the imagination.

E-*rotic* love scenes are explicit, leave nothing to the imagination, and are high in volume per the overall word count. E-rated titles might contain material that some readers find objectionable—in other words, almost anything goes, sexually. E-rated titles are the most graphic titles we carry in terms of both sexual language and descriptiveness in these works of literature.

X-*treme* titles differ from E-rated titles only in plot premise and storyline execution. Stories designated with the letter X tend to contain difficult or controversial subject matter not for the faint of heart.

Also by Hannah Murray

Knockout

The Devil and Ms. Johnson

Tooth and Nailed

About the Author

Hannah Murray started reading romances in junior high, hoarding her allowance to buy them and hiding them from her mother. She's been dreaming up stories of her own for years and finally decided to write them down. Being published is a lifelong dream come true, and even her mother is thrilled for her—she knew about the romances all along. Hannah lives in southern Texas in a very small house with a very large dog, where the battle for supremacy rages daily. The dog usually wins. When not catering to his needs, she can usually be found writing, reading, or doing anything else that allows her to put off the housework for one more day.

Hannah welcomes comments from readers. You can find her website and email address on her author bio page at www.ellorascave.com.

Tell Us What You Think

We appreciate hearing reader opinions about our books. You can email us at Comments@EllorasCave.com.

JANE AND THE SNEAKY DOM

Dedication

This book wouldn't have been possible without the love and support of a lot of people. The SPs and Pack Members, who cheered me on. Cole, who suffered through all of my rewrites and never failed to be honest and objective. Eric, who helped me stay sane. And Shimmy, Amy, AJ and Chuck, who not only believed in me, but nagged, whined, begged and bullied until I believed in me, too.

Y'all are the best friends a strange little girl like me could ever have. Big love!

Chapter One

Jane Denning took a sip of her margarita, licked the salt from her lip and tried to find the words to let the perfectly groomed, well-educated, handsome, charming man across the table know he was being dumped.

With a sigh that was more weariness than regret, she studied the classic profile of Harris Clayton, the Third—he always emphasized the "Third", as if it made him more important somehow—as he delivered his drink order to the waitress. He was movie star gorgeous, with gilded locks falling with just the right amount of casual disarray over his tanned forehead. He had a nice body—good chest, great legs that proclaimed his sincere affection for jogging. There was also a really fine cock under those Gap khakis and Tommy Hilfiger boxers. On paper, he was perfect. In reality, he was so boring she wanted to scream.

Jane snapped back to attention as Harris completed his explanation to the beleaguered waitress of what made a truly remarkable Harvey Wallbanger and turned his attention back to her. He flashed a smile of such warmth and desire she felt her stomach clench in guilt over the fact she was about to cut him off at the knees.

"So, darling," he reached across the table, took her hand in his and began stroking the backs of her knuckles. "What was so urgent you couldn't wait until dinner tomorrow night?"

Jane noted the glint in his Paul Newman blue eyes, and barely restrained rolling her own in response. God, he thought she couldn't wait to have him in her bed again. She forced a smile and, in what she hoped was a not-so-subtle gesture of rejection, pulled her hand away from his stroking fingers to pick up her margarita again. She took another fortifying sip, a deep breath and bit the bullet.

"Harris," she said, with her patented break-up smile, "I think it's time we stopped kidding ourselves about this relationship, don't you?"

A genuinely puzzled look came into those vapid baby blues. "What do you mean, sweetheart?"

"Well, we've been seeing each other for a few weeks now," Jane began, then stopped for a big gulp of margarita and a very deep breath. Harris' confused smile only made her more nervous. "And I think it's time we looked at the situation realistically." She blew out a breath. There. That was clear, right?

Apparently not.

Harris' face broke out in a toothy grin, showing off his newly acquired caps and latched onto her hand again.

"Oh darling, I know exactly what you mean." He squeezed her hand. "In fact, I was going to speak to you about it at dinner tomorrow night, but I didn't think you'd be ready this soon."

Jane opened her mouth to respond, and then shut it again when she realized she had no idea what to say. Harris ignored her floundering trout expression and kept talking.

"I think it would work best if we moved you into my condo on Lake Michigan. Not that your apartment isn't perfectly…quaint." He gave her a pained smile and kept rolling. "I just think the condo will better suit our lifestyle. Plus, there's no room for my Bowflex in your place."

Jane drained the rest of the margarita in one swallow and reclaimed her hand to signal the waitress for another. "Harris," she began, "I think we have a misunderstanding here." The polite, inquiring look on his face put a hitch in her stride, but she rode over it and opened her mouth. "I wasn't talking about moving in together. I was talking about breaking up."

"Breaking up?" Now *he* looked like a floundering trout.

"Yes, Harris, breaking up." She spoke gently, softly. Much like you'd speak to a man with fifty pounds of dynamite strapped to his chest. "I realized after the other night that things weren't going to work out between us."

Harris blinked, confused. "You mean the night we spent together in your apartment? In your bed?"

Jane winced. His voice rose when he was agitated, and about thirty people heard his last comment, including the waitress who was delivering a second margarita. "Yes. I realized from your reaction to my apartment, my things, we're just too different." More like she realized it when he couldn't manage to find her clit, but there was no need to humiliate the guy.

Immediately, his expression cleared and the toothpaste-ad grin was back. "Is that all that's holding you back, darling?" He shook his head indulgently. It made her feel nine years old again. "Jane, I understand you enjoy those bright colors and..." he waved his hand vaguely, "casual style. But really, sweets, you'll find a soothing palate of cream tones and simple art much more relaxing and efficient. And those objects and knickknacks you like to leave lying around?" He made a sound that, coming from a less perfection-oriented man she'd have termed a snort. "Darling, they just collect dust. My allergies, you know."

Jane realized it might be necessary to humiliate him. "Harris, I'm not just talking about the color and knickknacks. I don't think that we're compatible, and I think if you really think about the other night, you'll understand what I'm talking about." Hoping that would do it, she took a sip of her fresh drink.

"You mean the fact that you're not a very sexual person?" He smiled indulgently as she choked, spraying salt and tequila on the table in front of her. "Sweetheart, I know you aren't very experienced, but trust me, you'll do better with some practice. I can be patient."

Okay, things were getting serious now. She forgot about not wanting to humiliate and narrowed her eyes on him. "Harris, you're out of your mind. I'm actually a very sexual person, with the normal amount of experience for a thirty-one year old woman. And maybe you can be patient, but I can't."

For the first time since he'd sat down, Harris showed signs of actually listening to her. "What are you talking about?"

"I'm talking about your inability to figure out from body language, suggestion and outright direction what a woman wants in bed. Here's a hint," she leaned across the table and lowered her voice. "When a woman says, 'my clit is higher up than that', it generally means she wants you to do more than say, 'so it is' and continue drooling on her thigh."

He stiffened up like a poker. "I hardly think it's my fault if you were dissatisfied." His chest puffed out. "I can assure you, none of my previous bed partners were. There must be something wrong with you."

Jane nodded, gathering her purse from the back of her chair. "You're absolutely right." She pulled a twenty from her wallet and dropped it on the table. "It's my fault for going to bed with a dweeb more worried about how the sex was going to muss his hair than with getting me off. And what's wrong with me," she continued, relishing the way his jaw dropped as she rose and shouldered her purse, "is that your money and looks just aren't enough for me to ignore the fact that you couldn't fuck your way out of a paper bag." She sent him the smile that had earned her the nickname Barracuda in college. "Goodbye, Harris. I hope you find what you're looking for." She turned on her heel and walked away, leaving him sputtering and choking on his perfect Harvey Wallbanger.

* * * * *

"Oh my God!" Lacey Johnson's cupid-bow mouth was hanging open as she stared at Jane. "You actually said that in a *restaurant*? What if someone had overheard you?"

Jane shrugged. They were hunkered down on her living room floor, surrounded by a variety of half-empty potato chip bags and two pints of rapidly melting ice cream. She had on her oldest pair of flannel pajamas, her hair in a ponytail, and her face scrubbed clean of cosmetics. Lacey, her oldest friend and downstairs neighbor, was in similar attire of ratty sweats and droopy socks. They were performing their time-honored ritual for ending a bad day—eating like pigs.

Jane spooned up more Moose Tracks ice cream. Around a mouthful of fudge and vanilla, she said, "Someone probably did; it was packed in there. But who cared at that point? I just wanted to get out of there before I decked him for telling me he'd be patient." She snorted, coughing when ice cream went up her nose. When she could breathe again, she pointed her spoon at Lacey. "One more crack about my 'quaint' apartment or lack of sexuality, I'd have done it, and bugger the consequences."

Lacey grinned. "Well, I think the paper bag crack was probably just as effective, and you didn't have to ruin your manicure by punching him." She slurped her mint chocolate chip milkshake. "What's going on with you anyway? Lately you seem to be going through men at a rate of about two a month. You date them, maybe sleep with them once, then out they go. What's the deal?"

Jane sighed and put the ice cream aside. She pulled her knees to her chest and wrapped her arms around them. "I'm not sure. I'm just getting so bored, so fast. I mean, I meet a nice guy, we go to lunch, dinner, maybe the theatre. Then I sleep with them and I never want to see them again." She flipped her hair out of her eyes and settled her chin on her knees. "It might be because I haven't been able to come with any of them."

Lacey's doe-brown eyes went wide, and she put her milkshake aside. "None of them? Wow." She thought about it for a minute, her face puckered in a frown that made her look like Tinkerbell in a snit. "Why do you think that is?"

"God, I don't know!" Jane let go of her knees to stretch full-length on the floor. She stared at her ceiling for a minute, soothed by the swirls of color and glitter she'd painted and pasted there herself. "If I knew, don't you think it's something I would have fixed by now?"

Lacey scooted around the pile of potato chip bags and ice cream cartons on the floor to stretch out beside Jane. "Well, let's look at the problem practically. What have these guys all had in common?"

"You mean besides the fact they all needed a map to find their way around a pussy?"

"Yes." Lacey rolled her eyes, then rolled over to lay on her stomach. She propped her chin on her hands and looked at Jane, eyes serious. "C'mon, no jokes. What did they all have in common?"

Jane sighed deeply, and then flipped herself over so her pose mirrored her friend's. She began to count off the men on her fingers. "Before Harris, there was Mark, the investment banker. Drove a BMW and wore Prada suits."

Lacey straightened with interest. "Did he call the BMW a Beemer?"

"Yes! Don't you hate that? Now don't interrupt, I have to concentrate." Jane bit her lip and stared at the Jackson Pollock print on her wall, trying to recall which loser came before Mark. "Oh, I know! It was Jeremy, the DotCom millionaire who thought he was James Bond." She tilted her friend a look. "Shaken, not stirred."

She ignored Lacey's giggle and continued. "Before him there was Kenneth in advertising, George the sports medicine specialist, and Donald, who, of all things, owned a company that manufactures rubber bath duckies." Jane held up her hand, fingers splayed. "Five losers in four and a half months, and nary a tingle from any one of them. So," she turned her head in her palm and eyed Lacey. "What's the diagnosis, Madam Freud?"

"Vell," crooned Lacey in bad attempt at a German accent, "I sink you haf bin looking for zee wrong kind of man, dalink. Zey are all too, how you say, vaneella."

"Vanilla?" Jane frowned. "What are you talking about?"

"Vat I meen iz," Lacey cleared her throat. "What I mean is, they're all simple, nice guys who appreciate money and prestige, and don't know how to let their hair down and have a good time, right?"

Jane nodded. "That pretty much describes the whole bunch."

"Yep. And when you can't let your hair down out of the bedroom, it stands to reason, with a few exceptions, of course, that the action under the sheets is going to be pretty much the same." Lacey reached back for her melted shake and slurped some up the straw. "What you need, darlin', is a little adventure."

"Well, no shit." Jane twisted around until she could reach her own bowl. She made a face at the melted mess, and traded it for the ridged potato chips. "Obviously, I can't keep dating the walking dead or I'll never have another orgasm that isn't self-induced." She crunched for a minute. "You know what I think the problem is?"

Lacey slurped more milkshake. "What?"

"Well, the problem with the vanilla men is that I'm not vanilla anymore." She munched more potato chips. "I used to be vanilla. I mean, I used to be perfectly happy with Beemer-driving stockbrokers, or advertising executives who talked for hours about how to market flavored water to yuppies." She paused with a chip halfway to her mouth. "Do we have yuppies anymore?"

Lacey was chasing a hunk of ice cream in her glass and didn't look up. "I think they were in the 80s. I don't know what we call them now."

"Anyway," Jane popped the chip into her mouth. "The problem is I'm just not happy with that kind of guy anymore. I want somebody who'll push me a little, someone who wants to take charge for a change." She frowned. "That didn't make any sense."

"No, it totally did." Lacey abandoned her milkshake and heaved herself around until she was sitting cross-legged, facing Jane. "You've always been a very passionate woman, you've just always channeled it into making the store a success. And now that it is, you don't have anywhere to put that energy."

Jane chewed thoughtfully. It was true that for the past seven years, she'd worked nearly night and day to make a go of the business. Chicago had nearly three million residents, and over two hundred bookstores within the city proper. Some were major conglomerates like Barnes and Noble, others small independent shops that were often highly specialized. When she'd graduated from college with a small inheritance from her grandfather, she'd known exactly what she wanted to do with it. It had been seven years of the hardest work she could have ever imagined, but Denning Books was now a downtown institution. It drew New York Times bestselling authors and major publishers, along with the self-published and struggling writers. She'd gained a reputation for ferreting out the best unknowns, making it one of the most popular bookstores in town for the casual reader and literary critic alike.

It was immensely satisfying, but it now nearly ran itself. She was no longer needed in the day-to-day operations. She'd hired a wonderful manager to handle all but the most important tasks of running the business, and though she kept her fingers fully in the pie, it didn't require the energy it once had.

"I guess I always took charge when I was working so hard with the store, even in my personal life." Jane shoved the chips out of the way and sat up. "These guys are exactly like all the others I've dated since college. They let me call the shots, let me decide the where, when and how of everything from where we ate dinner to when we went to bed. To what we did in bed."

"And now that you don't have to be so in control at the store," Lacey picked up the thought, "it's not doing it for you in bed anymore." She pointed, "You don't want to be in control, you want someone to take control of you."

Jane stared at Lacey for a moment then shook her head. "Nah, that's probably not it." She reached for the bag of potato chips.

"No, don't dismiss this." Lacey shoved the bag behind her back, out of Jane's reach, and grasped her hand. "I really think we're onto something here. Look, when you were working eighty hours a week at the store, what did you do with your free time?" She waved a hand. "Besides bang the cosmically boring."

Jane pouted over the out-of-reach chips for a moment, then relented. "All right, let's see. I wrote in my journal, like always. Worked out, read, went to the occasional movie."

"What did you read?"

Jane thought. "I guess it was mostly romance novels," she mused. "You know, the historical ones where the virgin marries the charming but aloof viscount to save somebody's reputation, or money, or estate in Scotland. They bumble along for about two hundred pages, something tragic happens, they realize they love each other, and live happily ever after."

"And what are you reading now?"

Jane snaked one arm behind Lacey's back, snatched the chips, and popped one in her mouth smugly. "Still romance, but it's way hotter. More like erotica, but still with the happily ever after of a romance novel."

Lacey's brows disappeared under her spiky blonde bangs. "Erotica? Interesting," she murmured, one finger tapping her lips as she thought. "What kinds of stories are we talking about here?"

Jane stretched out on her side. "Well, there are all kinds—it's a very expansive genre. Contemporary, historical, some fantasy and science fiction. But they're all *really* steamy."

Lacey had a thoughtful look on her face. "What kind of steamy? Like, *The Thorn Birds* steamy, or *9 1/2 Weeks* steamy?"

Jane shoved the chips to the side and sat back up. "*9 1/2 Weeks,* definitely. Sometimes I swear I could come just from reading one." She rolled her eyes dramatically.

Lacey grinned. "So, out of all the ones that you've read, which ones get you going the most?"

Jane frowned, thinking. "Well, I've read a few vampire ones, a couple with werewolves and other supernatural creatures. Oh, and some futuristic, other-world ones that were mega hot. But the ones I've liked best are the contemporary ones with regular human characters. Seems more real, less like a fantasy." She paused, and then laughed. "There was one that got me so fired up I almost called the stockbroker for a quickie."

Lacey blinked. "Wow. So what was it about?"

Jane giggled and leaned in, automatically assuming the international pose of girlfriends about to dish. "It's about this couple who're having trouble in the bedroom. They really love each other, but they haven't exactly been burning up the sheets, know what I mean? So he sort of takes drastic measures to light the fires."

Lacey leaned in, mirroring Jane's pose. "What does he do?"

"Well," Jane lowered her voice. "He tells her that he loves her and wants to marry her, but he doesn't want her answer yet. And that he wants her to do whatever he tells her to for the next twenty-four hours, and then she can give him her answer."

"Ohmigosh," Lacey breathed. "What does he tell her to do?"

Jane scooted closer. "Well, he basically dominates her sexually." She gestured vaguely with her hands. "Like, he puts her in a certain position and tells her not to move, even when he's going down on her." She paused, frowning. "I think he spanks her a couple of times." She rolled her eyes at Lacey. "It was so hot. I couldn't believe I was getting so worked up over a book."

Lacey took a deep breath and let it out slowly. "I'm getting worked up just listening to you talk about it." She paused, narrowing her eyes at Jane. "The other books you liked, did they all have this domination theme in them?"

Jane blinked, surprised. "Yeah, now that I think about it, they did. And several of them had, like, bondage and spanking and stuff."

Lacey leaned back and grinned. "Well, there you go."

"Huh?"

"You want to be dominated in bed, and maybe even out of it, too," Lacey's grin got bigger. "Didn't you figure that out when a story got you hotter than the stockbroker?"

Chapter Two

Lacey was out of her mind. Jane just kept repeating the phrase like a mantra as she got dressed to go to the store early the next morning. Chanted it to herself as she trotted down the stairs and out of the renovated townhouse that housed her apartment. Muttered it under her breath during the entire twenty minutes it took for her to walk to the Michigan Avenue entrance of Denning Books. At just after six in the morning, the neighborhood was just beginning to wake up, the sun just beginning to lighten the eastern sky. So there wasn't much happening on the street to distract her from her thoughts.

Jane shook her head as she unlocked the door and made her way across the expanse of ebony marble that made up the entryway to the store. Once across the entry, she pushed open the double glass doors and entered the store itself, and stopped, distracted from her thoughts, and just looked. Sometimes it amazed her; this was all hers. The gleaming hardwood floors with colorful rugs scattered here and there, the elegant curve of the circular wrap desk dominating the entrance. The comfortable seating areas tucked into cozy corners, the café that served flavored coffees, warm pastries and sandwiches. And all those books. Books on anthropology, zygotes and everything in between.

She felt a smile spread across her face, and could almost feel the quiet building beaming back at her. She loved being here before the staff arrived, though she rarely managed to make it in before the 7:30 a.m. weekday opening. But after Lacey's little theory last night, sleep had been elusive. And since she'd used the fact that none of her workout clothes were clean as an excuse to avoid the early morning gym crowd, her only options left were pacing her apartment and thinking or coming in to work. And she'd done enough thinking, thank you very much.

Giving herself a slight shake, Jane started up the curving staircase leading to the second floor and made her way through the research volumes and study tables to her private office. Furnished with a sturdy desk in rough-hewn Indian rosewood, deep leather chairs, and painted a tomato red, the office was the only place in the world where she felt as comfortable as when in her own apartment. She could have easily installed a home office, since most of what she did these days consisted of phone calls and paperwork, but she liked being at the store. And the overstuffed sofa in the corner, upholstered in a bright apple green and plumped with pillows, made it possible to take the occasional nap when the workday ran long.

Jane dropped her battered leather briefcase to the floor beside the desk, grabbed the stack of paperwork waiting for her in the IN box, and settled down to work.

Five hours later she had a raging headache from trying to enter the impossibly small numbers on the latest invoice from Ingrams into her computer, felt just a little jittery and had to pee from the four lattes she'd had sent up from the café, and could still hear Lacey's voice in her mind like a sound bite on a loop—"You want to be dominated, you want to be dominated". The phrase had taken on a singsong quality in her head that was threatening to make her crazy. Even turning on her favorite zone-out CD, Jimmy Hendrix, hadn't done the trick. During *Foxy Lady*, when Jimmy crooned, "Here I come, baby. I'm comin' to getcha", the loop had started all over again.

Her private office line rang, interrupting her fifth attempt to reach Lacey telepathically and curse her to eternal hellfire for putting this idea in her brain. Jane snatched it up as the first ring trailed away. "What?"

A long silence greeted her. "Well, aren't we in a perky mood this morning?"

Jane hissed into the phone at the sound of Lacey's voice. "Don't you start with me, you daughter of Satan. This is all your fault."

"What is?"

"You know."

"Do not."

"Do too."

"Do NOT!"

"Do TOO!"

"DO N—okay, this could go on for a while." Jane could almost see Lacy plowing her fingers through her spiky blonde hair in frustration. "Why don't you tell me what you think is all my fault, and we'll go from there?"

All the fight drained out of her like air from a leaky balloon, and with a groan, Jane let her head drop to the desk with a thud. "It's your fault I can't concentrate and can only think about being tied up and driven to multiple orgasms."

There was silence on the line for a moment. Then, "Well, slap my ass and call me Judy."

"Oh, God. That sounds good too." Jane stared at her computer screen, the numbers of the spreadsheet blurring together so they made no sense. Not that they were making a lot of sense earlier.

"Wow." Lacey let out a low whistle.

"Yeah, wow." Jane sighed. "Look, there's no way I'm going to get any work done here today. Can you take a break, meet me in the café for lunch?"

"I'm at a good stopping point." An independent web designer, Lacey worked from home most days. "And I want to continue this very interesting conversation, Judy."

Jane grinned into the phone, good spirits restored. "Don't be fresh. Ten minutes?"

"Be there or be square."

Jane hung up, suddenly ravenous, and headed for the café, a chicken salad sandwich and a conversation that would either rid her of the notion of being dominated once and for all, or send her running out looking for something in leather.

When Jane arrived in the café, she ordered her sandwich and a tuna on rye for Lacey, along with coffee for both of them and then headed toward the small grouping of tables near the crackling fireplace. There were a few people in the café, but since the lunch rush was still a good hour away, there were plenty of empty tables, and she chose one in a secluded corner. God knew she didn't need any patrons overhearing this particular conversation.

She tapped her fingers impatiently and kept an eye on the door to the café's street entrance. Within minutes, it flew open, and Lacey danced in. Her pixie face was flushed from the cold, her eyes bright and her hair tousled by the wind. She spotted Jane immediately and made her way to the table, peeling off her coat as she walked.

Lacey grinned at her companion as she sat down, tossing her coat over the empty third chair. "So, Judy. What's going on?"

Jane rolled her eyes. "Don't call me Judy. Seriously, Lace. What am I going to do?"

Lacey nodded her thanks to the waitress who was delivering their coffee and waited for her to walk out of earshot before answering. She picked up her cup and took a tentative sip, savoring the steaming brew. "What do you want to do?"

Jane ignored her coffee, her eyes narrowing into slits of glowing blue and practically growled. "I want to get laid, dammit."

Lacey grinned. "There," she said in a bad Spanish accent, "I cannot help you."

Jane blew out a breath. "Well, what am I supposed to do? You can't just drop a bomb on me like the one you let go last night and then not help me figure out how to make it happen!"

Lacey raised one delicate fairy eyebrow. "So, you've decided to go with the whole 'dominated in bed' thing?"

Jane heaved a beleaguered sigh. "Yes." She held up a hand, as if to make a pledge. "I, Jane Elizabeth Denning, do hereby admit to needing a man to take control in the bedroom." She let her hand fall with a thump to the table. "Now will you please help me figure out how to find someone to do it?" Her voice rose, agitation making her heedless of listening ears. "I mean, it's not like I can walk into a club on a Saturday night and announce that I'm looking for someone to tie me down and fuck me."

Lacey shushed her, looking around the room to make sure no one had overheard, and grinned. "Actually, that's a probably a pretty surefire method." She waved a hand as Jane opened her mouth to protest. "But I can see how that might get you some fairly undesirable candidates, and since you're already thirty-one, we don't have a lot of time to spend on the selection process."

Jane stuck out her tongue. "Fuck you. You're only four months behind me, so don't act all smug that you're still thirty." She took a sip of her coffee, then propped her chin on her palm. "Okay, we need a game plan here, pal. How am I going to pull this off?"

"Well, I guess we need to figure out what you're looking for, and go from there." Lacey leaned forward, keeping her voice low so that Jane had to lean in to hear her. "I mean, are we looking for a one-night stand here, or a long-term thing?"

Jane frowned. "Well, I'd say one-night stand, but I could certainly adjust my thinking if he's any good."

"Okay, so we're flexible." Lacey sat back a little as the waitress delivered their sandwiches, then leaned back in. "Any particular physical type?"

Jane shrugged. "Well, I don't want a dweeb. I mean, he has to be strong enough physically and mentally to actually dominate me. But if you mean any particular hair or eye color, I don't really think it's important." Jane chewed her lip thoughtfully for a minute. "But I have to be attracted to him, because I'm not going to have sex with any old goober just for the sake of trying this."

Lacey nodded. "Agreed." She took a bite of sandwich and chewed thoughtfully. "Tan ou fink of adyboby ou wad?"

Jane starred at her. "I have no idea what the hell you just said. Was that English?"

Lacey held up a hand, chewed frantically, and swallowed. "I said, can you think of anybody you want?"

Jane's expression cleared. "Oh. No, of course not. That's the point. All my life I've looked for guys I could control, not ones that could control me. If they could control me, I never even saw them. My radar has been tuned for the controllable, and I don't know how to switch it over so it picks up the controlling."

Lacey was chewing again. "You're George," she mumbled around a mouthful of food. But at least Jane could understand her this time.

Jane blinked, confused. "What do you mean, I'm George?"

"Remember on *Seinfeld* when George decided that everything he'd ever done was wrong, so that in order to be right, he had to do the opposite?" Jane nodded. "Well, you're George. Since all these years you've been looking at the wrong kind of guy, you're going to have to do the opposite of what you'd normally do, and you'll find the right kind of guy."

"I'm getting a headache." Jane closed her eyes for a minute then took a deep breath. "First of all," she began, "please don't compare me to bumbling, bald sitcom characters," she sighed. "Second, you may have a point."

"Yep," Lacey was nodding her head. "Gotta do the opposite."

Jane straightened in her chair. "Okay," she said briskly. "If I'm going to do the opposite, I've got to go to a place I don't normally go to, where I can meet a guy and not do what I would normally do. But where?"

Lacey pushed aside her sandwich and turned her attention back to the conversation. "How 'bout The Blue Note, tonight? It's Friday, there should be a pretty good crowd."

The Blue Note was a club downtown. It wasn't one of Jane's regular hangouts, but she'd been there once or twice for a change of pace. Unlike a lot of the clubs in the area, it was neither new nor flashy, and didn't cater to the hip and trendy. It was a hole in the wall that'd been around since the days of Al Capone, and the secret door that proclaimed its history as a onetime speakeasy was still in place. They had live blues several nights a week, and a great selection of prerecorded music when there wasn't a band. The atmosphere was dark, smoky and sultry, and there was no way she'd be running into any stockbrokers there.

Jane nodded thoughtfully. "Not a bad idea. I'm sure not going to run into any dweebs there, and it's a far cry from the martini bars and coffeehouses where I've met most of my recent losers. But how am I going to approach someone?"

Lacey shook her head. "You're not approaching anyone, Jane. Remember, this is about you not being in control for a change, and that includes you letting guys approach you, instead of the other way around." She pointed a finger at Jane. "Opposite, remember?"

"Okay." Jane blew out a breath. "But I have to have some control over the selection process. I mean, there are a lot of freaks and psychos out there. I can't just say 'yee-haw' to the first controlling asshole who comes along."

Lacey hmmed in agreement. "Well, of course you have ultimate veto power. Like you said, you have to at least be attracted to the guy. And you don't have to sleep with him tonight, anyway. You could always just set up a real date and see how it goes."

Jane nodded thoughtfully. "Okay, that sounds good. Are you coming with me?"

Lacey looked at her with surprise. "Well, duh. I've got to make sure you're following the plan. Besides, you might chicken out and not go at all."

Jane rolled her eyes. "Well, there's little danger of that. I really want this to work. I'm so horny I could hump a Buick." Then her eyes narrowed to blue slits. "However, if this doesn't work, I'm going to make your life hell for the next few thousand years."

Lacey grinned, brown eyes flashing. "Baby, if I'm right—and I usually am—you're going to be thanking me for the rest of your days." She wiped her fingers on her napkin and tossed it onto the remnants of her lunch. She nodded at the sandwich that Jane hadn't touched. "Do you want to eat? I'll wait for you."

Jane shook her head and pushed back her chair. "No, I'm not really hungry." She stood abruptly. "I'm heading upstairs to grab my purse, then I'm going to go shopping to find some sexy little number to wear tonight. Saks is having a sale—want to come, or do you have to get back to work?"

Lacey leapt to her feet. "Well, I'm working on that CPA's website, but it can wait." She hooked her arm companionably through Jane's. "Let's go, Judy."

Jane giggled as they headed for the stairs, her mind already occupied with the coming evening. She was so wrapped up in thoughts of the perfect little black dress, that she never even noticed the grass green eyes that tracked her out the door.

Ian MacInnes sat in the easy chair next to the fireplace and tried to concentrate on breathing normally. That was perhaps the most intriguing, exciting and downright titillating conversation he'd ever had the good fortune to overhear.

He'd noticed the brunette the moment she flew into the café from the adjoining bookstore. She was stunning. On the taller side, about five foot seven or eight, with flawless ivory skin and plenty of attitude. The details of her figure were camouflaged under worn denim and a long-sleeve knit shirt the color of ripe cherries, but she moved with the ease and grace of a woman who was used to using her body, and he caught intriguing glimpses of hidden curves as she moved across the room.

He watched her as she placed an order at the counter, then headed to a table just behind him and off to his left, moving out of his line of vision. The high-backed fireplace chair he was sitting in hid her from view, but he could almost feel the nervous energy pumping off her in waves. As he wondered at the cause of it, a petite blonde with a pixie face blew in with the wind, and after a quick glance around the room, made a beeline for the brunette's table.

Even though he could no longer see her, the brunette's image remained firm in his memory. He'd only gotten a cursory look before she'd moved out of his line of sight, but years in the military had trained him to observe details quickly, and he had no trouble bringing her image, fully formed and detailed, to his mind. Her hair was shoulder-length, thick and a true, rich brown, without the blonde or red highlights woman with brown hair usually had. He gave a brief thought to wondering how that hair would look spread across his pillow, and the image was so pleasing that he held onto it while he mentally catalogued the rest of her. Her face wasn't round or soft, but made up of angles and sharp curves, giving her a slightly exotic look. Sharp cheekbones, eyes that turned up slightly at the corners and a chin coming to a sharp little point. It was a face that might have been too harsh and too sharp, if it wasn't softened by the lush contours of her mouth. It was unpainted and full, and the image of that mouth wrapped around his cock had the fit of his slacks suddenly changing.

He'd seen her toss her head back as she'd strode past him to the table, and he mentally followed the elegant sweep of her neck to the curve of her shoulder, the wide neck of her shirt having slipped a little. He felt an almost uncontrollable urge to nibble, just there, along that soft curve, covered in milk-white skin.

He'd been entertaining himself by absently listening to the rise and fall of her voice, indistinct though it might be, and enjoying his coffee, when suddenly the voice was no longer indistinct or low. The words carried clearly to his ears. "I can't just walk into a bar and announce I'm looking for someone to tie me up and fuck me!" He'd nearly choked on his coffee, his eyes watering as he tried to keep from spewing the drink into his lap. Once he'd gotten control of himself, the voices behind him had once again dropped to a low murmur, and he'd been unable to keep from listening in earnest.

He'd silently scooted his chair back a few inches and slightly to the left, so the winged back of the chair no longer served as a sound barrier, and he had no trouble hearing her talk to her friend. And he'd been so absolutely stunned by the turn of the conversation, he was still sitting there, in shock, five minutes after they'd gone.

The brunette's name was Jane, and apparently, she wanted to give surrendering control in the bedroom a try.

Ian grinned to himself, ignoring the speculative glances that he earned from the other inhabitants of the café as he stood. He was aware, as he always was, of the eyes on him. His training demanded he be aware and alert to his surroundings, but as his mind was still on the brunette and her plans for the evening, he only registered it on an automatic level. Normally he was amused and entertained by the speculative looks and coy glances he drew from women. He knew that at six-foot two-inches, two hundred and sixty pounds, he was a change of pace from the soft, out of shape businessmen one usually encountered in the Chicago financial district. The twelve years he'd spent in military intelligence had required intense physical conditioning, and it had become so ingrained that he'd continued to train after resigning his commission to work in the private sector. His body retained the hard, muscled look of a physical laborer, even though most of his work was done behind a desk these days. The only real change in his appearance since becoming a civilian again was his hair. Once kept ruthlessly short, he now let the raven locks grow to just below his collar. After so many years of keeping it short, he enjoyed having it brush against his neck.

He felt it lift a little in the wind as he stepped out onto the sidewalk. April in Chicago was not a comfortable time to be without a coat, but he ignored the cold as easily as he ignored the lunch-hour crowds that were beginning to spill out on to the street. He made his way easily through the throngs of people, moving by rote as his mind continued to replay the conversation in the café. He didn't have to think about it much—if the delectable Jane was looking for someone to take control, he'd be happy to apply for the job.

He suddenly tossed his head back and laughed, startling several men on the street and drawing interested glances from the women. He continued to grin as he picked up the pace, wanting to get back to the office to make sure he didn't need to work late. It looked like he was going to a blues club tonight.

Chapter Three

Jane took a deep breath and let it out slowly as she surveyed the club from a corner booth. There was no live band tonight, but the DJ kept the music moving, and if the crowd on the dance floor was any indication, no one seemed to care where it came from. Stevie Ray Vaughn was crooning about the crying sky and the joint, as they say, was jumping.

Jane tried not to fidget as she waiting for Lacey to make the return trip from the ladies' room. She'd dressed very carefully for tonight, and she knew she looked good, but she had a case of the jitters and couldn't seem to sit still. The slim column of flame-colored silk shifted and slid over her skin with every tiny movement, the Lycra it was blended with clinging to hardened nipples and tense thighs. It was doing nothing to combat her nervousness, rather, it only made her skin tingle with a sensitivity that was driving her crazy. The dress had seemed like a good idea that afternoon at Saks. It came to just below the knee, with wide-set straps that left her upper chest and arms bare, and the back dipped nearly down to her waist, making it impossible to wear a bra. Thankfully, the designer had taken into account that someone with curves might want to buy it and had included built-in support. It suited her figure, making her look like a 40s pinup girl, so she'd continued the slight retro theme with chunky high-heeled shoes and seamed stockings. Her only concession to modern conveniences was that the stockings were thigh-highs and required no garters to keep them in place.

A woman who was most comfortable in worn jeans and ratty T-shirts, she felt somewhat on edge just because of the clothes. That, added to the whole reason for this outing, had her feeling so jumpy that she figured if someone did ask her to dance, she'd probably leap right out of her skin.

Jane gave a sigh of relief as she spotted Lacey heading back her way, drinks in hand. Apparently, she'd stopped by the bar on the way back from the bathroom. As soon as she was within reach, Jane snatched one of the glasses from her hand and downed it in one swallow. Her eyes teared up and her throat closed off as the whiskey hit her stomach, but it made her feel just the slightest bit steadier, and at least it took her mind off the throb of her own pulse.

Lacey merely shoved the empty glass to the side and slid into the booth. "Little liquid courage, darling?"

Jane turned to her friend. "I'm in a bar to pick up a guy. And not just any guy—one that I'm supposed to ask to tie me up, or hold me down, or whatever. Dominate me. This is perhaps the craziest idea ever conceived, and I don't think I've ever been this turned on in my entire life." She grinned at Lacey. "I might as well have not even worn panties for all the good they're doing me right now."

Lacey rolled her eyes. "I don't know why I thought you'd be nervous about this."

Jane laughed. "I am nervous. But I'm also excited." She grabbed Lacey's hand in a vise grip. "Just think I might actually get laid tonight! By a man who knows what he's doing! To whom I don't have to tell the names of various female body parts and what to do with them!"

Lacey peeled Jane's fingers off hers. "You are way too worked up about this. If you don't calm down, you're going to end up freaking some poor guy out."

"You're right." Jane held up her hands. "I'll calm down. And hey, I think we should set a time limit on this thing."

Lacey's face turned quizzical. "What kind of time limit?"

Jane huffed out a breath. "Well, if I don't find Mr. Tie-Me-Up-And-Do-Me within," she glanced at her watch, "two hours, then we split and go find another opposite place. I don't want to waste time."

Lacey threw up her hands. "Fine. Two hours it is." She shook her head, muttering under her breath, "I've created a monster."

One hour and forty-five minutes later, Jane's enthusiasm for the project had gone the way of the dodo, and she was ready to pack it in. She'd danced with no fewer than seven different men, and she'd wager her grandmother's pearls she could walk all over every one of them. So much for avoiding the dweebs. She was tired, more than a little tipsy from the three additional whiskeys she'd had over the course of the night, and her feet hurt.

She leaned against the bar, waiting for the bartender to close out her tab and for Lacey to emerge from the bathroom, when she got that creepy, itchy feeling between her shoulder blades, signaling someone was watching her. She wasn't going to turn around. It was probably dweeb number four, the one who'd spent every minute of the two dances she'd given him talking about his golf handicap and the hair plugs he was considering, and she had no desire to encourage him further. But the itch wasn't going away, so she risked one swift glance over her shoulder. And nearly swallowed her tongue.

He was leaning against the corner booth where she'd been sitting for most of the night. In fact, if he had been there five minutes ago, she would have tripped over him in her rush to get away from dweeb number seven. She felt her mouth go dry at the thought, and began a mental inventory of the most promising prospect she'd encountered all night.

His feet were encased in engineer boots, and crossed casually at the ankles. Long legs led to lean hips, and a simple, white, button-down shirt that was tucked neatly into the waistband of faded button fly Levis. The sleeves were rolled to his forearms, and as she watched, he pulled his hands from his pockets and crossed his arms over his chest. She drew in an involuntary breath as the motion pulled the shirt taut across broad shoulders and bulging biceps, then let it out in one long, shaky sigh as she caught sight of the ridge of his collarbones through the open neck of his shirt. She had a horrible weakness for shoulders and collarbones on a man. She strained to see if she could get a better look, but his collar was in the way, so she moved up the strong, tanned column of his throat, over the solid jaw, the slash of his cheekbones. She took in the hair that brushed his collar, and so black it shone almost blue in the light, and just a little too long to be respectable. But it was his eyes, green as Ireland and locked on her, that had the noise and confusion of the bar fading away.

As she watched, he slowly straightened from his perch and began walking toward her. His arms fell to his sides, the motion of his body pulling his shirt open just a little bit at the neck, and she spotted his collarbones. Jesus, they were amazing.

"Hey."

Jane started and turned, the voice at her side breaking the spell cast by his unwavering gaze. "Lacey."

"So, you ready to go, or what?" Lacey was concentrating on getting her purse strap untangled, but looked up when she didn't get an answer. "Jane? What's up?"

For some reason her mouth didn't want to form words, so she just looked back across the room, and Lacey followed her gaze. Her eyes widened almost comically as she saw the hunk heading across the room. "Wow. Is he coming over here for you?"

Jane nodded automatically, not taking her eyes off the stranger. "I think so."

"Well, then I'm just going to find an empty stool at the bar and order myself another cocktail."

Jane nodded again. "Okay." She barely noticed when Lacey moved away. She continued to follow his progress across the room. Never once did he take his eyes off her as he moved easily through the crowd. He came to a stop about two feet in front of her, forcing her to look up to keep her eyes on his face. Sweet Jesus in the morning, he was gorgeous.

He simply stood there for a moment, his eyes on her face, his expression inscrutable, then the corners of his mouth tilted up in the barest hint of a smile. He held out a hand, palm up and said, "Dance with me."

It was more command than request, and a lesser man would have been treated to a withering glare and a snide putdown. But this man was every fantasy she'd ever had come to gorgeous, heart-thumping life, and there was no way she was turning him down. Added to that, she was playing the opposite game tonight. Besides, she was a strong, independent woman with a healthy sexuality and a strong sense of herself, and she could handle anything that Tall, Dark and Delicious here had in mind.

So, instead of cutting him off at the knees, she gave him a slow smile and put her hand in his. She had to suppress a shudder at the touch of his hand as he led her to the dance floor. His skin was warm and dry, and somehow generated sparks that shot up her arm and settled in her nipples. Since his back was to her as he led them to the center of the dance floor, she risked a quick glance down. Yep, they were standing at attention. The only other time she could remember them being this hard was the time she'd gone skinny-dipping in February.

He stopped in the middle of the floor, turned and smoothly pulled her into his arms. He tucked her hand close to his chest, cuddled in his bigger one, and slid the other hand along her back, moving her in close and leaving a tingling trail in its wake.

The DJ chose that moment to segue into a smooth, mellow Bonnie Raitt ballad, one of her favorites. As he began to lead her in the slow rhythm of the dance, her nipples were forced into contact with his chest, and she drew in a breath. She'd never been one of those women with supersensitive nipples, but they were making up for lost time tonight. The sway of their bodies caused them to rasp, continuously, back and forth along his chest, and before Bonnie even made it though the first verse, she could feel her womb clench and her pussy drench with wet heat.

It occurred to her that while she was a strong woman with a healthy sexuality and strong sense of herself, maybe, just maybe, she was in trouble here.

He was just too yummy. She stood in the circle of his arms, barely swaying to the beat of the music and stared up into his face. It was a strong face, with bold features and bronze skin that only made the green of his eyes seem brighter. And the way he was looking at her made every rational and half-hearted second thought fly right out of her head.

He never took his eyes off hers, the way a man will do when he's unsure of his moves or of a woman's reactions. No, his gaze was steady and unwavering, and the heavy-lidded sensuality of it made *her* want to look away, the intensity of the moment was almost too much to bear. But she couldn't—her brain couldn't make the connection necessary to tell her eyes to move.

They stood there, swaying gently to the beat of the music, the rest of the room fading into a haze in her peripheral vision. He continued to watch her, the hand he held on her back continuously stroking so that her skin broke out in gooseflesh and her nipples puckered even tighter. The hand holding hers to his chest wasn't idle—his thumb was sliding back and forth, back and forth, over her wrist and she knew her pulse pounded like a jackrabbit under her skin. She also knew by the slumberous, slightly satisfied look in his eyes he knew it too.

After what seemed like an eternity, he finally shifted his eyes from hers. She thought it might cause the intensity of him to ease a little, but as his gaze began to lazily rove over her, it only continued to build. She watched him as his gaze skimmed over her hair, piled into a loose twist that left several strands to trail along her neck, felt the impact of those eyes as they catalogued her face. She sucked in an involuntary breath as he halted his perusal at the base of her throat, and knew that he could see the hammer of her pulse beating beneath the delicate skin.

He continued his slow perusal of her body, taking in the rise of her breasts above the square bodice of the dress, the slope of her bare shoulders and arms. She felt his eyes on her as a physical touch; everywhere he looked, she tingled. By the time he finally looked back into her eyes, she felt as though she'd been stroked by invisible hands and her heartbeat was thudding so loud in her ears, that when he spoke, she had to concentrate to hear him.

"What's your name?" She saw his lips form the words, and heard the faint echo of them over the music and the thumping of her own heart. But her entire body had gone on alert when she heard his voice. Deep and slightly gravelly, it had the same effect on her nipples as Lake Michigan in February. And her underwear would likely never be dry again.

She had to swallow before answering. "Jane," she managed, in a voice that sounded too throaty, too needy, to be hers. She tried clearing her throat, but it didn't help much. "What's yours?"

He smiled at the breathy quality of her response, his eyes going heavy-lidded and sensual. "Ian," he replied, and stroked his hand up her back to loosely clasp the back of her neck. He seemed to absorb her involuntary shudder and his fingers began a slow stroke over her skin. "You seem a little restless tonight, Jane."

Jane had to fight to keep her eyes open, his hand felt so good on her neck. She licked lips gone suddenly dry, and felt her heart rate increase as his eyes tracked the movement. "What do you mean?"

His gaze stayed on her mouth. "I mean you've danced with quite a few men since you arrived, but you didn't seem to be having a good time." He flicked his gaze back to hers. "Didn't you want to dance with all of them?"

"Not particularly, no." God, if he kept stroking her neck for much longer, she was going to melt into a puddle right at his feet.

He tilted his head to the side in question. "Then why did you?"

Jane answered automatically, without thinking. "'Cause I'm doing the opposite."

Ian quirked a brow. "What's the opposite?"

It occurred to Jane in some small corner of her brain that it might be a good idea to censor her response to that question. He was yummy, sexy, and if the ridge in his jeans was any indication, hung like a horse, but he was still a stranger. She decided to give him part of the truth, and edit out the more interesting, possibly damaging, details. "Usually I pick the guys I want to dance with, what to dance to. Everything."

That one midnight brow inched up a little higher. "Nothing wrong with that, is there?"

Jane felt her mouth quirk up in a smile at the blatant humor in his voice. "Not usually, but it hasn't been working out so well lately. So," she gave a little half shrug, "I'm doing the opposite—letting someone else call a few shots for a change."

The humor remained in his voice, but the sensuality that had never really left seemed to kick up a notch. "And how's that working out right now?"

Suddenly, Jane felt the thrill of this new adventure overtake her, and decided caution was for sissies. She let the sensual smile that wanted to emerge spread over her face, and lowered one eye in a slow wink. "Ask me in the morning."

This time both brows made the climb up his forehead. "That doesn't sound like you're letting someone else call the shots, now does it?"

She shrugged. "So I'm a beginner. There're bound to be a few hitches along the way."

"You sure you know what you're doing?"

Jane grinned, despite the very real clutch of trepidation in her belly at the predatory gleam in his eye. "I doubt it. But what's life without a little risk?"

That fabulous mouth of his spread into a grin, and Jane felt her head go just the tiniest bit lighter at the sheer carnality of it. "Well," he purred, "in that case." He tightened his arms, gathering her even closer, and bent his head.

Jane had time to think, "Oh, sweet Jesus," as his head blocked out the dim light of the room, and then his mouth was on hers. Her eyes slid shut, and the ability to form rational thought floated away.

He didn't cajole, didn't seduce. He conquered. His mouth slanted over hers with a small twist, pressing her lips just slightly apart, and his tongue slid past her teeth like hot, wet silk. She gave a little involuntary moan as the sensation seemed to arrow straight to her pelvis and she rose up on her toes opening her mouth wider. He took instant advantage and immediate control of the kiss. The hand on the back of her neck clamped down, holding her head immobile, and the sensation of being restrained only seemed to intensify the arousal pooling like lava in her belly.

The other hand, still holding her right one in a loose clasp against his chest, tightened and slowly dragged her hand across his body, the backs of his knuckles catching her nipples and making her whimper, until he could reach her other hand. Without letting go of her right hand, he gathered the left from where it was clenched on his shoulder so he had both of her hands firmly in his one.

He lifted his head briefly, and she opened her eyes to find him staring at her mouth, his breath coming fast and hard. He moved his hand from her neck, and felt him take both of her hands and pull them behind her, so they rested in the small of her back. He cuffed her wrists in one big hand, not pulling, not hurting, but holding her immobile. Then he wrapped the other hand in her hair, tilted her head and dove back into her mouth.

Jane groaned, certain she'd never been so turned on by a kiss in her entire life. She could feel her shoulders pulling slightly, unused to the position. Her scalp stung slightly where his hand twisted in her hair. Her lips felt slightly bruised from the force of his grinding down on them. And her panties were so wet that she'd have sworn they squished.

Jane gave a fleeting thought to the oddity of her response. That this man, with his emerald eyes and artist's hands, could wrest control over her body with a few smooth, practiced moves, struck her as alarming, even dangerous. But the thought was gone as quickly as it came, and then she could only concentrate on the rising heat in her body.

Jane whimpered into his mouth. She could feel the pressure and tension gathering in her pelvis as he took the kiss deeper. There was no subtlety or seduction in the kiss anymore; he fucked her mouth with his tongue, and she could feel the smooth muscles of her pussy clench in response, the flood of moisture as it grasped at nothing. The sheer carnality and aggression of his marauding mouth and restraining hands brought her to the brink of satisfaction within moments. Her clit throbbed, her nipples tingled, and she knew that the orgasm was going to hit her like a freight train. The very small part of her brain still capable of rational thought goggled at the prospect. She, Jane Denning, was about to have an orgasm just from a kiss and a little restraint.

Or maybe not. It was right there, shimmering just out of her grasp, but it wasn't enough—she needed more. Jane whimpered again, the sound absorbed by his mouth, as she tried to move against his hold. He tightened his grip, keeping her in place and she nearly wept from frustration. Her legs shifted restlessly, straining to get just a little bit of pressure, just a little bit of friction, to her aching clit. She wasn't going to get there without it, and oh, she wanted that orgasm. She could almost taste it, it was so close, and she thought she'd cry if he didn't let her have it.

She could hear the soft, almost panicked little cries, but she didn't realize they came from her. She could feel the pressure of his hands on her wrists, but didn't realize that she was twisting in his hold. All she knew, all she felt, was the orgasm he was holding just out of reach, like a treat he wanted her to beg for. And she'd do it—if he let go of her mouth for two seconds she'd be begging with all the breath left in her lungs.

She strained to get closer, for the teeny bit of extra contact it would take for her to reach nirvana, and he finally seemed to get the hint. He shifted his grip on her hands, tilted her pelvis and slid one jean-covered leg between hers. Instantly, the gathering storm within her spun out of control. Her womb clenched, her nipples stabbed into his chest and with a long, keening moan that went no further than his mouth, she exploded.

The racking shudders went on and on, spurred on by the hard friction of his leg against her cleft. His teeth closed over her bottom lip and nipped, the slight sting setting off a fresh round of spasms in her aching pussy. Jane hung suspended in the safe cradle of his arms, sparks going off behind her eyes, fighting to draw breath as he drew the orgasm out with deliberate skill.

When the spasms and shivers finally faded, he gave her mouth one last lick, a tiny nip and pulled back. Jane felt him release her hair, felt him take her hands in both of his and draw them around her body so that her palms rested lightly on his chest. She kept her eyes closed as he began a slow massage of her shoulders and upper arms, and only then did she become aware of the slight ache in her muscles.

"How're you doing?" He bent his head and spoke directly into her ear, and the low rumble of his voice was enough to have one more convulsive shiver racing through her.

"Hmmmmm." Since it was so close, and her head felt too heavy for her neck, she rested her forehead on his chest.

Absently, she noted his heartbeat seemed awfully fast. "I'm good," she sighed. "How're you?"

She felt him smile against the side of her neck, and his hands paused in their stroking. He curved his palms around the balls of her shoulders and pulled her back slightly. He grinned at the look of sleepy satisfaction on her face. Grasping one of her limp hands in his, he dragged it down, down his chest, past his belt buckle, to the hard ridge of his cock. "How do I feel?" he rumbled, his voice deepening with lust.

Jane purred, her eyes going wide and greedy as she felt that thick, pulsing curve of flesh. His hand pressed on hers briefly, then released the pressure, giving her the choice of leaving it there or removing it. But her fingers had already begun to curl and stroke, and her tongue snuck out to swipe along swollen lips as she felt renewed desire curl in her belly. She flattened her palm and stroked down the length of him in one firm stroke, and watched his eyes darken and narrow in response.

She licked her lips again. "Like about seven to eight inches, and hard as a pike."

His features were now tight with lust; his eyes almost black with it, and the grin spreading over his face had a definite edge. "The pike part is right."

With renewed lust heating her blood, she answered his grin with one of her own. "And the seven to eight?"

"Is something we can't really verify on the dance floor," he growled.

Jane looked around, somehow surprised to find herself in the middle of a crowded dance floor with her hand on a total stranger's dick. "Ohmigosh, I can't believe I forgot we were in public." She turned back to him with eyes gone wild with humor. "Does that make me an exhibitionist?"

He gave a short bark of laughter. He pulled her fingers away from his fly, curling them in his and lifting them to his lips. He brushed a quick kiss across her knuckles. "No, but the smart money says you will be if you keep that up much longer."

Jane smiled and slid her free hand to toy with the hair curling at his collar. "Well, as crazy I'm feeling right now, I just don't think I'm ready to show the Friday night crowd what color panties I wear. So, since I'm supposed to be letting someone else call the shots…" She trailed one finger over the shell of his ear, leaned in to nip ever so slightly at the ridge of that fabulous collarbone, "got any ideas?"

Ian's eyes glittered. "Your place or mine?"

Chapter Four

The next fifteen minutes were pretty much a blur to Jane. They paid their respective bar bills, gathered their coats and were speeding away in Ian's Land Rover before she knew it.

"What was that about back there?"

Jane made an effort to get her mind off the throbbing pulse between her thighs. "Huh? What was what?"

"That whole sign language thing with your friend, back at the bar."

"Oh! She was just making sure I was leaving with you because I wanted to, and to tell me to make sure to call her in the morning."

Both eyebrows shot up. "You got all that from a shrug, a smile and a phone pantomime?"

Jane nodded. "Girlfriend code."

Ian smiled, turning his attention back to the road. "And was she satisfied that you're acting of your own free will?"

Jane swallowed heavily at the husky timbre of his voice. Her own sounded rusty to her ears when she answered. "I think so."

He grinned and winked. "You can call her in the morning."

Jane grinned back, though the tension in her was beginning to climb to uncomfortable levels once more. The look in Lacey's eyes had been a lot more envious than worried. "Oh, I'm sure she'll call me if I forget."

"Hope it won't be too early." He sent her a slow smile. "It's going to take me a while before I'm through."

Jane turned to look at him, and felt a quick one-two punch in her belly when she saw his gaze intent on her. She felt as though her head was floating about six inches above her neck when he looked at her like that. Like a hungry wolf eyeing a particularly tasty meal. She shivered.

"Cold?" He reached out with one broad hand, intending to turn up the heat. Her throaty reply stayed his hand in midair.

"Not exactly," she drawled.

He arched one raven brow. "Turned on?" he purred.

She flicked out her tongue to wet her lips, smiling as his eyes tracked the movement. "Exactly."

Ian grinned, feral and sharp. "How turned on?" She must have looked as blank as she suddenly felt, because he elaborated. "Is your pussy wet, are your nipples hard?" His voice lowered seductively. "Is your cunt just aching to have me inside, thick and hard, filling you up?"

Jane couldn't help the involuntary moan that escaped at the image he painted. She actually felt her pussy clench down and pull, seeking something to fill it.

In between panting breaths she managed to utter a "Sweet baby Jesus, yes" and dimly heard his answering chuckle. She licked lips gone suddenly dry. "Are we almost there?"

Her eyes were pretty much crossed with lust, but she caught the gleam in his with no trouble. "Impatient, aren't we?" he purred.

Jane gulped in a deep breath. "Cowboy, I'm about six words and two potholes away from having this party without you." She slanted him a look that would've had a lesser man swerving to the curb due to the sudden southern migration of his blood.

Ian merely grinned. "Baby, I don't have that far to go to catch up to you."

"Just the same, I'd prefer an escort for this particular fete. Think you can drive a little faster?" The slightly superior tone and delicately arched brow took all of Jane's concentration, but she was pretty sure she pulled it off. Then she blinked, surprised, as they swung to the curb in front of her building. She didn't think she'd ever been so glad to see home in her entire life.

Ian switched off the ignition and climbed out of the car. She sat, in a state of suspended arousal, and watched him walk around the hood of the Rover to open her door. The wind flirted with the raven locks brushing his collar and gave his dark skin a healthy, ruddy cast. Even through the tinted windshield, she could see the sensual intent in those green eyes. Jesus, he was bee-yoo-ti-ful.

Jane watched him as he reached out and opened her door. "Well?" He held out a hand. "Thought you were in a bit of a rush?"

She shook her head clear of the lust clouding it to grab his hand and all but leapt from the car and into his arms. She wound both arms around his shoulders and buried her face in the smooth skin of his throat. "You look like a pretty strong guy to me." She took a delicate nip of one delicious collarbone. "Like you keep in shape, work out regularly." She followed the nip with a slow lick, and felt him shudder in response.

His arms had come around her automatically when she flew from the Rover, and now they tightened, lifting her up on her toes. "I can hold my own."

Jane tipped back her head and grinned at him. She shifted her grip on his shoulders, bounced once on her toes, and boosted herself up to wrap her legs around his waist. His hands automatically caught her under her thighs. She gave one brief prayer of thanksgiving that her new dress was a Lycra blend and didn't rip, then concentrated on the thrills to be had in this new position. "Think you're strong enough to make it to my apartment without dropping me?"

Ian lifted one sardonic brow in mock question, though it was hard to pull off with his face so tight with lust. "Doesn't feel like there's anything wrong with your legs," he rumbled. He shifted his hands, stroking up her thighs before clamping them firmly on her butt under the dress, bared by her skimpy thong and thigh-high stockings. She felt herself go faint and barely managed to bite back a moan as the motion brought her burning cleft into firm contact with his cock.

She brought his face back into focus with an effort. "No, nothing wrong with my legs," she panted. "But I'm pretty sure I can't walk and do this at the same time." Keeping her gaze locked on his, she slithered one hand between their bodies, thumbed open the top two buttons of his fly, and wrapped her fingers firmly around the base of his cock.

Ian staggered a bit then seemed to gather himself. He lifted one booted foot and kicked the car door shut, making them both shudder as the motion lifted her even higher on his hips and had her hand clenching convulsively on his dick. He bounced her once, getting a firm grip on her ass, then started toward the front door of the brownstone as fast as he could.

The lock gave them some trouble. She wouldn't let go of him long enough to dig her keys out of her bag, so he was forced to pin her to the wall with his weight in order to free his hands for the search. He fumbled with the small glittery purse, his hands feeling about six times their normal size in his haste, and by the time he located her key ring they were both panting for air.

He fought the key into the lock and pushed open the door with such force that it slammed into the wall. He wasted no time in gathering her up and propelling them into the hallway. He caught the door with his foot and kicked it shut, then looked around. There were two doors, one on either side of the narrow hall, and a staircase that led to a second floor.

"Which way is yours?"

"Hmmm?" Jane was busy testing the crispness of his pubic hair with her nails.

"Jane!" The harsh bark snapped her attention back to him, and she looked into his face to find him breathing hard, nostrils flared, his pupils dilated so that only a sliver of green remained. She didn't think she'd ever seen such a look of need, and had a moment's fear that she might be biting off more than she could chew.

"Which. Way. To. Your. Apartment?" He sounded as though he was biting the words off.

"Oh." She glanced around the hallway as if seeing it for the first time. Her eyes lit on the stairway. "Up." She looked back at him. "I'm up."

"That makes two of us," he muttered, and, moving as quickly as his rock-hard cock and armful of wriggly female would allow, started up the stairs.

Jane gave a low chuckle and swiped her tongue across his Adam's apple. "You are indeed up," she purred, savoring the salty taste of his skin. She could feel her eyes wanting to cross as he began taking the steps two at a time. The jogging motion was rocking her aching clit right against the back of her own hand, which was still tucked into his fly. She was half tempted to turn her wrist and finish herself off, but she resisted the urge. After the way he'd sent her flying on the dance floor with just a kiss, she couldn't wait to see what he could do with a bed.

Five minutes later she was remembering the old adage, "Be careful what you wish for."

They'd gotten through her front door and to the bedroom without bumping into too many walls, and he'd plopped her with little ceremony into the middle of her bed. She'd been expecting him to follow her down and gobble her up like Little Red Riding Hood, so to say that she'd been surprised when he just stood there was a bit of an understatement.

Jane cleared her throat. "Have you changed your mind?"

Ian shook his head slowly, looking down at her from the side of the bed. She'd fallen back onto her elbows when he dropped her, and now she realized that the position thrust her breasts into sharp relief. Which was fine when he was all over her, but now that it seemed his blood had cooled it left her feeling a tad vulnerable.

"No."

"Well, then the condoms are in the nightstand."

"I haven't changed my mind," he said slowly, and he came down on one knee, bracing his hands on either side of her head and bearing her back into the pillows. He gathered her hands in his, bringing them together above her head and stretching them toward the headboard. "I just think a little change of pace is in order."

Jane gasped at the sensation as he dropped his head to nuzzle the side of her neck. "What do you mean?"

Ian stroked his tongue against the pulse in her neck, and she felt his lips curve into a smile as she shuddered in reaction. "What I mean," he rumbled into her ear, "is I have a plan for you. But in order for it to work, you have to trust me." He picked his head up to look into her eyes. "Can you do that for me?"

She stared up at him, her brain struggling to process what he'd said. "Trust you?" she rasped. "Trust you how?"

"Trust me not to hurt you. Trust me to give you pleasure." He lowered his forehead to rest on hers. "Trust me to control you."

She swallowed heavily, watching his eyes carefully. She saw nothing but earnest desire in his emerald gaze. "What if you do something that I don't like?"

He kept his gaze steady on hers. "Then you'll tell me to stop, and I will."

"Just like that?"

"Just like that." He continued to watch her, waiting. His hands continued to hold hers pinned to the bed, but his grip was light, and she knew if she tugged away, he'd let her go.

He waited patiently while she wrestled with herself. She knew her every thought, her every doubt, would be written all over her face. She never could play poker, especially when it came to relationships. She knew he could read the indecision warring with the longing, and that he could easily tip the scales in his favor. But he simply waited, holding her down, for her to decide.

And the fact she knew he'd respect any choice she made gave her the courage to make the one she wanted.

Jane licked her lips. "Okay."

He didn't move, his expression didn't change, not even the slightest bit. "Okay, what?"

She gave a tiny half shrug within the cage of his arms. "Okay, you can go ahead with your plan."

Ian's mouth remained unsmiling, his gaze steady and intense. "Jane, I need you to tell me that you're going to trust me. I don't want there to be any misunderstandings between us."

Jane hitched in an unsteady breath. "You'll stop if I say to, right?" At his solemn nod, she let the breath hiss back out of her lungs. "Okay. I trust you."

He smiled then, a slow, easy expression that made his eyes light up and softened the hard planes of his face. "Good girl," he murmured. He swooped down, captured her mouth in a hard kiss. She moaned, arching up into his body, then blinked in surprise when he sprang up as though he'd been lifted straight off her.

His face loomed over hers just long enough for him to say "Don't move," then he was gone again, heading into the adjoining bath. She turned her head to watch him walk—Christ, what an ass. Keeping that tush in focus and that thought in her head was helping to settle the butterflies that had shown up the minute she'd promised to trust him.

His very fine butt disappeared into the bathroom. The light clicked on, and she heard him rummaging around. She frowned. What was in the bathroom that he needed? Her mind spun with possibilities, and the butterflies in her belly turned to frogs and nearly had her hopping out of bed.

Before she could make a break for it, he was back. He strode past the bed and over to her chest of drawers. He dug around the top drawer for a second, and then he was looming over her again, grinning. "Going somewhere?" He waggled his eyebrows Groucho Marx style.

Jane scowled, irritated at being so easily read. "No."

If anything, his grin got bigger. "Liar."

She rolled her eyes. "Okay, so I was considering making a break for it." She turned her gaze to the coverlet and watched her fingers worry a loose thread.

There was suppressed laughter in his voice. "Baby, it's your apartment."

"I know that." She tugged firmly at the thread and watched an appliquéd flower unravel.

"Jane. Look at me." She kept her eyes firmly down, winding the growing length of thread around her fingertip. She felt the mattress give as he sat on the edge of the bed, and kept her gaze resolutely on her own hand. "Jane." He gripped her chin, forcing her face up to his. She reluctantly met his serious gaze with her wary one.

"Do you want me?"

She swallowed. "Yes."

"Okay, so what's changed in the last ten minutes?"

"Well," Jane shrugged. "The whole 'trust me' thing's got me kinda spooked."

His fingers gentled on her skin and his voice softened. "What about it is worrying you? Are you afraid that I won't stop when you ask me to?"

She shook her head. "No, that's not it." And it wasn't. She somehow knew that if she asked him to stop, he would, no matter the consequences to himself.

"Then what is it?"

She sighed before drawing in a deep breath. "I just don't trust very easily, that's all. It's a little new for me."

"Ah," Ian relaxed, that easy grin stealing back over his face. "You've had easy and it hasn't been that great, remember?" He leaned in, his mouth a breath away from hers. "Maybe a challenge is just what you need. Unless," he gave a little shrug, his mouth brushing hers ever so slightly with the motion, "you're too scared."

Jane narrowed her eyes, ignoring the little flares of heat that the brush of his lips had ignited. She knew, on an intellectual level, that he was deliberately baiting her with that bit about being too scared. It didn't matter—she was pretty much hardwired to pick up the gauntlet. She raised one eyebrow in a look she knew had reduced countless other men into stammering idiots. "I'm not too scared. I can handle anything you can dish out."

Ian just grinned wider, his eyes glowing with approval. "Good. Then how does this dress come off?"

Chapter Five

Jane reached for the zipper tucked into the side seam, but his fingers stayed hers and worked the fastening free himself. He scooched the hem up her thighs, up over her hips and at his quiet murmur, she raised her arms so he could tug it all the way over her head. He leaned down to the footboard, draping the delicate fabric over the bench at the foot of the bed, then turned back to her.

She'd never felt as turned on in the whole of her life as when he looked at her, laying there nearly naked. Propped up on her elbows as she was, her breasts were thrust forward, and her heaving breath was causing a little bounce that, if the heat in his gaze was anything to go by, he thoroughly approved of. He took in her bare breasts, the slight curve of her belly, the flare of her hips bisected by the strings of her thong. He traced one finger over the elasticized lace holding her stocking up at her thigh, and she shivered at the slight caress.

He looked back at her face, a satisfied smile curving his mouth at the need he saw there. He swooped in for a quick kiss, a flash of teeth and tongue that sent her senses reeling, and then he was standing again. She felt him draw her right hand over her head, towards the post of the bed, but she couldn't manage to focus on what he was doing. God, her body felt like it was on fire, and they hadn't even gotten to the heavy petting! That orgasm in the club had barely taken the edge off, and now her body was screaming with the need for more.

Through the haze of her vision, she watched him circle the bed to her left side. He drew her other hand towards the bedpost, and she watched in a kind of appalled fascination as he took one of her silk stockings, the ones that cost a small fortune at the priciest boutique in town, and used it to bind her wrist to the post. She started to extend her other hand to reach out and stop him, only to come up short when she couldn't move it. Her head swiveled around on the pillow, and blinked numbly at the sight of her right wrist wrapped in expensive lingerie, latched to the bedpost.

She turned her head back to find him finished with his task, and she opened her mouth to blast him for ruining a brand new pair of very expensive stockings. Her mouth went dry and the words slipped quietly away into oblivion when she saw him reach for the buttons on his shirt. He began stripping quickly and efficiently, a man in a serious hurry to be naked, but the speed and lack of pageantry of the act did nothing to detract from the sheer virility and beauty of the man performing it.

Good golly, Miss Molly. Jane swallowed heavily as she felt her heart begin a slow, heavy beat in her breast. He was just so…everything she'd ever fantasized about in the dark.

The simple white button-down shirt gave way to a chest liberally sprinkled with ebony hair. Not the "rug of luuuv" type that only reminded her of her mother's fake mink coat, but a subtle, almost delicate fan across the breastbone, tapering into a silky line that delineated six-pack abs to disappear beneath the button fly of his jeans. Jane was entertaining thoughts of tracing that gorgeous little happy trail with her tongue when he distracted her. He pulled the shirt completely free from his waistband and peeled it completely off, and she got her first real look at his shoulders.

The part of her brain that had continued to function up until that point simply shut down at the sight of those shoulders. They were broad and tanned, with a layer of muscle that rippled when he shed the shirt and tossed it across the room. His collarbones stood in sharp relief against the heavy muscle of his torso and flowed into the perfection of his shoulders in a way that made her mouth water and her palms itch. She tried to lift her hands, just to glide them over that glorious combination of bone and muscle. The resistance of the silk stockings binding her hands brought her back to reality with a thump.

She blinked, her eyes snapping back to his face, to find him staring at her. An indulgent, amused smile tipped the corners of his mouth, his hands resting on the waistband of his jeans. The top two buttons were still undone, and the shadow of what was behind the remaining three was driving her crazy. "You still with me, darlin'? Thought I'd lost you there for a minute."

Jane gulped air into starving lungs. "Oh, I'm still here." She swallowed, her eyes now riveted to the long, tapered fingers resting on his fly. She nodded in his direction. "Do you plan to leave those on?"

The smile grew to a full-fledged grin. "Oh, they're coming off. I was just waiting to make sure you were paying attention." He flicked a finger, and the placket opened a little more. He raised one eyebrow. "You paying attention?"

Jane nodded and struggled for something witty and sophisticated to say. Something that would have him peeling out of worn denim in record time and pouncing on her like Yogi on a picnic basket. What came out was, "Yuh-huh."

"Good." The fingers moved again, and buttons began to give way. Flick—pop. Flick—pop. Flick—pop. Jane watched, riveted, as each button slid free, and then he was shoving the jeans off his hips and down his legs and kicking them across the room, and she really couldn't breathe because the bottom half of him was even better than the top half.

He didn't give her a lot of time to take in the sights. One quick dip into her nightstand drawer for a condom and he was looming over her again. He dropped the little foil packet between her breasts and braced his elbows on either side of her head, then set his mouth to hers.

Jane moaned at the wet heat of his tongue sliding across her lips and past her teeth, her hips automatically arching into his. The sound of arousal turned into one of frustration as he held himself away from her, denying her the contact that she craved. The frustration was only intensified as she tried to wrap her arms around his neck and was brought up short once again by the bindings at her wrist.

She wrenched her mouth away from his and tried to catch her breath. "Untie me."

He slid his mouth across her check, under her jaw and nipped at her ear. "Why?"

She arched up, trying to bring her pelvis into contact with all that delicious hard flesh, and whimpered in frustration when his hands caught her hips and pressed them back into the mattress. "Because," she wailed, "this is no good. I can't touch you!"

His tongue flicked out over her earlobe, then dipped briefly into her ear, making her purr and shiver in reaction. "But I can touch you," he breathed.

She groaned at the wash of warm air over her sensitized skin. "But you're not touching me enough!"

Ian chuckled, the sound vibrating against the skin of her neck. "Did anyone ever tell you," he dragged his tongue in one slow swipe across the pulse pounding in the base of her neck and caused the breath to wheeze out of her throat, "that patience is a virtue?"

Her eyes popped wide as his teeth closed in a stinging nip on the flesh of her shoulder, then drifted shut when he soothed the tiny hurt with a swipe of his tongue. "It may be a virtue," she managed thickly, "but it's never been one of mine."

"Well, then how about we get this show on the road?"

Jane had approximately two seconds to process that statement, then her brain ceased to function as he began to devour her. It seemed that his hands, his mouth, were suddenly everywhere. He pushed her ample breasts together with his hands, kneading them roughly. The firm touch sent heat and moisture flooding to her pussy, and she was sure her eyes rolled all the way back into her head when that glorious mouth latched onto one nipple and suckled strongly.

Her hips arched hard off the bed, straining to get close, but his hands immediately left her breasts to clamp back over them and hold her down, and she dimly heard the wild, keening noises coming out of her own throat. She pushed hard against his hands, the restless heat building inside her aching to get out, but he held her easily. He nipped sharply at her nipple, and the shock of that stinging caress wound the tension and lust inside her even tighter, until she was moving restlessly under his hands, heaving, straining for release.

The torture of his lips at her nipple, his hands biting into her hips, had her head tossing on the pillow and sobs breaking out of her throat. She tried to scissor her legs around Ian's hips in a desperate move to get some friction where she needed it most, but quick as lightning he pinned her legs with his. Instead of cooling her heated blood, the added sensation of restraint, of being controlled, sent her spiraling into orgasm with a scream.

When the fireworks in her head faded and she regained her sense of sight, she forced her eyes open to find him staring down at her with a mixture of tenderness, awe and sheer lust.

"What?" she managed through parched lips.

He shook his head, amazed. "You really liked that, didn't you?"

Jane managed a shaky grin. "What was your first clue?"

Ian grinned back. "Oh, I don't know. Maybe the fact that you shook so hard I had to let go or bite down to hang on. And considering where I was at the time," he flicked her nipple, still damp from his mouth, with a fingertip, "I figured letting go was the wise choice."

Jane chuckled and tried to ignore the little zing that his touch sent flying through her already overloaded system. "Thanks for that. I would've missed it if you'd bitten it off."

"Don't mention it." He shifted slightly above her, propping his elbows on either side of her head so that he leaned in close. "You recovered yet?"

Jane felt her pussy clench involuntarily at the look in his eyes. "Getting there."

"Good." He shifted his lower body, and she felt him settle his legs on either side of hers, his cock prodding her belly. It felt like a brand—hot and pulsing with eager life—and she felt her cunt begin to flood in earnest at the idea of holding that glorious thing inside her body.

She saw his eyes go sharp, his nostrils flare, and she knew that he was picking up the signs of her renewed arousal. Unsure if she should be relived or worried that he was so tuned into her, she licked her lips, tugging restlessly at her bonds.

His eyes followed the movement, and he frowned. "Are your arms okay?"

Jane smiled at him. The fact that he thought to ask about her comfort when he'd had no orgasms to her two made her slightly more relaxed with her submissive position. "They're fine."

He smiled back. "Excellent. Then I think we'll leave them that way for a little bit longer."

Jane arched a brow. "Really? While we do what, exactly?"

His gaze took on a decidedly predatory gleam. He moved his hand into her line of vision, and when she focused she saw that he held the condom that he'd placed on her chest earlier. It had fallen to the bed, and now he ripped it open with his teeth.

Her breath caught in her throat as he levered himself off her to rest on his heels, his knees bracketing her hips and his legs holding hers closed. Automatically she looked to his groin, and felt her eyes go huge and her breathing stop. God, he looked delicious—and huge—she was way off with that estimate of seven to eight. If she'd had any doubts about how much he wanted her, one look at the engorged, throbbing cock currently resting on her belly would've put them to rest in a big hurry.

He was so hard he throbbed, the plum-colored head bobbing gently. She suddenly wished she wasn't tied, because the urge to taste him was nearly overwhelming. While she watched, he seemed to grow even harder, thickening even further until she began to worry that he'd split her open. She watched him roll on the condom, following the movement of his hands as they trailed down to the root. She could see his balls underneath, drawn high and tight underneath the rigid stalk of his cock, and knew her waiting time was just about over.

She blinked, startled, and latched onto the stockings binding her hands for balance as he slipped his hands under her knees, shifted himself around a bit, and suddenly her panties were on the floor, her ankles were on his shoulders and he was looming over her once again.

She gulped in a breath and offered up a quick prayer of thanksgiving that he was finally getting around to it. Then she ceased to think or breathe as she felt him reach between her splayed legs, slipping one finger into the core of her. She heard him give a grunt of satisfaction at the slick liquid he found there, and she shuddered as the roughness of his callused finger abraded her cunt, made swollen and sensitive by her recent climax.

Ian, who had been staring fascinated at the pink, damp flesh of her pussy, now fixed that emerald gaze on her. He removed his finger, giving her clit an upward flick as he went, smiling at the ragged groan and convulsive twitch of her limbs. Through slitted eyes she watched him lean further over her, forcing her knees high, opening her further for his invasion.

He gripped the base of his latex-covered cock in one hand and slid the head gently around her swollen cunt. He kept his eyes on her expressive face as he fitted the broad head to her opening, nudging it just inside.

Her muscles instinctively clamped down, trying to draw him further inside, and the convulsive movement had him slipping fractionally deeper before he stopped with a shiver.

Jane groaned and tried to arch up, desperate to capture more of that hard flesh within her body. But her position left her very little leverage, and she only succeeded in frustrating herself further when he pulled away.

"God!" She sobbed, her head tossing on the pillow. "What are you waiting for?"

"Look at me." She ignored the command, continuing to strain upwards and sob out in need.

"Jane! Look at me!" The crack of his voice caught her attention, and her eyes popped open to find him staring down at her, eyes glittering

"What?" she panted, chest heaving with the effort of drawing breath.

"I want to watch you," he growled, "when I do this." And with that, his hips coiled and he drove his full length into her with one thrust.

Jane's back arched and her breath escaped in a strangled scream. He didn't give her any time to recover from the shock of him fully inside her, stretching her, but immediately set a hard, driving rhythm that had the headboard thumping against the wall and the breath exploding out of her lungs on a thin cry with every thrust. And through it all, he held her gaze, his eyes drilling into hers.

The tension coiled tight in her belly, each thrust pulling her further and further towards the edge of madness. Her eyes remained locked on his, unable to look away, and she saw his eyes go impossibly darker, his face pull tight as he put even more force behind his driving hips.

He gathered her body up in his arms, sliding them under her back to grip her shoulders from underneath. The position forced her legs even higher, and she gave a thin scream as the new angle put him right at the mouth of her womb. He leaned down even further, pressing her knees to her shoulders, rubbing her over sensitized nipples with the hair on his chest. He nipped her lower lip sharply, never taking his eyes off her face and said in that dark, magic voice, "Come."

At that, all the tension gathering inside her suddenly reached flashpoint, and with a keening cry, she exploded. Her head went back in a hard arch, her eyes starring blindly at the headboard, little lights exploding like flashbulbs in her vision. The shuddering convulsions went on and on, seemingly endless. She dimly heard his answering shout, felt his fingers bite into her shoulders as he stiffened and hardened even further inside her. His orgasm seemed to kick hers into high gear, setting off a fresh round of spasms so strong she felt her entire pelvis clench down.

After what could have been hours or minutes—it was hard to tell time when none of her brain cells were functioning—Jane opened her eyes. She laid there, her fingers flexing on the stockings holding her to the bed, her knees almost next to her ears and struggled to catch her breath. Her heart was racing like Secretariat and she had little spots dancing in front of her eyes, like someone had just taken a close-up photo with a real bright flash.

She could feel Ian as a dead weight pressing her into the mattress, but she was too relaxed to care much. His face was turned into her neck, and she could feel the stubble on his jaw abrading her skin. She thought absently about whisker burn, but couldn't bring herself be overly concerned about it.

She sighed heavily, more content and satisfied than she'd been in months, and he stirred.

Ian levered himself up on his elbows, pulling his face out of the curve of her neck to look down at her with lazy satisfaction. "How's it going?" he rumbled.

She felt her lips curve into a slightly sappy, dreamy smile. "Oh, it's going just peachy." She managed to summon the energy to lift one brow and tugged at her bound hands. "But I think my hands are starting to go numb. Mind untying me?"

He grinned, a somewhat evil glint in his gaze. "Oh, I wouldn't want your hands to go numb." He shifted his weight to one side and began working the knots free with one hand. "But don't get any ideas about going anywhere. I'm not done with you yet."

Jane could only stare up at him, mute with the sudden onslaught of renewed lust. She could feel him, hard inside her despite his recent climax, and she felt her pussy clench in response. She managed to find her voice as he finished untying her second hand. "Oh. Well, if you insist..."

"Oh, I do." He massaged her wrists slightly, rubbing circulation back into her limbs. He kept his eyes on her face. "How about a shower?"

Jane swallowed her disappointment. "Oh, sure. Go ahead, there are fresh towels in the cabinet next to the sink."

"Good." He lifted himself off her, sliding free of her clasping, clinging sex and setting off aftershocks with the delicious friction. He gripped her hands, and automatically she allowed him to pull her to her feet to stand beside the bed, blinking up at him in bemused lust. Then she squealed, startled, when he bent down and lifted her into a fireman's carry over his shoulder and strode towards the bathroom.

"What're you doing?" she squawked.

"Taking a shower. You can wash my back." He smacked her ass, and she jumped, rubbing her butt against the side of his face. He turned and nipped at the reddening cheek.

Oh, boy, she thought as she bounced against his back on the way to the bathroom. She just might be in trouble.

* * * * *

Jane was not a person who woke easily. She did it in stages, grumbling and grousing, resisting consciousness with the same intensity that most women used for a half-off sale at

Neiman's, until the process of trying to go back to sleep finally woke her up.

Having a man in her bed didn't make much of a difference in that routine. So when the alarm buzzed the following morning, she swung out with a fist, aiming as always for the snooze bar and twelve more minutes of precious oblivion. She felt her fist connect with something, but the DJ kept talking. She frowned and struck out again. And jackknifed straight up in bed when she heard, "Are you trying to tell me something?"

"God!" She panted, staring at him with wide eyes. "You scared the shit out of me!"

"Sorry," he grinned, scruffy and amused and gorgeous in the morning light. "But you hit me, so I figure we're even."

"Eek." Jane winced. "I'm really sorry about that. I was aiming for the alarm."

"So I gathered." He reached out and flicked the alarm off himself, then his arms extended up toward the headboard, muscle and sinew moving over bone and drawing her eye as he stretched. Her eye was drawn and caught by the sheet draped over his rangy form. It rested low across his abdomen. She could just see the ridges of his hipbones above the concealing cloth, and the shadow of his penis underneath it. As she watched, the sheet began to twitch and move as the flesh underneath woke up. Her eyes flew to his to find him watching her, all traces of amusement gone from his face, replaced by hard and urgent lust.

She goggled. "Again? What're you mainlining Viagra while I'm not looking?"

That startled a half laugh out of him. "No need to, honey. This," he gestured to his lap, "is a natural high." He shrugged. "Although I will say that after last night, I'm a little surprised myself."

Frankly, Jane was stunned that either of them was capable of movement this morning. They'd had each other no fewer than four times in the night. By the end, the orgasms had just been rolling together, one after the other, until it was impossible to tell where the endings and beginnings were. Finally, at four a.m., they'd collapsed, exhausted and satiated, in a sweaty tangled heap in the middle of the bed.

Ian moved suddenly, snaking out an arm and locking it around her waist. He tugged, and caught off balance, she tumbled toward him, landing draped over his chest. She planted her hands instinctively for balance as she fell, her hands landing on his pectoral muscles.

The way she landed brought her face within inches of his, her lips a mere pucker away. And despite the excesses of the night, she felt her blood quicken at the feel of him under her.

He slid one hard palm in a slow caress over her bare ass, holding her gaze as he slipped one finger between her legs. She gasped as he dipped his finger into the damp flesh of her pussy. She was tender and swollen from the mad frenzy of lust they'd indulged in during the night, and his rough finger felt huge.

Ian stroked carefully, watching her face as she broke out in shivers. "Are you too sore?" he murmured, lust deepening his voice to a dark rumble.

Jane gasped as the first finger was joined by a second, and she struggled to keep his face in focus. "I'm a little tender." Her eyes all but crossed as he scissored his fingers inside her, stretching her tender flesh wide. "But I'm game," she managed.

She caught the flash of his grin through the haze of her vision. "Good," he rumbled. He slid his fingers out of her slowly, watching her face carefully for signs of genuine discomfort. She moaned and her flesh clamped down on his withdrawing fingers, her body grasping to keep him in place. His face hardened with lust, and he slid her up the few inches necessary to bring her mouth to his.

She moaned into his mouth, sucking frantically on his tongue as her pussy tried to suck his fingers back into its heated depths. Her hips surged in helpless need, seeking firmer, deeper contact. His hands left her briefly, and she felt him fumble a condom on. She gave a brief prayer of thanksgiving that at least one of them was thinking clearly, then gasped, still clinging to his mouth, as he shifted his hands to her hips, lifted her slightly and plunged firmly inside her.

Jane cried out, breaking the kiss and arching her back. Her legs automatically slid to bracket his hips, and she pushed herself up with her hands on his chest, sliding even more firmly onto the erection filling her.

She opened her eyes slightly, looking down into Ian's. Her pussy clenched involuntarily around his invading cock, and she watched his eyes close as he groaned at the sensation. She felt a sense of power fill her at the sight of his lust. Her lips curved into a smile as old as Eve, and she began to move.

Slowly, she slid up his cock, until only the very head was still lodged in her cunt. Then back down, so that every inch of him was held in the tight clasp of her body and his balls nestled in the curve of her ass. Then slowly up again, and back down. She kept the pace slow, the rhythm languid, so that she could feel every delicious inch. Her body began to respond. Tissues swollen from the night's activities thickened and moistened with renewed arousal, and her pace began to quicken as her blood heated.

She kept her eyes on his face, watching the need darken his eyes and tighten his features. She brought her hands up to cup her own flesh, plucking at the hardening nipples, and felt him twitch and surge inside her even as he moaned at the sight. Keeping her eyes on him, she brought one hand to her mouth. She licked the tip of her index finger then trailed it down the center of her body to the moist, bare cleft that clung to him so tenaciously. His eyes followed the travels of that finger as she brought it to her clit and teased them both by flicking the hard little nub gently.

They both gasped as her pussy spasmed in reaction, and suddenly Jane could feel her orgasm hovering just beyond reach. She knew that a few hard strokes of her clit would finish it, but she didn't want to come that fast. She wanted to draw it out. So she kept her touch light and teasing, and her eyes on his, gauging his reactions.

She began riding him faster, her breath coming in pants as she fought to keep her eyes open and on his. She watched his eyes half-close, his chest heave with the effort to draw breath. Her fingers began to move faster on her clit, and she gave a whimpering little cry as her orgasm bore down on her.

Quick as a snake, his right hand released its bruising grip on her hip and snatched her hand away from her clit, holding it high. Her eyes flew open in shock, and instinctively moved her other hand to take its place. Before she could move two inches, he had it in his grip, holding her hands wide, away from her torso in an inexorable hold.

Jane cried out in frustration, tugging fruitlessly at her hands. She stared down at him in shock and confusion. "Ian," she moaned. "I want to come."

"Not yet," he growled. His hips surged, driving high into her and lifting her knees off the bed so that she was fully impaled on his cock. Her head went back on a gasp, and her hips surged frantically.

"Ian," she sobbed, hips pumping frantically. "Please!"

Her eyes nearly crossed as he suddenly sat upright on the bed, wrapping his arms around her back, taking her hands with him so that he held them pinned at the small of her back. He gathered her as close as possible, crushing her breasts to his chest, and in one quick, pussy-jarring move slid his legs underneath him so that he was kneeling on the bed. He began thrusting again, short, heavy digs of his cock that tormented her sensitized sheath.

She moaned, agonized, as she felt the coil of tension in her pelvis wind even tighter, pushing her inexorably closer to orgasm. "Ian," she whimpered, her body battered by the relentless pounding of his hips. She was so wet that she could hear her pussy trying to suck him back in with each thrust. She strained toward him, arching her back in the effort to get closer so that her hair brushed over his hands where they grasped hers at the small of her back.

In a flash, he grasped the tangled locks and held on, holding her neck in its dramatic arch. The position thrust her breasts forward, the motion of their bodies bouncing them almost right in front of Ian's face. He took immediate advantage, clamping his mouth onto one pouting nipple and suckling hard.

Jane began sobbing uncontrollably. Between the heavy pounding of his cock in her cunt, his mouth at her breast and the strangely erotic sensation of her hair caught in his hands, she was right on the edge. She could almost *taste* the orgasm, it was so close, but still she couldn't seem to go over.

She felt him growl around her nipple, the vibration kicking her already overloaded system into an even higher gear. "Ian," she cried out, her voice cracking.

She felt him lick a path from her nipple to the base of her throat, where she knew her pulse pounded like a jackrabbit. "Tell me what you want, Jane." His voice was so low, so guttural, that it was almost without sound, and she had to strain to understand him. "Tell me, and I'll let you."

She sobbed, fighting to find the words. He bit lightly at her collarbone, and she shuddered from the added stimulation. "Tell me, Jane."

Jane brought her scattered senses into focus and fought to speak. "I want to come," she managed. "Please, let me come!"

Ian dragged his tongue up to her ear, flicked the lobe, and said, "Come," in a growl, just before he set his teeth to her neck and bit down—hard.

Jane's eyes few wide at the command, the sudden sensation of his teeth in her skin, and then rolled back into her head as her body went supernova. Her clit exploded, and sparks went off in her vision as she felt her womb clamp down in hard, rhythmic spasms. She felt him suddenly grow bigger and harder inside her, stretching her impossibly wide and setting off a fresh round of spasms before the first had even fully subsided.

She heard his muffled shout of satisfaction as his teeth still sunk into her neck, and savored the feel of him pulsing inside her. As completely focused as she was, the sound of her bedroom door opening barely registered. But Lacey's cheerful voice brought her crashing back to earth.

"Hey girl—you awake? I brought bagels..." Jane's eyes popped wide-open. Even though her back was to the door, her head was still bent almost completely back by Ian's grip on her hair. So she had a perfect upside-down view of Lacey, standing in the doorway, bakery bag in one hand and her jaw on the floor.

Even as she was struggling to focus enough to form words, Lacey was scrambling, juggling the bakery bag and fumbling for the doorknob. "Umm...I'll just take these to the kitchen." She waved the bag in the air like a banner. "You just..."She gestured wildly with the bag, hitting herself in the face, "take your time." Rubbing her nose, she pulled the door closed behind her, and Jane could hear her footsteps fade down the hall.

Ian released his death grip on her hair and hands, easing her back to lie on the bed, her head nearly resting on the footboard. He brushed her hair back from her face, grinning into her stunned expression. "Well," he rumbled, "do you think she brought enough bagels for me, too?"

Chapter Six

Fifteen minutes later, Jane tightened the sash on her robe and headed down the hall towards the kitchen. Ian was using the shower, and considering how much time men usually spent on personal grooming, she figured she had ten minutes, maybe fifteen at the outside, to talk to Lacey before he joined them.

She walked into the kitchen, her features schooled into a mask of polite indifference, to find Lacey sitting at the small dinette table by the window. She'd made coffee, and was calmly sipping the steaming brew from a mug that proclaimed "Do I Look Like a Fucking Morning Person to You?" and nibbling on a poppy seed bagel spread thick with cream cheese. She turned her head to look at Jane, her face devoid of expression.

Jane walked to the table and began rummaging in the bakery bag. "Did you get any blueberry?" she asked, keeping her head down and allowing her hair to curtain her face.

"Should be some in there." Lacey took a bite of bagel, a small sip of coffee.

"Great," Jane enthused, tugging the bagel from the bottom of the bag and sitting down across from Lacey. She tore off a hunk, dipped in into the container of cream cheese on the table between them and popped it into her mouth.

Lacey set down her cup, carefully slid her bagel to the side. Jane finished chewing, and folded her hands on the table in front of her.

Their eyes met across the table and held for a long moment. "So," Lacey finally said, sounding for all the world like she was making a dentist appointment. "What's new with you?"

The question hung in the air while they stared at each other, pokerfaced. Then Lacey's left eyebrow twitched. Jane's nose wiggled. A giggle escaped Lacey's lips, and she quickly choked it back and folded her lips as if to contain any further outbursts. Jane quickly turned the chuckle tickling her throat into a cough.

They continued to stare at each other, gamely trying to contain themselves, for about another fifteen seconds. Then Jane giggled, snorting a little as she tried to contain it. Lacey giggled back, quickly putting her hand over her mouth to stifle the sound. Jane's shoulders started to shake, and suddenly they were laughing out loud.

Jane gasped for air, howling with mirth and hanging onto the edge of the table to keep herself upright in her seat. "Oh Jesus, Lace!" she wheezed. "If you could have seen the look on your face when you walked into that room!"

Lacey screamed with laughter, sliding out of the chair and hitting the floor with a thump. "Oh my God, I KNOW!" She clutched her stomach and fell over to her back, laughing so hard she could hardly speak. "I mean, I couldn't *move,* I was just so *stunned*!"

Jane laughed so hard she saw spots in front of her eyes. She let go of the table to clutch her aching sides, and slid to the floor. She rolled when she hit the tile so she ended up on her back, looking up through the glass tabletop of her dinette set.

"How do you think I felt?" she managed to squeak out between guffaws. "I mean, I was in the middle of *coming* when you walked in! Jaysus, woman—don't you knock?"

Lacey was doubled over with fresh spasms of laughter. "I didn't…I didn't" she gasped, trying to speak through the giggles. "I didn't think you'd still be *doing it*!" she finally shouted, and sent them both into fresh gales of laughter.

Jane had herself pretty much under control when she opened her eyes and let out a short, shrill scream. Lying on her back as she was, she was looking straight up through the tabletop, into Ian's face as he peered at her through the glass. He'd gotten dressed, though his shirt was left unbuttoned and his hair was still damp from the shower.

"Did you have whiskey instead of coffee?" he queried, and Jane began chuckling anew. Lacey was still rolling back and forth on the floor, clutching her sides and howling, and showing no sign of slowing down.

Jane struggled to get herself under control, scooting out from under the table on her backside. Ian reached down with two hands and hauled her up by her shoulders, and she leaned against him weakly, her body still racked with giggles. "Sorry," she gasped, gulping air into her aching lungs. "Private joke."

He grinned, one eyebrow lifting. "Private, indeed," he said, and held her up when she began giggling all over again.

By the time she'd managed to stop laughing, Lacey had come out from under the table and was sitting in her chair again, drinking coffee and only emitting the occasional muffled snort. Jane wiped her eyes, pushing away from Ian's supporting hold to go get two more coffee mugs from the cabinet.

"Lacey, this is Ian," she said over her shoulder. "Ian, my best friend and downstairs neighbor, Lacey Johnson."

Lacey grinned at him over her coffee cup. "Meetcha," she chortled.

Ian grinned back at her and took a seat at the table. "Likewise." He grabbed a cinnamon raisin bagel from the bag at his elbow and snagged the cream cheese. "I generally like to know the names of the women who see me having sex."

Jane set the coffee cups down on the table with a thunk. "Don't make me laugh again, my ribs hurt as it is." She grabbed the coffeepot from the counter and poured two cups. She looked at Ian. "Do you want cream or sugar?"

He shook his head. "Black is fine." He picked up the cup, which had "PMS is a Valid Defense" emblazoned on it, and took a sip. "Mmmm, that's good." He snagged another bite of bagel, and then gestured to her with his cup. "What're you doing the rest of today?"

Jane blinked, a little startled by the question. "Ahh—I need to go into work for a little bit, maybe hit the gym." She shrugged. "Housecleaning, errands. Typical Saturday stuff. Why?"

He took another sip of coffee, holding her gaze. "Have lunch with me."

She felt the butterflies that had started up in her stomach at his question morph into leaping frogs. "I don't really know if I'll have time. It's already after nine."

He didn't look away, didn't so much as blink. "It'll be a late lunch. Two o'clock." He set down his cup and began buttoning his shirt. "You can clean house afterwards." That one eyebrow made the climb towards his hairline. "Right?"

She took a breath, tried to let it out slowly and smoothly, and sound as casual as possible when she felt anything but. "Okay. Where?"

He didn't smile, but his eyes took on a satisfied gleam. "I'll pick you up. Here or at work?"

Jane's brain did some fast calculations. "Umm, work, I think."

"Okay," he said. He waited a beat then said, "Where is work?"

"Oh!" She gave a little laugh that didn't quite feel natural. "I, ah, work at Denning Books, over on Michigan." She shrugged, clearing her throat. "I actually own it."

"Really?" He grinned, delighted. "It's one of my favorite spots. I have lunch in your café at least twice a week."

Jane grinned back at him, froggy stomach forgotten. She was ridiculously pleased that he knew of her business.

Ian stood, taking a last gulp of coffee and finished buttoning his shirt. He held out a hand. "Walk me to the door."

The frogs came back at the command in his voice, but she saw her hand extend to be enfolded in his. He took his eyes off her to glance at Lacey. He grinned. "Lacey, it was a pleasure to meet you."

Lacey chuckled, eyes dancing. "Oh believe me, the pleasure was all mine."

Ian laughed in response then tugged Jane toward the living room. He stopped at the front door, running his hands from her shoulders to elbows and back again in a soothing caress. "So, I'll come by the store at two?"

Jane nodded, her throat suddenly too tight to speak.

"You okay?" he asked, searching her face.

"Yes, I'm fine," she managed with what she knew was a nervous twitter and a less than steady smile.

He cupped her face in his hands, forcing her eyes up to meet his. "Trust me, remember? I won't hurt you."

She continued to smile, although a shiver ran through her. "Of course you won't, don't be silly. I'll see you at two."

He searched her face for a minute longer, then nodded, apparently satisfied with what he found there. "Okay." He leaned in for a swift, hard kiss then opened the door. He paused, flicked a finger at the point of her chin. "I'm nowhere near done with you, Jane." And with a quick wink, the door closed behind him.

Jane was still staring at the closed door when she heard Lacey speak behind her.

"Girrrrrrrrl," she drew out the word, "you are in trouble with a capital T with that one."

Jane let out a shaky laugh and turned to see her friend leaning against the kitchen doorway. "What're you talking about? I'm not in trouble," she scoffed.

Lacey nodded, lips pursed. "Sure sweetie, you just keep telling yourself that." She pointed. "But that man is different from your usual fare, and I'm telling you that you could fall for this one."

Jane shook her head, walking past Lacey to pick up her coffee cup in both hands. "No, it's just sex. That's all."

"Oh really?" Lacey turned in the doorway to face the kitchen. "Then why does he want to meet you for lunch?"

Jane rolled her eyes. "Honestly, Lace. He just wants to get laid again." She shrugged. "I'll probably sleep with him one more time, then call it off."

"Why?" Lacey demanded. "What I saw of his technique was pretty impressive."

Jane smiled, a cat-snacking-on-canary smile, and Lacey nodded. "See, that smile proves it. So if he's good in bed, handsome as all sin and wants to see you again, why the *hell* would you call it off unless you were worried about maybe falling for this guy?"

Jane set her coffee cup on the counter with a sharp *clack*. "I just don't think we're all that compatible that's all." She turned on the faucet and rinsed her cup, then placed it in the dishwasher. She busied herself wiping the already spotless counters for a few moments, then set the rag aside and turned to Lacey.

"I just think it's better to stay a little detached, that's all. That way, nobody gets hurt. Okay?"

Lacey held up her hands in surrender. "Okay. But when you're ready to admit that he's trouble with a capital T, you know my number."

Jane sighed. "Yes, I do. Now, if you don't mind, I need to get to the gym if I'm going to get any work done at the store before Ian picks me up for lunch." She started down the hall to the bathroom. "I'll see you later?" she called over her shoulder.

"Sure," Lacey responded, heading toward the door. "With a capital T," she muttered under her breath.

"I heard that!" Jane hollered, and slammed the bathroom door.

*****

Ian grinned to himself as he climbed into the Rover and fit the key to the ignition. The well-maintained engine leapt to life on the first crank, despite having spent the night in the elements rather than its space in his garage. He shifted smoothly into gear and headed down the street, kicking up slush as he went. The day was already beginning to turn warm, melting the light dusting of snow that had fallen and formed the night before.

He looked up to the crisp, cloudless sky, considering. If it stayed sunny, he just might try to take Jane to Navy Pier for lunch, maybe a walk along the lake. They'd have to eat inside—nobody was goofy enough to try patio dining in Chicago until at least mid-May—but a walk along the shore might give him some time to get to know her a little, figure out what made her tick.

He wasn't fooling himself—he knew she'd enjoyed his company, knew she'd *loved* the sex—but the momentary look of blind panic in her eyes when he'd suggested lunch was telling. She figured him for a one-night stand. A few hours of hot, sweaty sex, a friendly cup of coffee and a vague promise from him to call her sometime, and he'd be out the door and out of her life. Well, if that's what Ms. Denning was hoping for, she was out of luck. That may be what other men had done, may have been what she'd been looking for when she brought him home, but he had other ideas. He'd had too good a time with her both in bed and out to leave it with a "You were the best, baby".

It wasn't just the sex—though God knows that was hot enough to have him crawling to her on hands and knees for another taste—but he had a feeling that once he got to know her, he would genuinely like who she was. The way she was able to laugh at Lacey catching them going at it like drunken minks showed him that she didn't take herself too seriously. A lot of women would have panicked and been painfully embarrassed. He had no doubt that she was a little embarrassed by it—after all, she'd hustled him into the shower as fast as she could, then gone out to talk to her friend. He'd been tempted to follow, see how she'd handle the situation, but in the end had decided to leave them to it.

So he'd showered faster than he ever had in his life—just hit the high points with the soap and skipped washing his hair altogether—dressed hurriedly and headed out to the kitchen. Finding them on the floor, rolling with laughter, had made him grin with relief that there would be no awkward silences and fumbling explanations to deliver. He chuckled, thinking of the way Jane had screamed out when she'd seen his face on the other side of the glass tabletop.

He liked her friend, too. He gathered from her easy familiarity in Jane's apartment—and key to the front door—that they were close.

He frowned as he stopped for a red light. Jane really had seemed put off by his invitation to lunch, and he wondered at the cause. He was a likeable enough guy, he knew, and women generally weren't eager to show him the door in the morning. Judging by the conversation that he'd overheard in the café, she hadn't been having a very good time in the sack with her previous partners. Thus the whole "opposite" experiment, and her willingness to let him all but devour her before they even got out of the club. And he knew that she'd had a good time last night—he'd lost count of the orgasms she'd had, her body squeezing his cock rhythmically each time and threatening his own tenuous control.

Lost in the memory of the sweet clasp of her velvet pussy, he jumped a foot when a horn blasted rudely from behind him. He glanced up and found that the light had turned while he'd been reliving the best sex of his life. He shifted into gear and accelerated through the intersection, his thoughts once again turning to her obvious reluctance to see him again.

The only thing that he could figure is that he made her nervous. Which, he thought with a satisfied smile, was just fine with him. If he made her nervous, that meant she felt something for him, even if it was just crazed lust. After all, that was a good part of his feelings for her—they hadn't known each other long enough for much more. But what he had seen of her outside the bedroom, he liked. She had humor—he'd seen that firsthand this morning. And she must have a brain—she didn't run one of the most popular bookstores in town on looks. Starting a business took brains, guts and a bit of a gambler's heart. He was banking on her having all three. He'd spent enough time in the café and bookstore of Denning Books in the six months since his move to the city to know that the stock was extensive, the layout comfortable and the marketing clever. And since she didn't strike him as a woman who would bust her ass to build a business only to leave the reputation and future of that business in the hands of others, he'd bet that all of that fell under her control.

Ian hit the remote to raise the door on the garage under his townhome, pulling the Rover smoothly into place. He shut off the engine and climbed from the car, whistling. He gave his other vehicle an affectionate pat on its gleaming fender as he walked by, then stepped through the door into his kitchen.

He moved through the rooms of the house by rote, the rubber soles of his boots a muffled thump on the wooden floors as he made his way to the open stairway leading to the second floor. He took them two at a time, unbuttoning his shirt as he went. He strode through the bedroom without pause, and went directly into the connecting bath. The shower he'd had at Jane's had been more to give her time with Lacey than for personal grooming, and he had a full day ahead. He stripped methodically, his mind focused on his upcoming meeting with Jane. He reached into the large shower stall, flicked on the water, stepping into the stream without waiting for the water to heat.

He ignored the chill as he began to lather the soap, his hands running over his body quickly and efficiently. He washed his hair the same way—with economy of motion and without conscious thought. He was going over possible scenarios for lunch in his head, the routine task of grooming secondary.

He didn't think she'd be open to coming back to his place for lunch, though he would've liked to fix her a private meal. He was actually a fairly accomplished cook, having learned by necessity. Military food was necessary on a mission—when he was stationed stateside he'd forgone the mess hall for meals in his own quarters, and had developed an affinity for creative cooking. But considering her edginess at the thought of a public lunch, that particular scenario would have to wait until he could slip a little further past her defenses. So, Navy Pier was his next choice.

He knew of a seafood place and a family dining type restaurant on the Pier itself—either one of them would be casual enough to put her at ease. They'd be able to talk, but not too intimately, which should help her to relax and let down her guard a little. Then he'd suggest a walk after the meal. It was good for digestion, after all. He didn't think she'd fall for that lame line, but she'd be hard-pressed to find a reason to refuse, so he was fairly certain he could talk her into it.

He cut off the water and reached for a towel, wrapping it around his hips as he stepped out of the stall. Without bothering to dry off completely, he walked back into the bedroom. He dressed quickly in crisp khakis and a cotton T-shirt the color of blackberries, then headed to his home office down the hall.

While most of his home was decorated with an eye for comfort and color, his office was strictly business. The workstation was a sweep of dark wood that took up half the wall and looked out onto the street through a bay window. The computer equipment was state of the art, with various gadgets and gizmos that ensured the highest security for the system that money could buy. In his business, information was power, and he was very good at gathering it and using it to his advantage.

And since he had a few hours before he could put his plan to wear down the defenses of Ms. Jane Denning into effect, he figured the time would be best spent in gathering as much information on her as possible.

He sat at the keyboard, flexed his fingers and logged on.

Chapter Seven

Ian walked into the bookstore at precisely fifteen minutes to two. He figured Jane would be in the café, ready to plead her case for having lunch on her own turf. She was a smart cookie—he'd bet his vintage Shelby GT 500 that she knew the advantage of being the home team. But he was no slouch in the strategy department himself, thanks to Uncle Sam's extensive training program, and he was going to get her on neutral territory. Then shuffle her to his turf as quick as he could.

A quick look around the crowded café yielded no sign of her, and a brief tour of the main area of the store also proved fruitless. He checked his watch—2:01. Time to roust Jane from wherever she was hiding.

He strode up to the information desk and turned his sexiest smile on the college-age blonde in Lisa Lobe glasses manning the counter. "Hi," he rumbled, letting his voice stay low and intimate. "I was hoping you could help me," he glanced pointedly at the brass nametag pinned to her shoulder, "Maggie."

The smile and the voice had the desired effect, as the blonde's eyes went bug-wide behind the narrow glasses and her cheeks flushed. "Umm...can I help you, sir?" Her voice gave a little squeak at the end and if possible, her face turned an even brighter shade of pink.

Ian grinned. "I hope so." He rested one elbow on the counter and leaned in conspiratorially. "I'm looking for someone who works here, but I can't find her." He glanced at his watch. "I was supposed to meet her a few minutes ago, and I'm afraid she might have left." He let the smile turn sheepish. "I'm running a bit late."

If possible, Maggie's eyes went even wider. "Oh, I'm sure she wouldn't leave just because you were a few minutes late!" Ian's grin grew even bigger at the dreamy quality of her voice, and she blushed even harder. She used one finger to push her glasses up onto her nose, straightened in the chair and folded her hands on the desk.

"Umm…if you give me the name of the person you're looking for, I can tell you if she's still here." She made a valiant effort to keep her voice businesslike and professional, like her speech professor was always instructing, but she figured she'd blown it by sighing at the end. But jeez—how often did a guy who looked like *him* smile at *her*?

"That'd be great," he enthused, and turned to lean on the counter with both arms. Her pulse hit aerobic level as she watched those fabulous green eyes crinkle at the corners. She lost herself in the masculine glow for a second, and then shook herself as she realized he was still talking. She tuned back in to hear him say, "…know where Jane Denning is?"

"Oh, Ms. Denning! Sure she's here." Maggie rested her chin on her hand, thinking how cool it was that his hair was long. A lot of guys looked silly with long hair, but he looked great—a little like Jason Patric, from *The Lost Boys*. Her roommate was really into vampire movies—they'd watched that one at least a dozen times since Christmas.

Ian waited a beat, then realized she was done talking. "Do you know where she is?" he prompted.

"Oh!" Maggie sat back up, the blush heating her skin again. She fiddled with the pens in the Muppets pencil holder, looking at him over the rim of her glasses. "She's probably in her office. It's on the second floor." She pointed to the stairs past the café entrance.

"Thanks, Maggie." He winked, gave a little wave and started towards the stairs.

Maggie watched him go, thinking that Ms. Denning must be the luckiest woman on earth.

Ian took the stairs two at a time, found himself in a wide-open space with racks of books and study tables. There were people at most of the tables, with books spread out in front of them and having lively discussions with study partners. It sure beat a library, where silence was a premium and the librarians weren't nearly as cute as the woman in the office at the end of the room.

Her door was open, and she was pacing back and forth. She held the receiver of an old rotary desk phone to her ear, and had the base in her other hand. Whenever she turned, she swept her arm out to the side to flick the cord out of her path. Since her attention was on her conversation, and she hadn't yet noticed his approach, he took the opportunity to study her thoroughly.

She'd dressed for the day in worn jeans and a simple black V-neck sweater that she probably thought made her look sexless and unappealing. Instead, the jeans hugged the supple curves of her hips and ass, while the sweater showcased the slim strength of her shoulders and showed just a teasing hint of cleavage. And since he already knew how she was put together under those clothes, the outfit fell far short of the frumpy image she was probably trying to project. Hell, after last night, he'd probably find sackcloth and ashes appealing on her.

She turned again, swinging the cord in front of her. The movement caused her hair to swing out from her face. She looked amazing—pissed off, but amazing. Her annoyance at whoever was on the other end of the phone had brought a flush to her cheeks and a sparkle to her eyes. Her wide, mobile mouth was set in a grim line, and he wondered at the cause.

He moved closer, into the doorway of her office, and shut out the noise of the study room so he could concentrate on what she was saying.

"Jack, I don't think you're hearing me." Her voice was clipped, cool and sharp as a blade. A far cry from the "do me, Big Daddy" tone of the night before. But they both suited her.

She paused briefly in her pacing, then resumed with an agitated twitch of her hips. "Jack, stop talking. No. STOP. TALKING. Thank you. Now, as I was saying," she blew her hair out of her face. "When I ordered your line of holiday cards, Christmas ornaments and winter-themed gift items, it was with the understanding that they would actually be in the store for the holiday season. Since they arrived just in time for Groundhog Day, I felt perfectly justified in refusing the shipment."

She set the heavy base of the phone on the desk with a thunk. The old-fashioned bells inside it rang slightly with the force of it. "I'm not paying for it. I don't plan on paying for it. And if you try to make me pay for it, you'll only be making my attorney earn his retainer. Now, I have several vendors to speak to this afternoon who are actually interested in getting me the merchandise I order in a timely fashion, and your whiny voice and bitchy attitude are making my head hurt."

Without bothering to say goodbye, she let the handset drop into the cradle from a good twelve inches, the resulting *clang* making her smile in satisfaction.

The smile flew off her face and she let out a short scream when he drawled, "Wrong number?"

"Jesus!" Jane fell back against the corner of the desk, one hand at her throat. "What're you, part ghost?"

He grinned. "Nah. You were just too busy reaming your vendor a new orifice to notice me coming."

She snorted. "Former vendor, you mean. He'll be lucky if I order a pencil from him after this." She straightened, pushing her sleeves to her elbows like a fighter preparing for a bout. She cleared her throat. "So, are you ready to eat?"

"In a minute." Since it didn't look like an invitation to enter would be forthcoming, he pushed off the doorframe and came into the room. He took his time wandering through, making note of the details of her space.

He'd noticed this morning that she liked bright colors. Her apartment was an artist's palate, a hodgepodge of styles and disciplines that somehow managed to meld into an interesting and comfortable space. Her office space was no different.

The walls were painted a brash tomato red, the long windowless wall taken up by black metal shelves that seemed to float on the surface of the wall. The shelves held knickknacks in a rainbow of colors and shapes, and books of various genres and age. The other walls were peppered with framed art and personal photographs. He recognized Lacey in several of them, and chuckled over a shot of the two of them hanging upside-down by their knees from a tree, laughing like loons.

Her desk was made of dark, rough wood and took up one end of the room. It was a cluttered mass of paperwork, manila folders, post-it notes and discarded food wrappers. It made his organized, military-trained soul shudder to think about trying to find anything in that mess.

A divan sat in a corner, some bright green color that he was sure had a fancy designer name, with comfortable-looking pillows and a jewel-toned throw tossed carelessly over the end. Since looking at it gave him ideas that he was pretty sure she'd object to at this stage of the game, he turned back to her.

She hadn't moved from the corner of the desk, just turned her head to follow his progress throughout the room. She had her hands tucked into her pockets, one eyebrow quirked at him in question.

He grinned at her, unrepentant at having invaded her office. "I like your space."

She grinned back. "Thanks. So," she pushed off from the desk and took a few steps towards the door. She gestured with her hand. "Do you want to get something to eat in the café?"

Ian shook his head, still grinning. He'd known she'd go for the café. "Now, that's not really a lunch break, eating where you work. I want to take you some place where we can talk, relax."

"Oh, that's really not necessary," she protested. "The café is just fine."

"Sure it is," he countered, and crossed to take her hand. "It's always necessary to treat a pretty woman to a nice meal." He raised her hand to his lips, just barely brushing a kiss across the knuckles, and felt her pulse quicken ever so slightly under his fingertips.

He knew she fought it, but still he saw the slight softening of her eyes. "Okay," she relented. "Let me get my coat."

He reached for the jacket on the ebony hall tree next to the office door. "Allow me," he rumbled, and held it out for her to slip her arms into. She did so with a wary glance over her shoulder, as if she couldn't quite figure out what he was up to. He hid his grin as he settled the coat onto her shoulders. Good. Off balance was just where he wanted her.

* * * * *

Jane knew that Ian was amused at her not so subtle attempts to put further distance between them, but she just couldn't seem to help it. She could admit to herself, in a very quiet corner of her consciousness where it didn't interfere with the rest of her brain, that he made her very nervous.

She watched him out of the corner of her eye as he propelled the Rover smoothly through the Saturday afternoon traffic. He was an unusual man, in her experience. He didn't appear threatened by her intelligence, rather, he seemed to enjoy it. He didn't try to make himself seem more important or appealing by bragging about himself and his accomplishments. Most men were only too eager to regale a new woman with tales of their prowess in both the boardroom and the bedroom. Well, so far she didn't even know what he did for a living, and his bedroom prowess had already been proven beyond a shadow of a doubt.

She cleared her throat, determined to brazen the afternoon out, no matter how jumpy her stomach was. "So where're we headed for lunch?"

He flicked on his blinker and switched lanes, turning toward the lake. "I thought we'd try Navy Pier." He glanced at her briefly before turning his attention back to the road. "Any objections?"

Jane shrugged. "No, not really. But it's kind of a tourist trap, isn't it?"

Ian chuckled. "So? I just moved here six months ago, I'm still sort of a tourist. And I happen to like tourist traps. They're fun. Besides, there'll be precious few tourists hanging around the Pier in April."

He had a point there. They were silent for a few moments as Ian negotiated the construction that seemed to be a permanent fixture along the lakefront. Then he pulled up at the valet station across the street from the main entrance. A jacketed attendant opened her door and his, and they clambered out into the frigid air.

They moved as quickly as they could then, eager to get out of the biting wind. It blew sharp and cold from the lake, so they hustled across the street and into the building as soon as the attendant passed Ian his claim ticket. After a brief discussion, they settled on the seafood restaurant.

The restaurant was busy, but since it was after the usual lunchtime rush, they were seated right away in a corner booth. Once the waiter had taken their orders, Jane felt her nervousness coming back, full force. He was just sitting there across the table, watching her and sipping his beer. She suppressed the urge to fidget and raised her own beer to her mouth for a long drink. The fact that his eyes tracked the movement and seemed to lock onto her mouth had the butterflies in her belly turning to liquid heat, but really didn't do anything to put her more at ease.

Just when she thought she might scream from the tension, he spoke.

"So," he put his bottle down. "How come you're so nervous?"

Jane choked, having just taken another fortifying sip of Corona. Through watering eyes, she saw him rise out of the booth to come around her side. He thumped her on the back a few times, then returned to his seat.

"Go down the wrong pipe?"

She glared at him, coughing. When she could speak again, she rasped, "You did that on purpose, didn't you?"

He grinned. "Well, I didn't think you were going to choke."

She rolled her eyes, still coughing. When she had it under control and could speak, she said, "Well, now you know. If I'm drinking beer and someone shocks me, I choke."

He titled his head to the side, curious. "Why did that question shock you?"

Jane raised one brow. "Most people are polite enough not to ask it."

He shrugged and sipped beer. "Well, I want to know the answer more than I care about making a social faux pas." He waited a beat, then, "Are you going to deny that you're nervous?"

Jane could feel herself blushing, but met his eyes steadily. "Well, that would just make me a liar, and an obvious one at that."

He nodded, toasting her with his beer bottle. "So what's the answer?"

Jane stuck her tongue out at him, laughing when he crossed his eyes in response. "C'mon, Jane. Is it just new guy nerves or something more?"

She was saved from answering right away by the waiter bearing down on them with two huge platters, piled high with steaming crab legs. He set them down with a clatter, and she busied herself for a moment with her napkin and utensils. When she had no more to do, she raised her head to find him still looking at her expectantly.

"You know," he said conversationally, ripping into a crustacean with a crack, "you didn't strike me as a coward."

Instantly insulted, she stiffened up like a poker. "I am *not* a coward," she spat. Then slumped back into the cushioned back of the booth. "I'm just a little out of my element with you, that's all." She stared morosely into her plate.

"How do you figure?"

Jane rolled her eyes, then picked up her own crunchers and set to work. Bad mood or no, not much interfered with her ability to enjoy a meal. "Well, most guys I go out with aren't so…" she gestured expansively with her fork, "you know, pushy. Commanding. Take charge."

Ian snorted. "Well, if you don't like 'take charge', why did you fuck my brains out all night long?"

Jane choked out a laugh. The waiter, who had been delivering a fresh round of Corona with lime, tripped over his own feet and fell headlong into the table. Only Ian's quick reflexes saved the beer from shattering into the crab legs.

Once the waiter had scurried away, Jane took a pull of her fresh beer, and tucked back into her meal. "I never said I don't like 'take charge'," she mumbled around a mouthful of spicy crab and melted butter. "Just that I'm not used to it. I don't know how to operate with someone else calling the shots."

Ian chewed thoughtfully. "Does this have anything to do with that whole 'do the opposite' thing you were talking about last night?"

She swallowed hastily. "Ohmigosh, I'd forgotten that I told you about that."

"Well?"

She nodded, tossing her empty shells on the discard plate. "Yeah, it has something to do with that."

When she didn't say anything further, just kept eating, he chuckled. "Am I going to have to tickle it out of you?"

She flicked a sidelong glance. "Those kinds of threats will get you stuck with the check." She wiped her fingers on the wet naps, watching him. He met her gaze squarely, and it was the amused patience in his expression that made her relent.

"All right." She added the used wet naps to the pile of empty crab shells. "You met Lacey this morning. She and I were talking the other night, and we were kind of trying to figure out why my love life has been in the crapper lately."

She ignored his choked laugh, pulling her feet underneath her and getting comfortable in the corner of the booth. "Well, we sort of came to the conclusion, in a roundabout kind of way, that part of the problem may be in the men I've been picking."

"Let me guess." Ian wiped his own fingers clean and settled back. "They were not 'take charge'?"

Jane grinned, thinking of the stockbroker and the marketing executive. "No," she chortled, shaking her head, "they were not 'take charge'."

"Thus, a change of tactic."

She nodded. "Yep. So, we decided to try a little experiment for the night. We went to the club to see if I could not be in charge, pick a guy who was and have a better time than I've been having." She winced, suddenly realizing how that sounded. "That didn't sound quite as insulting in my head as it did out loud."

Ian laughed, the rough masculine sound sending a chill down her spine. "Don't worry, I'm not offended. I've never been happier to be 'take charge'."

Jane laughed, relieved. "Anyway," she continued, "I'm usually the one in charge of everything, which seems to work great in business but not so great socially." She shrugged, her fingers worrying the hem of her sweater. "So I tried something different."

Ian nodded. "Well, I imagine that a woman in her—what, early thirties?" She nodded. "A woman in her early thirties running a successful business would have become accustomed to having her word taken as law. For example, the errant vendor you were ripping into this afternoon."

Jane snorted. "I was hardly ripping into him."

He leaned forward and snagged her hands in his. "Darling, you were tearing his throat out. Bloodlessly." He tugged her hands to his mouth and brushed a swift kiss across her knuckles. "It made me horny as hell to watch."

Jane was amazed to feel herself blush. "Really?"

Ian chuckled. She looked like a sixteen-year-old at the prom, all sparkling eyes and flushed cheeks. He lowered his voice intimately. "Oh, yeah." He winked, then released her hands and sat back.

"So," he swigged his beer, hoping it would put out the sudden fire in his gut. "The experiment worked—we both had a great time. So why the nervousness?"

Jane struggled to make her brain work. It was amazing, a kiss on her hand, a sly little wink, and all she could think about was crawling in his lap and devouring him. "Well, I guess I'm just not used to giving up control to a man."

"But you liked it, right? Submitting in bed?"

Jane rolled her eyes. "Once again, denying that would just make me a liar—an obvious one. I *really* liked it. But," she looked at him pointedly, "I'm a big girl, and I know I don't always get what I like or what I want."

"Why not?" He held up a hand as she opened her mouth to blast him. "No, just hear me out. Why can't we both have what we want here? You make me laugh. God knows you make me hot, and you don't seem to be having all that terrible a time right now. So, give me one good reason why we can't expand on last night and see where it takes us?"

Jane stared at him, incredulous. "Well for one thing, I don't even know your last name!"

He grinned. "It's MacInnes. What else?"

She threw her hands up. "It's not just your name—I don't know anything about you!"

He nodded. "Point to the lady. I'm thirty-seven. My mother's name is Rosa, my father's name is Michael. They live in New Jersey. I've got two sisters, one older, one younger. The younger one is a junior at Vassar—straight As. The older one lives in Schenectady with her husband the accountant and their two kids—fourteen-year-old twins that they named Matthew and Michael. Damned if I can tell which one is which."

Jane folded her arms across her chest and raised a brow. "Well, that tells me a great deal about your family, but precious little about you. Try again."

He grinned. "Didn't think I'd be able to slip that by you. Okay, I'm formerly with military intelligence. I became a civilian again after a particularly nasty expedition in a country you've probably never heard of. I moved to Chicago because I like the bustle of a large city but didn't want to live in New York. Too much opportunity for my mother to drop in from Jersey and tell me she's not getting any younger and all she desires in the winter of her life is more grandchildren to dote on."

Jane let out a sharp crack of laughter, startling their waiter into bobbling the cheesecake they'd ordered for dessert. "Sounds like my mother." She took a bite of the creamy confection and hummed her approval. "What else?"

Ian pulled his gaze away from Jane's mouth with effort. "Well, once I moved here I bought a townhouse, found some office space overlooking the lake and set up shop as a security consultant. Thanks to Uncle Sam, I have quite a bit of useful knowledge when it comes to keeping both people and information safe from prying eyes."

She raised an eyebrow. "Doing rather well, are we?"

He toasted her with a forkful of dessert. "Can't complain."

She polished off her cheesecake, setting her fork down with a sigh of repletion. "That was fabulous."

He goggled at her plate. "Did you finish already?"

She grinned, used to people's reactions to her appetite. "I like to eat."

He stared at her out of heavy-lidded, sensual eyes. "So do I," he murmured, and she shivered at the sensual promise in his tone.

"So, what's the verdict?" He forked up more cheesecake.

Jane sighed. "Well, I just don't know."

"Oh, come on. Look," he said, setting his fork down and pushing his plate to the side. "I like you. A lot. You're funny, smart, sexy and hell on wheels in the sack. And," he pointed, "if you're honest with yourself, you'll admit that you like me, too." He waited for her reluctant nod then plowed on. "So what is really bothering you about seeing me again? It can't be the 'take charge' thing, since we've already established that you like it."

"Aha! I do like it, but I like it in *bed*. I sure as hell wouldn't like being dominated in other areas of my life, and my general experience has been that the way a person is in bed is a good indicator of how they conduct themselves in other areas of their lives."

"Bullshit."

Jane blinked. "Huh?"

"I said, bullshit." Ian signaled the waiter for the check. Then he leaned across the table, lowering his voice. "You were submissive as hell in bed last night—you let me tie you up and tease you until you were begging for me to fuck you. And this afternoon you ripped Jack the Lazy Vendor a new asshole. So don't tell me that bedroom behavior is an automatic indicator of personality."

"Oh." Jane grimaced. "Okay, point for you."

"Here's another one." He took her hand, waiting until she looked up to meet his eyes. "I know that you've got responsibilities and ambitions for the store, and I have no intention of interfering with that. Hell, I'm building a business of my own—I know how hard it is, how much energy it takes, and I'm busy enough without worrying about taking on your burdens. So you can lay to rest any fears that I'm wanting to control your life."

Jane waited a beat, then drawled, "But...?"

"But," Ian repeated, "I do like to have control in the bedroom. I love knowing that the tiger lady that I saw in the store today purrs like kitten for me in bed. There's nothing sexier than a strong woman in surrender."

He straightened slightly to allow the waiter to deliver the bill then leaned back in when he'd gone. "So, I have a proposal for you. Let's extend the experiment a little, into say, a trial period."

Jane blinked. "A trial period?"

Ian nodded. "A thirty-day get-to-know-each-other trial period. We'll date—spend as much time together as our respective busy schedules allow. We'll make love—and further explore the concept of you giving up control in the bedroom. And if at the end of the thirty days you figure out that you really don't like me or want to be dominated in bed, and I figure out that I don't like you and you snore and hog the covers, then we'll call it a day and no hard feelings."

She narrowed her eyes, wary of a trap "And would there be rules governing this trial period?"

He grinned at her. "I hate to call them rules. We'll think of them as guidelines. And really, there's only one."

"And that would be...?"

"That when we're in the bedroom—or engaged in sexual activity—I'm in charge. You do whatever I say."

Jane laughed, a tight, nervous sound that no one would mistake for genuine humor. "Well, that's convenient for you, isn't it?"

Ian shook his head, suddenly very serious. "Necessary. If you're going to give sexual submission a try, then you have to do it, not just talk about it or play at it when it's convenient."

Jane swallowed heavily, suddenly dry-mouthed. She went to take a fortifying sip of beer, scowling at the bottle when she realized it was empty. Holding it in her hands, she fiddled with the label. "You said 'in the bedroom or engaged in sexual activity'. Now, I'm not a prude who only expects sex to be missionary style under the covers with the lights out, but what does that mean?"

Ian leaned forward, his voice lowered to a sensual rumble. "It means I'm not restricting myself to only fucking you in a bed. Now, I don't actually have a plan about this—there's no script to follow here. Part of the getting-to-know-you end of the experiment is my discovering what your fantasies are—the deep dark ones that you only tell your girlfriends after a pitcher of margaritas—and making them come true safely."

Jane thought of a few of her fantasies and visibly shivered. Still, it might not be such a great idea to make all of them come true. She might fantasize about having sex in the middle of the head table at the Chicago Women in Business awards dinner, but it would definitely not be good for her career.

She took a deep breath as another thought occurred to her. "Say I agree to this, to doing whatever you say in the bedroom—or wherever. What happens if I don't *want* to do what you say? What happens if I get freaked out, or scared, or just plain can't do whatever it is you want me to do?"

He shrugged. "Then we won't do it. The purpose of all this is to explore a part of your sexuality that I suspect you've had buried for a long time. The last thing I want to do is make you do something that you truly don't want to do, or even make you do something that makes you so uncomfortable or worried that you can't enjoy yourself. But you have to give it a shot—you can't automatically say no to everything just because you can."

Jane puzzled over that for a minute. "Okay."

"So," Ian continued, "let's say this—anything that I ask, you at least give it serious consideration. If after thinking it through, you find that you really don't like the idea—and I mean really don't like it. Not just that it makes you nervous or a little bit scared, but you *really* hate it, or it *really* freaks you out—then you get to veto."

Jane nodded, thoughtful. "Okay." She took a deep, steadying breath. "Okay, I guess I can handle that. But just so we're clear on something—nobody *makes* me do anything. Anything I do, I do it because *I* want to. Got it?"

He grinned, winked. "Absolutely. What about birth control?"

She blinked, startled by the abrupt change of topic. "Uh, we use it, of course."

"Naturally," he agreed. "My question is what kind?"

"Well, I'm on the pill," she mused, "but that doesn't address the disease issue."

"True." He paused a moment, thoughtful. "I actually just had a physical a month ago, including a full STD panel. I'm clean."

She looked at him, considering. "I had one two weeks ago. Just got the word yesterday everything's fine. Are you saying you want to ditch the condoms?"

He shrugged. "It's an idea."

"I've never had sex without a condom."

He grinned. "Me neither, and I'd really like to try it with you. But it's up to you—if you don't feel safe, we can keep the condoms."

She thought for a moment. "No, we can try it without, I'm okay with that. As long as I can see your medical results."

"Not a problem," he said. "They're back at the house." He tugged his wallet out of his pocket, dropped several bills on the table. He slid out of the booth, tucked his wallet back in his pocket, and held out a hand. "Do we have a deal?"

Jane took a deep breath and placed her hand in his. She looked into his eyes, felt the impact of what she was agreeing to all the way down to her toes. "Deal," she said breathlessly. "So…what do we do now?"

She squeaked in surprise when he tightened his grip and tugged, pulling her out of the booth and into his arms. He planted a hard, biting kiss on her mouth. "Now," he rumbled, his face hard with lust, "we skip the walk on the beach I had in mind in favor of seeing how you look on my silk sheets." He lifted a brow. "That's good with you, yes?"

Jane gulped at the look in his eye. "Do I really have a choice?"

Ian's eyes narrowed and his grip on her waist tightened. "Jane, you always have a choice. All you ever have to say is no, got it?"

Jane licked her lips. "Yeah, but the thing is," she wound her arms around his neck and pulled herself up so that the ridge of his cock nestled into the notch of her thighs. "I don't want to say no. I was kind of hoping that you'd just drag me back to your lair and have your wicked way with me." She peeked up at him from under her lashes and licked her lips again.

A flush spread over his tight cheekbones and his eyes took on a feral glitter. "Well, in that case…" He shifted, bent and hoisted her over one shoulder so fast that she had to grab onto his belt to keep her balance. "Let's get started."

Jane grinned at his backside, thinking this might be a pretty good deal she'd gotten herself into. The last thing she saw as they strode out of the restaurant was the startled, shocked faces of their waiter and the remaining few diners.

Chapter Eight

Twenty minutes later she found herself in the master suite of Ian's townhouse, flat on her back, naked, blindfolded and more turned on than she could ever remember being. She was also alone. He'd dumped her on the bed, stripped her in record time and proceeded to blindfold her with a silk necktie. He'd ordered her to stay, then walked out of the room. And she was sorely temped to rip off the blindfold, hunt him down and pinch him black and blue for leaving her in such a state. She could do it, too. He hadn't tied her down this time, just told her to stay. Which somehow was more arousing than actually being tied.

She lay there fuming, wondering how she could ever have been nuts enough to agree to this "obedience in the bedroom" scheme. She was so preoccupied with thoughts of exacting vengeance that she didn't realize he'd come into the room again until his hand landed on her thigh with a light slap. It didn't hurt, but she jumped, startled.

"I can hear you thinking," he murmured, his voice rich with amusement. "Considering bolting again?"

"No," she practically growled. "Thinking of ways to torture you for leaving me up here while you check your messages, or whatever it was you were doing. I mean, I'm *naked* here—you're supposed to DO stuff to me!"

Now the laughter was audible in his tone. "Oh, I wouldn't worry. I plan on doing a great many things to you." She felt him lean down, close to her ear. "I need you to stay very, very still for me Jane." He licked the shell of her ear softly, delicately. "Can you do that for me?" he whispered. She let out a whimper and nodded frantically, her blood heating at the raw sexuality in his tone. "Good girl," he whispered. "Now remember—perfectly still."

Jane lay there, concentrating on keeping her limbs as still as possible. But she couldn't help the fine tremors that shook her muscles almost imperceptibly. She strained to hear him, to detect any sound in the room, but all she could hear was the pounding of her own heart.

Where was he?

* * * * *

Ian simply stood next to the bed and looked at Jane as she struggled to obey his command. God, she was just beautiful. He loved being able to look at all of her, knowing that she couldn't see him doing it. He didn't have to rein in the emotion that he knew was obvious on his face, in his eyes. He was beginning to care about this woman very much. But he was being careful to keep from overwhelming her, knowing that she wasn't ready to hear it.

But with her blindfolded, he didn't have to hold back. He let his eyes roam over her freely, taking in her sleek limbs, the high curves of her breasts. They quivered with her breathing, the tips already puckered and begging for his mouth. He took in the smooth skin of her torso, the gentle curve of her belly. He loved that it wasn't concave, loved that he couldn't count her ribs through her skin. He knew that she worked out—she'd mentioned the gym that morning—and that she was strong, but she didn't have the hard edge of too much exercise and not enough food that some women seemed to strive for. She was all gorgeous curves and supple skin, the way a woman should be. Her hips flared into sweetly rounded thighs, thighs that he knew were plenty strong enough to wrap around him and hang on for the ride. Right now, those thighs were clenched in an effort to remain still, and the plump, bare flesh between them drew his eyes.

He'd been with women who'd shaved or waxed their pussy before, and he'd always found the experience extremely erotic. It had been a nice surprise to find her smooth and bare. It made going down on a woman better, more intimate. The lack of a barrier of hair made the flesh there more sensitive to everything—the touch of his tongue, the wash of his breath over her skin. Thinking about it made him realize that through their marathon of sex the night before he'd forgotten that particular act, and though he'd had other ideas when he planned this, he thought he could improvise a little to correct that oversight.

He picked up the small, fine-haired brush that he'd pulled from one of his tech kits. The brush was for cleaning delicate electronic components, but he had other ideas for it. Being as quiet as possible, he opened the jar of gourmet honey, dipped the brush into the golden liquid. Watching her face carefully, he drew the brush over one plump pussy lip, carefully avoiding her swollen clit. She jumped at the contact, her legs shifting apart.

He lightly tapped her thigh with the end of the brush. "Ah ah ah. I said still, remember?"

She frowned, confused. "But..."

He tapped her leg again with the brush handle, hard enough this time to sting slightly. "But nothing. Still means still. So legs back together, please." He grinned as she complied. If the look on her face was any indication, she wasn't happy about it, but she did it.

He dipped the brush again and drew a line down the other lip to her thigh, then back up again. This time she did a better job of staying still, though her breathing became ragged. He continued to paint her pussy, dipping the brush over and over again, until her entire mound and the tops of her thighs glistened with a combination of her juices and the honey.

Ian put the brush and jar aside and surveyed his work. Her thighs were moving slightly, flexing with the effort of remaining still, spreading the combination of honey and her own cream around. Her chest was heaving with every breath, and he could feel the fine tremors that shook her muscles. Her skin was dewy with a slight sheen of perspiration, and the scent of her arousal filled the room.

He leaned over her, bracing his hands on either side of her hips, and bent low so his face was mere inches from her pussy. He saw her hips surge slightly before she suppressed the movement, and grinned. He could tell by the flush of her skin and the sharp scent of her cunt that she was already riding the fine edge of control. He knew that the order to remain still made her hot, so hot that she was ready to explode from just the faint touch of the brush on her pussy. He'd been careful to avoid her clit, knowing that the slightest touch of the swollen, throbbing little nub would likely send her screaming over the edge, and he had a lot more fun in mind before he let that happen.

He bent closer, inhaling the intoxicating scent of her, and blew lightly on the glistening flesh of her mound. A strangled scream escaped her lips, and her head began to toss mindlessly on the pillow.

"Remember Jane," he forced steel into his voice. "Keep your body perfectly still, or we'll have to start all over again. I don't think you want that, do you?" His only answer was an agonized groan. He lowered his voice to a growl. "Do you?"

"Nooooooo," she cried, her head stilling on the pillow. "God, Ian, you're *killing* me!"

"Oh darlin'," he rumbled, "I'm just getting started."

He reached down to the glass of ice he'd brought along with the honey. Slowly, because he didn't want the ice to clink and clue her in, he fished out a cube. He didn't want it to drip on her, so he wiped it off on the edge of the sheet, soaking up any excess water. Then he held it between thumb and forefinger, and carefully, oh so carefully, touched it to her cunt.

She reacted like she'd been shot, her breath exploding from her lungs in a wail, her hands clenching in the bed sheets as she fought to remain still. He ignored her gasping cries and drew it along her flesh, watching the honey crystallize on her skin as it reacted to the cold. He continued to swipe the cube over her skin, carefully avoiding her clit and watching her face to gauge her reactions, until it was almost melted and her skin was cool to the touch.

He tossed the sliver of ice aside and moved up to her head. She was nearly sobbing with need. He leaned down and touched his tongue to the bow in her upper lip, and she whimpered and tried to grasp it with her lips. He obliged, his mouth coming down hard on hers and driving his tongue into her mouth. She immediately began to suck on his tongue, those mindless cries still coming from her throat.

He broke the kiss, brushing one hand over her hair as he placed the other on her chest. Her heart felt like it would burst right through. "You okay?" he murmured.

"No," she sobbed. "Oh God, Ian. I need to move, I need to come. Please, please, please, let me come!"

Ian nipped her lower lip with his teeth. "You want to come, baby?"

"Yes!" she cried.

He smoothed one of his hands over her hip, lightly brushed a fingertip over her honey-covered mound. She twitched and moaned again, and suddenly he was aware of the hard length of his cock pressing against his fly. "You want to move?"

Jane groaned. "Yes!"

"Well," he mused, moving back to the foot of the bed and putting his hands on her knees. "Okay, I guess you've been good enough. You can move—but you can't come."

Her chest heaved, her breath coming in strained sobs, tears leaking from behind the tie blinding her. "Why?"

"Because." He forced her knees apart, pressing them flat on the bed so that her entire cunt was exposed to his gaze. She was beautiful, pink and plump, and so wet that there was a puddle forming under her. "Because," he continued, sliding up to wedge his shoulders between her thighs, "I said so. That was the deal, remember? What I say in the bedroom goes, and I'm telling you not to come."

He used his thumbs to part her folds and leaned close enough so that she could feel his breath on her. "Jane, do you understand?"

"Yes yes yes yes yes, I understand!" Her head tossed mindlessly on the bed.

"Good girl." Ian leaned closer, blew a gentle breath over her heated flesh. She flinched and moaned. He knew that if he touched her clit she'd go off like a rocket, so he slid his tongue in one long, slow glide up the outer edge of her cunt. Her hips surged to meet him, her wailing moan ringing in his ears. He tasted honey and her own spicy sweetness, and growled in satisfaction.

He began to devour her in earnest, licking and sucking and nipping at her flesh. She was pumping her hips mindlessly, her hands coming up to grip his hair, her wails constant now. He stayed away from her clit, instead suckling the plump lips of her cunt and sliding his tongue deep inside her. He slid two fingers into her clinging depths, twisting his wrist and sliding them in and out, as he raised his head to watch her face.

Her hair was a tangled, ratted mess, damp with sweat and tears. The blindfold had come loose and was slipping down her face. He doubted that she'd noticed, though—her eyes were clamped tightly shut. Mascara streaked her cheeks. Her breasts heaved with every breath, the nipples beaded tightly and flushed a dark red. He didn't think he'd ever seen anything so gorgeous.

"Baby," he rumbled, bringing his face down to her cunt for a slow lick that had her hips surging wildly, "do you want to come?"

"Oh, God, yes! Please please please please let me come!" she chanted, panting for air. "I'll do anything you want, just please *please* let me come!"

Ian brought his face to within a hairsbreadth of her clit. The small knot of nerves was blood red and throbbed visibly. He withdrew his fingers and she wailed in frustration, thinking he was going to withhold satisfaction from her yet again. Instead, he pressed three fingers to her opening, holding them just inside, and positioned his mouth over her clit. He hovered there, savoring the moment, then said "Come now for me, sweetheart. Now!" He thrust his fingers deep into her core, twisting them inside her and clamped his mouth over her clit.

She screamed, a high, keening sound that echoed throughout the room. Her back arched, her hands clenching in his hair and she exploded. He felt her cunt clamp down on his fingers in rhythmic pulls and tugs, and he growled, vibrating her clit and sending her flying even higher. It went on and on for long moments, and he continued to suck and thrust his fingers, drawing her pleasure out as long as he could. Finally, she went limp, her hands slipping from his hair to fall lifelessly to the bed.

Ian pulled his fingers from her grasping pussy, and she twitched and moaned slightly at the friction. Suddenly, he couldn't wait any longer to have her, and began shucking his clothes frantically, pausing only to grab a condom from his wallet.

She was still lying limp, her breathing ragged, her thighs spread wide. His cock throbbed with the need to be inside her, and he grabbed the pillows from the head of the bed. He piled them in the middle of the mattress, next to her limp and satiated form, and then picked her up as easily as he would a rag doll. She stirred as he placed her on her stomach on the pillows, propping her ass high.

He could see the plump, damp lips of her cunt peeking from between her thighs, the rounded cheeks of her ass. She pushed herself up on her elbows as he grasped her hips and angled them higher. "Ian," she groaned.

"I'm sorry, baby." He brought one hand to his cock, fitting the broad head to her swollen opening. "I can't wait any longer. I have to fuck you."

Jane pushed herself to her hands and looked at him over her shoulder. He knew how he looked, his face tight with lust, his eyes wild. He waited while she watched him, straining to hold back. If she truly didn't want him to take her, then he wouldn't. But God, he didn't know how he'd be able to stop.

For long moments, she simply watched his face. Then, when he'd begun to brace himself to back away from her, she moved. Still keeping her eyes on his face, she let her torso come to rest on the pillows and reached behind her with both hands. She wrapped her arms around her thighs, her fingers reaching behind her. He steeled himself for the feel of her hands pushing him away, but she didn't touch him. Her fingers instead grasped the lips of her pussy, and he watched as she pulled them apart, opening herself to him.

His gaze flew to her face. "Fuck me, Ian," she whispered. "I'm empty. I want you inside me, filling me up."

"Jesus," he rasped. "Baby, I'm going to fill you so full, you'll never be empty again." With that, he drove forward, impaling her deep on one thrust, and they both groaned at the exquisite feeling. Jane let go of her own flesh to brace herself, pushing her hips back to meet him.

He paused for a moment to savor the feeling of her wet heat surrounding him, and then began to move. He could already feel his balls drawing up—feel that feathery sensation along his spine that signaled his impending climax. He slid one hand under her belly to find her clit, determined that he'd take her with him. She groaned when he found it, pinching it between two fingers, and threw her head back on a gasp.

Ian leaned down and licked the side of her neck, his hips pumping faster. "I want you to come with me, sweetheart. Can you do that for me?"

Jane reached back with one hand and grasped his head, her hips pumping to meet his thrusts. "Yes, oh God! I'm going to come again."

Ian felt his balls draw up tight, and rubbed her clit harder. "Come now, baby. Come for me!"

She let out one long, keening wail, and he felt her cunt clamp down on him. He groaned, gave one final thrust and exploded. His hips jerked convulsively as he pumped into her, the smooth muscles of her cunt milking him, making him feel as though his head would blow clean off.

When it was over, he collapsed on her back, breathing as though he'd just run a marathon. He could feel her shuddering underneath him, aftershocks of her climax rippling along the still rigid length of his dick. "Jesus," he wheezed. "That damn near killed me."

He felt her go still. "You!" Her tone was incredulous. "It almost killed *you*? At least YOU got to move!"

He chuckled weakly and lifted off her, pulling his cock from her heated core. Carefully, he turned her over onto her back. "What, you didn't like it?"

She grinned at him. "Oh, I wouldn't say that."

He grinned back. "Didn't think so." He swung his legs off the bed and headed for the bathroom on shaky legs. He dealt with the condom and dampened a washcloth in the sink, then went back into the bedroom.

She hadn't moved, was still lying sprawled on her back, limbs akimbo, in a fabulous display of sexually satiated female. He stopped next to the bed and simply looked at her for a moment. "God, you're beautiful."

One blue eye popped open to peer at him. "You have got to be kidding me. My hair is a tangled, sweaty mess, my makeup is probably smeared over half my face and I'm breathing like a winded water buffalo. I look awful."

He shook his head. "While that's all true," he stepped back from her swinging fist, laughing, "all I have to do is think about how you got in that state and you're gorgeous."

"Well." She smoothed the sheet under her, not meeting his eyes. She ridiculously pleased that he wasn't turned off by her disheveled appearance. "I guess that's all right then."

Ian was still chuckling as he sat on the side of the bed. "I'm relieved. Here, scoot up here." He tugged her up so that she was lying nearer the head of the bed, pulling the pillows back up to their proper place and tucking them behind her. He held up the cloth. "It's going to be cold," he warned, then began to wash the remains of the honey and their lovemaking from her slit.

Jane sucked in a breath, the rough terrycloth abrading already sensitive tissues. But he was very gentle, thoroughly cleaning her mound and thighs, and the cold helped ease the aches and pains that were beginning to make themselves known.

He finished cleaning her and returned the washcloth to the bathroom, then slipped into bed beside her. She was yawning broadly, the lack of sleep from the night before catching up with her, and she nestled her head on his shoulder. "Maybe we could just take a little nap, okay?" she murmured, her eyes already drifting shut.

He reached down for the covers that had tangled at the foot of the bed during their romp, pulling them up over their naked bodies. "Sure, baby." He pulled the sheet up to her shoulder, pressed a kiss to her forehead. "Go to sleep."

"Don't go anywhere," she sighed.

He looked at her face, but her eyes were already closed and her breath had evened out in sleep. He pulled her closer to his side. "Don't you worry, darlin'," he pressed another kiss to the top of her head. "I'm not going anywhere."

He stared at the ceiling, his mind working feverishly as he savored the warm weight of her next to him. He'd suggested the getting-to-know-you experiment as a way to keep her in his bed, and to see if there could be something more between them. She was wary of anything more than sex, so he figured they'd start with that and see if there could be anything more. But now he was thinking he'd have to find a way to get her comfortable with the something more, and fast. Because he was very much afraid that he'd just tumbled head over heels in love with her.

He sighed. He'd never been in love before, and wasn't quite sure what to do about it. The only thing he knew for certain was that he couldn't tell her about it, not yet. She was already leery of him, of his motives, and a declaration of love when they'd only known each other for one day would only have her running for the hills. Better to take it slow, show her how good they could be together over the next month, and then declare himself when she was more certain of him.

His plan in place, he suddenly realized that he was exhausted. Fatigue pulled at him, his body unused to the demands that he'd put on it in the last twenty-four hours. He pulled the sheet up to his chest and turned slightly toward Jane, breathing in her scent. She snuggled closer in her sleep, and he felt his chest tighten with emotion. Yes, he was going to have to keep her, he thought sleepily. His last thought before oblivion claimed him was that he didn't think he could ever let her go.

Chapter Nine

Jane woke slowly, both out of habit and confusion. She was pretty sure the white walls and ceiling meant that she wasn't in her bed, but it took her a minute to remember exactly whose bed she was in. She shifted slightly, trying to get comfortable, and the twinge of discomfort in her thighs, as well as the arms that tightened around her middle, brought the memories flooding back.

She looked over her shoulder to find Ian still sleeping soundly, wrapped around her with his head tucked into her neck. Now that she was alert, she could feel the warmth of his breath stirring her hair, his muscled form pressing firmly along her back. The dim light that streamed in through the windows told her it was nearing twilight; they'd been asleep for just over an hour. She started to turn in his arms, to see his face fully, and he woke up.

She had to admire the way he did it—quickly and completely, with none of the yawning and stretching and grousing that usually accompanied her own journey from sleep to wake. One minute he was snuffling softly into her hair, the next he was staring at her from clear, bright eyes.

"Wow," she said. "You wake up quick."

Ian smiled, a sleepy sexy grin that had her heart doing handsprings in her chest. "Military training," he rumbled, his voice still rough from sleep. He reached up one hand to brush the tangle of her hair from her face and rolled to his back, bringing her to rest against his chest. "Sleep good?"

She nodded. "Yeah." She avoided his eyes, toying with his chest hair. "I'm sorry for conking out on you like that. I must've been more tired than I thought."

"Hey." He slipped a finger under her chin, forcing her gaze to meet his. "What is this? Are you embarrassed that you fell asleep?" She shrugged, a blush pinkening her cheeks. "Baby," he chuckled, "it's no big deal. I didn't give you a lot of time to sleep last night. It caught up with both of us."

Jane felt a genuine smile curve her lips, and she wriggled, feeling him hardening against her hip. "You feel pretty revived to me." Then she winced as they stuck together briefly. "And sticky."

He chuckled. "Well, I had enough energy to clean you, but I didn't feel like hopping in the shower. I figured we could do that together after we woke up." He lifted one raven brow in question. "Sound fun?"

Her grin turned sly and wicked. "Oh, I think we can do better than that." She moved suddenly, planting her hands on his shoulders and slithering over him so that he was flat on his back. The surprise in his eyes added to the zing in her blood, and she felt her body tighten with arousal. Unfortunately, she knew that she was too sore to do anything about it, but that didn't mean that she had to waste the lovely erection that was growing against her belly.

She leaned in and flicked his lip with her tongue, loving the smoky, spicy taste of him. She pulled back and winked. "You just stay right there, big guy, and leave the cleanup to me."

The surprise in his eyes had been replaced by amused heat, and he brought his arms up, folding them behind his head in a pose of lazy sensuality. "By all means," he rasped, stretching full-length on the king-sized bed. "Help yourself."

Jane grinned, trying to ignore the heat curling in her own belly. She moved her hands to the bed, bracing them on either side of his torso. "Hmmm," she murmured, her eyes flicking over the muscles that bunched and played over his chest and shoulders. Unable to resist, she lowered her lips to the ridge of his collarbone and licked. The salty taste of him went straight to her head like Kentucky whiskey, and she groaned.

She felt him tense under her, his breathing deepening as she made her way from his collarbone to the small copper nipples half hidden in the whorls of chest hair. She nibbled and licked and sucked to her heart's content, smiling at the groans and growls coming from his throat in a steady stream. She could feel his thighs flexing, shifting further apart, and his cock was prodding her belly insistently now.

When she just couldn't wait any longer, she left his nipples to trail her lips down his abdomen, smiling as she dragged her tongue across the silky line of hair that bisected his abs, then fanned out to circle his cock. She could taste dried sweat and the sweetness of the honey that he'd anointed her with. The hair of his groin was matted with it in some areas, and she spent long minutes making sure that she left no trace of honey behind.

She ignored the blind surge of his hips and the jutting erection next to her face, and trailed her tongue long the crease where leg met hip. The taste of him was stronger here, more potent, and her head swam with lust as she lapped him up.

But payback was payback, and she ignored her own rampant desire to devour him whole in favor of making him suffer. She swiped her tongue lower along his thigh, fighting back a chuckle as they moved further apart in encouragement. She could see his balls now, drawn tight against the base of his cock. Remembering the way he'd taken her from behind, the feel of his balls slapping against her swollen clit with every pounding thrust, she knew there was sure to be honey on that most sensitive of skin. She smiled. Well, she believed in being thorough.

When she delicately licked the tightly drawn skin, she thought he'd come off the bed. He arched so hard, that for a brief moment his weight was supported on his shoulders and heels, and she scrambled to keep her mouth on him and not get tossed to the floor. He collapsed back with a groan, his hands grasping her head. She hesitated, waiting to see what he would do, but he just tangled his fingers in her hair and held on. Testing, she snaked out her tongue for another lick. He tightened his hold on her scalp and growled, but otherwise didn't move.

Emboldened, she opened her mouth and carefully, tenderly sucked one testicle into the wet heat of her mouth. He gave a hoarse shout, hips pumping, fingers clenching, while she held him gently in the warm cave of her mouth and swiped him clean with her tongue. Then she switched to the other testicle and gave it the same loving treatment. By the time she was satisfied that she'd gotten all of the honey, his hips were surging and his fingers were clenching rhythmically in her hair.

She released him with one last lick and raised her head as far as his grip on her hair would allow. His face was a mask of agonized lust, rumbling groans were coming from his throat. He opened his eyes a slit, the blazing green drilling into hers. Holding his gaze, she reached out with her tongue and touched the tip to the drop of fluid that glistened on the head of his cock. He hissed out a breath, watching her savor the taste of him before reaching her tongue out for another.

His hands clenched tighter in her hair, pulling her head further onto his cock. "More," he growled, the word garbled and barely intelligible with lust. He tugged again, bringing her lips to settle on the swollen head. She flicked her tongue out to tease the slit in the head of his cock. It was weeping pre-cum continuously now, and she lapped at it like a cat at cream.

"Oh Jesus," he groaned, his head going back against the pillow. "You're killing me here."

Jane smiled, sly and female. "I can stop if you like," she purred.

His eyes snapped open to lock on hers, the green of his iris now almost swallowed by black. "Don't. You. Dare." He fisted his hands tighter in her hair. "Suck."

She gave him a slow wink. "Yes, sir," she murmured. She shifted her weight, grasped the base of his cock in one hand, and sucked him deep.

She heard his hoarse shout, felt his body arch and his hands clench painfully in her hair, but all her concentration was for the stalk of flesh invading her mouth. She set a steady rhythm, sucking strongly and stroking and swirling her tongue over the head on each pass. Within moments his hips were pumping steadily, driving more and more of him into her mouth until he was hitting the back of her throat. She stopped moving her head and let him do the work, concentrating on suppressing her gag reflex as he moved deeper.

His thrusts became frantic and choppy as his orgasm drew near, and she doubled her efforts, stroking him with her hand and humming. She knew the vibration would echo along his shaft. Shifting to keep her balance between his splayed legs, she slid the fingers of her free hand under his tightly drawn balls to rub, ever so gently, at the skin there. She felt him harden even further in her mouth, and braced herself.

Suddenly, his hands were dragging her head up instead of pushing it down. Jane blinked up at him, startled, and released him with a soft pop. "What is it? Did I hurt you?"

Ian's eyes seemed to blaze out of his face, his chest heaving like a bellows. "No," he panted. "But I'm going to come if you keep that up."

Jane smiled as she realized that he was stopping her not out of necessity, but out of courtesy. "So? What do you think I've been working for down here?" she murmured, and dipped back down to engulf him once again. She stroked down, then up, then back down. Tickled his balls, hummed, and with a hoarse shout, he erupted.

She continued to work him with her lips and tongue, using gentle suction and swirling licks to draw out his pleasure. He finally collapsed to the mattress with a grunt, his hands falling out of her hair to land limply at his sides. Jane crawled up to nestle in the curve of his arm and stroke his chest, feeling his heart thump a wild beat under her hand.

After long moments, he lifted his head and looked at her. "That was amazing."

Ridiculously pleased, she batted her lashes at him. "Why thank you, kind sir."

He leaned down to plant a hard kiss on her mouth. "I think I melted a few brain cells. Jeez, woman—were you trying to kill me?"

Jane laughed and snuggled closer, feeling giddy and lighthearted at the humor in his tone. "Oh, so dramatic! You're still here, aren't you?" She let her eyelids drift shut, content.

Ian snorted. "Barely." He looked down at her. "Hey, you going to sleep?"

"Hey," she protested without opening her eyes. "I worked hard! I deserve a rest."

"Yes, you did. And you do. But first…"

Jane squealed, eyes popping wide as he tumbled her to her back and planted her feet on his shoulders. She blinked, watched his wide grin disappear between her legs. Her eyes rolled back in her head, and she moaned.

"Well, if you insist…"

* * * * *

After a brief, sweaty tussle, that left her limp and exhausted with pleasure, they shared a shower in his luxuriously appointed bath. The huge walk-in shower was more than big enough for two, and they romped and played like children, splashing and laughing until the water ran cold.

Jane shivered as she stepped out of the stall, grabbing a towel off the warming rack and wrapping herself in it with a moan. "Wow, that's good. I need to get one of those warming rack things."

Ian stepped out behind her, shaking the water from his hair like a Labrador. He grinned as he reached for the remaining towel. "You can come over and use mine anytime." He toweled off briskly, then tossed the towel across the top of the shower door and strode into the bedroom. Jane stayed where she was, soaking up the heat from the towel and the steam in the room.

He came back in wearing loose sweatpants, slung low on his hips, and despite the fact that she was definitely too sore for another round, she felt her mouth water at the sight of all that bare male flesh.

He caught the look in her eye and grinned. "Don't even tempt me, darlin'. You're too sore and I barely have enough strength to stand." He shook out the robe he held in his hands, thick terrycloth in a blinding white that would set off his black hair and bronze skin to perfection. He held it up. "C'mon, lose the towel and wrap up in this. It'll keep you warm while we eat."

Jane unwrapped her towel, hanging it neatly over the bar before sliding her arms into the sleeves of the robe. He bundled it around her, tying the belt tight and rolling the cuffs so her hands peeked out from underneath.

He chuckled. "I think that's the best we can do. You look like you're drowning in that thing."

She looked down and laughed. The shoulder seams drifted half way past her arms, and the hem formed a puddle at her feet. She gathered the material in her hands, enough so she could walk without tripping, and glanced up at him with a wink. "Hey, it's warm."

He laughed again, dropping a quick kiss on her forehead. "God you're cute. C'mon." he beckoned, "let's get some pizza. You like anchovies?"

She made a face at his back. "Not on my pie, mister!" and hobbled out the door after him.

They settled at the kitchen counter with pizza—no anchovies—and ate like religious zealots just off a ritual fast. Ian's state of the art stainless steel, subzero refrigerator had yielded, after a quick and panicked search, three bottles of beer. Which they decided to split evenly to avoid a fight.

"So," Ian swigged beer and polished off his third slice. "What do you have going on the rest of this week?"

Jane shrugged and started work on her fourth slice. "Work mainly. I try not to stay out too late on the weeknights, because I like to workout early and then head to the store for a while. My hours are flexible, but I like to be there for a few hours every day, handle anything that comes up."

He nodded. "Sure, I get that."

She took a sip of beer. "Lacey and I usually hang out a couple nights a week—movies, facials, pedicures."

"Girl stuff."

"Well, we are girls."

He waggled his brows at her. "No argument there."

Jane laughed. "Other than that," she gestured with the beer, "not much going on."

Ian tore a paper towel off the roll on the counter and passed it to her before taking one for himself. "What about when you're seeing someone?"

Jane quirked a brow as she wiped her fingers. "Seeing someone?"

"C'mon, Janey. I know you haven't lived your entire life in a bubble—you've had dates before me, I'm sure. So what's your general routine when you're in a relationship?"

She settled back and curled up on the barstool. "Well, that depends on the relationship, I guess, and the guy. I mean, I've been involved with a lot of workaholics. So," she shrugged, "a lot of the time I spent with them was last minute, on-the-fly."

She regarded him warily. "Why do you ask?"

Ian suppressed a grin at the suspicion in her tone, and deliberately kept his manner mild. "No reason, I just wondered."

"Uh-huh." She didn't look convinced.

"Look," he wiped his fingers on the paper towel and tossed it on the nearly empty pizza box. "I'm just trying to figure out where we're headed here. I mean, I promised I wasn't going to interfere with your life or your routine, right? So I'm just trying to make sure that I don't do that."

Jane narrowed her eyes. "Hmmm. You know, that sounds reasonable, but I still don't quite buy it."

He let the grin through. "Are you always this suspicious?"

"Pretty much."

"Well, I promise that I don't have any motive for asking except to find out your schedule so that I don't accidentally come over to your place wearing leather pants and carrying handcuffs when your parents are over for dinner."

Jane choked on her beer, struggling to put the mental image of him in leather out of her head. She was too sore for more sex, dammit. "Well," she managed when the coughing subsided, "you don't have to worry about my folks. They live in Indiana."

"That's good to know."

She rolled her eyes at him. "Isn't it just?"

He laughed again, and stood, gathering up the remnants of their dinner and carrying them to a side door in the kitchen. He carried the trash through to the garage, and Jane got a glimpse of the Rover he'd driven last night and another vehicle mysteriously shrouded in a tarp before he returned. "So, what do you want to do now?" He wiggled his eyebrows suggestively.

Jane snorted. "Dream on, Bubba. I'm too sore to even *think* about more sex right now."

Ian glanced at his watch. "Well, it's still early. Wanna catch a movie?"

Jane nodded. "Sure, I guess." She looked down at her robe. "I'll have to change first."

"I threw your clothes in the wash earlier. I'll go switch 'em to the dryer; they should be done within a half hour." He gestured at the newspaper on the counter as he headed for the garage, and the laundry. "Why don't you see what's playing while I do that?"

Jane nodded, watched him go. She gathered the newspaper and started searching for the movie listings, a small knot of unease in her belly. As she flipped through the pages, she had the same thought she'd been having ever since he'd asked her to dance—she might be in trouble here.

Chapter Ten

Surprisingly, Jane didn't hear from Ian the next day. After their conversation in the kitchen, she'd figured that she'd be having to dodge him left and right. But he didn't call on Sunday. And by lunchtime on Monday, she was quietly freaking out.

"What the hell's wrong with you, girl?"

Lacey's question jerked Jane out of her musings. "What do you mean?" She avoided Lacey's gaze, using her fork to push what was left of the grilled red snapper she'd had for lunch.

"Hey, look at me." Lacey waited until she lifted her head grudgingly. "What's going on with you today? You're all moody and jumpy. You had crazy monkey sex all weekend; you should be mellow yellow."

"Not all weekend," Jane muttered, then could've cheerfully hacked out her own tongue as Lacey's gaze sharpened.

"So that's the problem!"

"I don't know what you're talking about."

"Ha! He hasn't called, has he?" Jane ignored her, took a sip of her iced tea. "*Has* he?"

Jane threw up her hands. "Fine! He didn't call. Happy now?"

Lacey's glance was admonishing. "Janey, please. Of course, I'm not happy when you're so obviously unhappy. What kind of a best friend would I be if your misery brought me joy?

"However, I'm *ecstatic* to know that I was right. You're in such deep trouble with this guy!"

Jane's face was mutinous. "Am not."

Lacey rolled her eyes. "That's very mature, Jane." She set her fork down. "Look, all I'm saying is that I've never seen you this way over a guy. You always treat new relationships so casually, you never get all twisted up and freaky like you are now."

Jane shrugged and resumed picking at her snapper. "I just expected him to call, that's all. Doesn't mean I'm in love with him or anything."

Lacey starred. "I never said anything about love. Ohmigosh, you're in *love with him*?"

Jane shushed her. "Keep your voice, down. And dammit, I just said I wasn't in love with him!"

Lacey was still staring. "I know, but jeez o peetes, Jane. I've never even heard you use the word love when it comes to a boyfriend. It's always been about the sex, or compatibility, or some other blah blah blah." She tapped her fingers on the table. "This guy is different, and you know it. Is it the opposite thing?"

"I don't really know! I mean, that's part of it I guess. The sex is amazing—I never knew letting someone else call the shots could be that wild."

"Don't remind me—I'm not getting any right now, remember?"

Jane grinned briefly at Lacey's pained look. "Trust me, if you ever get the chance, go for it." Her expression turned thoughtful. "If that was all it was, I think I'd be fine. But he's sweet, and funny, and considerate—for a total Alpha type, anyway. I mean, after we were done fucking each other's brains out on Saturday, I figured he'd be ready to hustle me out the door. Instead, we went to a movie, some silly slapstick comedy thing, and laughed our asses off. Then we went for ice cream."

She held her hands out, palms up. "What am I supposed to do with that?"

"Um, enjoy it?"

"I don't know how to enjoy it! Nobody's ever treated me that way before, like a girlfriend, you know? I've always been a lover or a companion. This girlfriend stuff is way more than I can handle."

"Jane." Lacey reached across the table to grasp her friend's hand, her tone quiet. "Maybe it's time you let someone treat you that way. Most of the guys you've been with haven't bothered to treat you special."

"I didn't *want* to be treated special!"

"I know. If they treat you special that means they care about you. If they care about you then you have to think about how you feel about them. Then before you know it, you're in a relationship. And I don't think you've ever been in one before."

Jane rolled her eyes. "Lacey, please. I've had lots of relationships."

Lacey shook her head. "No, you've had lots of encounters with men. I wouldn't call them relationships. For it to count as a relationship, you have to have gone out for more than a month, and you have to have met some of their friends. And," she held up a finger, "you have to have had a few dates where sex was not the end goal."

"Well, by that logic I'm not in a relationship with Ian. I've only seen him twice, and we've had sex both times. Great sex."

"I keep asking you not to remind me. And I didn't say you were in a relationship with Ian, I said you were heading in that direction. He took you to the movies and bought you ice cream. That, my darling girl, is a relationship building type date."

Lacey patted Jane's hand and picked up the dessert menu. "Now, if you don't chicken out, you might have something here." She opened the menu. "I think I'm in the mood for cheesecake."

"Wait, wait a minute." Jane snatched the menu from Lacey's hand, tossed it on the table. "What do you mean, if I don't chicken out? I don't chicken out, I've never chickened out!"

"Oh, please. You are the champion chicken-outer. And you don't like to take risks."

Genuinely hurt, Jane said, "How can you say that to me? I take risks all the time—huge risks. Look at the store. That was a major gamble, and I could've lost everything."

Lacey nodded. "But that's business, sugar. I'm talking about personal risk here."

"I've been skydiving! That's personal risk."

"I'm talking about personal *emotional* risk here, you twit. You've never once allowed yourself to care about a man enough to be vulnerable to him, risk having your heart broken."

"Well, who the hell wants to have their heart broken? I don't see anything wrong with protecting yourself against emotional trauma."

Lacey sighed. "There's something wrong with it when you allow it to get to the point where you won't even risk letting someone get close enough to you to treat you like a 'girlfriend', for heaven's sake."

She pointed a finger at Jane. "But this time, I think it's out of your hands. Here you are, all jumpy and crazy because he hasn't called."

Jane groaned, propping her chin on her hands. "I know, it's awful. How do people do this?"

Lacey shrugged. "It's hard. But when you find someone who makes you a better person when you're with them, well… That's the thing, isn't it?"

"I guess so." Jane waited a beat, then wailed. "We had such a good time on Saturday, why wouldn't he call?"

Lacey rolled her eyes, opened her mouth to answer, and then grinned as she heard the opening bars of *Havana Gila*. "Your cell phone's ringing, Janey."

"Oh!" Jane scrambled for her purse, cursing when she had to dig through several layers of junk to reach the ringing phone. She hit the talk button. "Hello? Oh, hello Ian. I wasn't expecting you to call."

Lacey rolled her eyes, grinning to herself as she hailed the waiter to order her cheesecake. Yep, she thought. Big trouble.

* * * * *

Ian chuckled to himself as he hung up the phone in his office. He doubted that Jane had any idea that she was transparent as glass.

"That her?"

Ian looked at his friend, and grinned. "Yep, that's her. The woman of my dreams, pal."

Devon Bannion chuckled. "Right, the woman of your dreams. You've seen her what, twice?"

"Sometimes that's all you need, Dev." Ian propped his feet on his desk and surveyed his friend. His handsome, rugged face was drawn with fatigue, jaw shadowed with beard, and even though he held himself with the erectness that only the military can teach you, he looked as though the effort cost him. "You look tired, man. Bad one this last time?"

Devon sighed, settling his rangy form into one of the leather club chairs in front of the desk. "They're always bad, man. I gotta admit, when I heard you were retiring, I didn't see how you were going to be able to live without the rush, the thrill of the game. But now…"

Ian watched his friend's face. "Getting burnt out?"

Devon let out a short bark of laughter. "That's an understatement." He rubbed broad palms over his face. "I'm thinking about hanging it up, Ian."

"Well," Ian said, "If you decide to do it, you've got a job waiting for you here. I can always use another guy with your particular skills, and right now I'm turning business away. Another pair of clever hands would likely double it. In fact," he decided, "what I could really use is a partner."

Devon settled back in the chair. "It's a tempting offer, believe me."

Ian watched his friend. Pals since their days of basic training, he knew Devon almost as well as he knew himself. If he was even considering leaving the military, Ian knew that the decision had been all but made and he was likely just waiting for the right time to make his move. Deciding not to push the issue, even though he could see the burnout in Dev, having been there himself, Ian shrugged. "Well, you know where to find me if you decide to take me up on it."

"Thanks, man, I just might do that. But enough about me. Tell me about this girl."

"Woman," Ian corrected. "Believe me, she's no girl."

"Oh, yeah?" Devon grinned, the fatigue fading from his face.

"Oh, yeah." Ian nodded. "She's it for me, man."

"It? Whatdaya mean, it?" Devon goggled, brown eyes wide with shock. "You mean *it* it? As in marriage, it?"

"Marriage, kids, house, dog, minivan…all of it." Ian leaned back in his chair, arms behind his head, and chuckled at the look of complete horror on his friend's face.

"Oh for sweet Lord's sake, Ian—tell me you're not trading in the Shelby for a damn minivan." Devon's voice cracked, fear on his face.

"Devon." Ian held a hand over his heart. "I may be in love, but I have not lost my mind." He shrugged. "The Rover's a good family car, maybe we'll just stick with that."

"Man, you're *killing* me here." Devon got up to pace, shoveling his hair back with both hands. The tawny strands simply fell back into his face, but he ignored it. "I can't believe you're talking about marriage after knowing this girl—excuse me, this *woman*—for a weekend." He stopped pacing, a thought suddenly occurring to him. "You have slept with her, right?"

Ian laughed. "Yes, I have. But even if I hadn't, I'd still be researching engagement rings."

Devon sat back down with a thump. "I don't get it, man. What makes her so special?"

Ian was still chuckling. "Well, let me tell you about our first date."

* * * * *

Twenty minutes later, Devon was howling with laughter. "Her friend walked in on you?" He wiped his streaming eyes, struggling to keep Ian in focus. "How'd she handle it? Wait, let me guess—screams and wails and embarrassed excuses?"

"You'd think, right? But no, she goes out to the kitchen and laughs her ass off with Lacey." Ian shook his head, a wide smile splitting his face. "Man, it was great. The two of them rolling around on the kitchen floor, laughing like loons. They started up all over again when I came in."

"Okay, so she might have something going for her," Devon grudgingly admitted. "How is she in the sack?"

Ian admonished his friend with a look. "Devon, please. I refuse to share the details of mine and my future bride's bedroom activities." He paused a moment. "She's amazing."

"Hotter than Gina Palmari?"

"Man, Gina Palmari was an ice cube compared to Jane."

Devon blinked. "Wow. What does she do?"

Ian snorted at the avid look on his friend's face. "She doesn't do anything out of the ordinary, she's just…I guess all the way there, you know? I mean, she's not thinking about how her hair looks, or if her ass is too big—all that stupid stuff that women think of during sex that kind of ruins it."

"Yeah." Devon frowned. "Why do they do that, anyway?"

Ian spread his palms. "What, like I'm the expert? The point is, she doesn't do that. Plus, the whole submissive thing she's got going on is a helluva turn-on."

Devon shook his head. "Yeah, I can't believe that. Does she know you overheard her in the café?"

"What am I, stupid?" Ian scoffed. "Hell no, she doesn't know I overheard her. I mean, I would've asked her out anyway, but knowing they were going to be at that club made it all happen a lot faster."

Devon nodded in agreement. "Did you run her?"

"Naturally. She's a pretty amazing woman—built that store on her own, made a success of it. Doesn't live like she could, funnels most of the profits back into the store. It shows, too. The place is great."

"I'm going to have to stop by while I'm in town. I can always use a cup of excellent coffee, and I want to get a look at this paragon you're going to marry."

"If you see her, don't let on about the marriage thing. I haven't exactly brought it up yet. I get the feeling she spooks easy."

Devon rose to his feet. "No problem. Besides, I know how she feels." He winked. "I've got some errands to take care of, and you're going to be late meeting wonder woman."

Ian grinned, came around the desk to give Devon a hard hug. "Don't be a stranger, man. I've missed you. Even if you stay in the game, I'd like to see more of you."

"You bet, man." With a last slap to the shoulder and a two-fingered salute, he was gone.

Ian sighed. He slipped his hands into his pockets and looked out the window at the bustle of the city. It was good to see Devon. The two of them had been like brothers in the unit, the natural bond they'd discovered in basic strengthened by the shared trials and dangers of the life they'd chosen. He hadn't realized how he'd missed that bond until he'd walked into the office, the wide, toothpaste grin and unruly tawny hair the same as always.

It would be great if Devon decided to leave the life. Ian knew better than most what that decision would cost him. It had taken him years of consideration and one disastrous final mission to make the decision. He didn't regret his time with the military; the training they'd given him was providing a very comfortable civilian life.

A civilian life that included a very delicious female, who was currently waiting for him across town. He turned from the window, shut down his computer and snagged his coat. He strode from the room, automatically hitting the lights and locks as he went.

As he rode the elevator to garage level, he thought about Jane's reaction to his call. She had definitely been expecting him to call before this, but she hid it pretty well. And he knew that she was expecting him to waltz in and take her straight to bed. That part of their relationship made sense to her—she was comfortable with it. In bed, she was open, willing—even vulnerable. But out of it—well, she wasn't quite so sure of herself or him.

She couldn't seem to understand his motives. It simply didn't occur to her that he'd want her for more than sex, that he enjoyed being with her and liked her as a person. Well, he was going to have to figure out a way to let her know, without spooking her too much, that he was in this for the long haul.

The most obvious way was to cut out the sex altogether and concentrate on showing her how compatible they were in other areas. But call him selfish, he wasn't going to give up the sex. Not only was it the best he'd ever had, but shelving the bedroom activities *would* spook her. The whole premise of the thirty-day trial he'd proposed was for her to explore giving up control sexually, see if it was something she liked. Eliminating sex would just give her an excuse to bail on him, and he wasn't about to let that happen.

No, he was going to have to get creative. Combine their experiment in dominance and submission with common date activities designed to show her how good they could be together. He tossed his keys from hand to hand as he stepped off the elevator at the garage level, running possible scenarios through his head. He fit the key into the door lock, but then paused as a thought occurred to him. He turned it over in his mind for a minute, looking for the flaws, possible problems. He grinned. That, he thought, was the perfect way to start. Ian chucked out loud. Oh, this was going to confuse the hell out of her.

* * * * *

He took her to the Lincoln Park Zoo. He almost lost it when he dragged her into the orangutan exhibit. The look on her face when she realized that "let's go see the monkeys" wasn't some euphemism for lascivious activities almost caused him to choke on his popcorn.

He pulled her through the exhibits, reading the informational plaques on the various species and laughing with her at the antics of the apes and monkeys. They spent four hours at the zoo, walking along the pond and talking. He bought her a stuffed ape from the souvenir shop and an ice cream cone.

All the walking gave them an appetite, so they found a little Italian place near the park and laughed over pasta and wine. He drove her home and stayed the night, taking her over and over again until she lost track how many times she came. The next morning he went to the corner bakery for croissants and served them to her in bed with orange juice and coffee.

When she was finished, he set the tray on the floor and had her for breakfast.

* * * * *

Over the next few weeks, he stuck to the plan of fun dates and hot sex. They went to an interleague game between the White Sox and Cubs at Wrigley Field, cheering with violent glee for opposite teams. By the time they made it back to his house, they were mindless with lust and devoured each other in his kitchen, unable to wait long enough to make it up the stairs.

He was working hard at keeping her off balance, knowing it was the key to his plan. It wasn't easy—she was a naturally suspicious woman, and he knew that she was confused by the lack of seriousness in their recent dates. He was deliberately keeping things light and fun. He knew she was likely racking her brain, trying to figure out his angle. It was something he was determined to keep her guessing on, at least until she was so deep in love with him she couldn't see straight.

Ian hung up the phone on a Saturday night, an idea forming in his head. She was still working—some problem was keeping her in the office—and he mulled an idea over. Obviously, his plans to take in a Bulls game were out the window. And now that his casual date plans had been scuttled, he began thinking that this might be the perfect time to step up the intensity a bit.

Chapter Eleven

Jane sat surrounded by a pile of papers in the middle of her office floor, frantically trying to find the February 5th gourmet coffee invoice. She'd been at it for over an hour, and her nerves were frayed. Her current state of panic had been helped along considerably by four espressos, and her staff was giving her a very wide berth.

"Dammit, where is that fuckin' thing?" she snarled, pawing at the pile. "Susie!" She hollered for her manager. "Susie, did you find the February file?"

Susie, a summa cum laude graduate from Northwestern and single mother of a rambunctious toddler, was wise enough to only poke her head in the door. A shock of jet-black hair, teased into spikes and tipped with blue led the way, followed by an angel's face that was accented by the barbell in her eyebrow and the row of diamond studs going up her left ear.

"I think you're sitting on it," she said, and disappeared back around the corner.

Jane shifted, cursing when she found the file tucked under her left butt cheek, and cursing even louder when it failed to yield the invoice.

She was in the middle of an inventive stream of insults aimed at the inventors of paper, invoices, filing systems and coffee when she heard, "Lose something, darling?"

She shrieked, papers flying in every direction, and she glared up at Ian. "You scared the shit out of me!"

He chuckled and shifted from his lounging position against the doorframe. Long strides carried him to the middle of the room, and he crouched down, lifting her face with a finger under the chin to drop a quick kiss on her lips. He looked around at the pile of papers. "What is all this?"

She huffed out a breath. "It's hopeless is what it is. I can't find the February invoice for the Café's coffee order, and I need it to prove that they charged me for twice what they actually delivered."

He began to shuffle papers. "What's it look like?"

She waved a hand. "Oh, don't even bother, Ian. I've been through that pile a hundred times, it's not in there." When he merely looked at her, eyebrow sardonically raised, she sighed and rolled her eyes. "Fine. It's rice paper-thin, with a blue border and a picture of a pile of coffee beans at the top. Says Gourmet Beanery."

He started shuffling papers again, and she took the opportunity to study him. Dressed head to toe in form-fitting black, his hair slightly tousled by the spring wind, she had to concentrate on her breathing. Lord, but he was fine. She watched the muscles of his shoulders and arms bunch and shift under his pullover, and tried not to drool.

Ian smiled, held up a paper with a blue border and a picture of pile of coffee beans. "This what you're looking for?"

Jane snatched it out of his hands, staring at it in disbelief. She looked up at his smirking face and scowled. "You know, I could learn to hate you for this."

He laughed. "What're you doing here so late, anyway?"

"Is it late?" Jane looked at her bare wrist. "I forgot my watch. What time is it?"

He glanced at the clock on the wall behind her. "After midnight. How long have you been here?"

"Since about four this afternoon." She looked around him to the doorway. "Susie, you don't have to babysit me. Go home."

Susie stepped into the doorway, purse and coat already in hand. "Are you sure? I can stick around for a while; my mom has Georgia for the night."

Jane waved a hand. "Go. I'll be fine, really."

"Okay." Susie shrugged into her coat. "Make her eat something, okay?" she said to Ian. "She had a half a slice of pizza and a grape soda at six. She's probably running on fumes by now."

"Will do." He smiled at her. "It was nice meeting you, Susie."

"Same here. See you tomorrow, Jane?"

"Okay. Say hi to your mom, and kiss Georgia for me."

Susie nodded and was gone with a wave. Jane looked at Ian. "I'm sorry, I didn't think to introduce you."

"We introduced ourselves, while you were in here insulting Juan Valdez's mother." He sat down cross-legged in front of her. "Who's Georgia?"

Jane was studying the coffee invoice. "Her little girl," she answered absently. "She's three."

"You like kids?" Ian asked.

"Sure, and Georgia's a pip. Cutest little thing this side of Hollywood, and smart as hell." She scowled at the invoice. "Dammit! I'm going to have to find the packing slip. The numbers on this are wrong, too."

"Whoa, slow down!" Ian grabbed her hand when she moved to stand up. "Where are you going?"

"I have to go down to receiving to look at the packing slips from February."

He shook his head. "You stay put. You've been at this for almost eight hours." He held up a hand, stilling the protest forming in her lips. "After you have a break, eat something, I'll go down and look with you. Deal?"

"Okay, fine. But I don't know what we're going to eat. The pizza is like, six hours old. Ick."

"Got it covered." He winked, then rose to his feet and went out the door. He reappeared a moment later, a basket in hand.

"A picnic?" She watched as he shoveled the stacks of paper out of the way and set down the basket.

"Not just any picnic," he said. "This is Michael MacInnes's Ultimate Romantic Picnic Surprise. Guaranteed to win the heart of any female, young or old."

She laughed. "Your father, right?"

"Right." He flipped the lid on the basket, and with a flourish pulled out a white tablecloth. She scooched out of the way so he could spread it on the floor, then sat back down and watched to see what else he'd bring out.

A bottle of champagne and two crystal flutes were next. Then pâté and crackers, caviar with toast points. A platter with fresh grapes and cheese, little slices of summer sausage. And a big silver bowl filled with juicy strawberries.

"Wow." She blinked at the spread laid out in front of her. "Your dad really knows his stuff."

"Actually, I made some modifications to the menu. My dad's formula calls for Haggis and beer. Somehow, I figured I'd probably do better with champagne and caviar."

"Wise move." She looked around. "But you missed something."

"What?"

She pointed. "No chocolate to go with the strawberries."

"Ah, you underestimate me." He held up a finger then reached into the basket once again. She laughed as he pulled out a blue enamel fondue pot, the scent of warm chocolate wafting to her nose. He placed it on the tablecloth next to the bowl of strawberries, dipped one in and held it to her lips.

"Hmmm," she bit into the fruit, closing her eyes as she chewed. "Now it's a romantic picnic."

He laughed, pulling matches from the basket and lighting the flame under the pot to keep the chocolate warm. He slid the basket behind him, out of the way. "What else would you like to try?"

"The caviar looks fabulous," she enthused, and reached for a toast point.

"Nope." He took her hand before she could reach the food, pressed a quick kiss to her fingers. He grinned at her confused look. "I'm going to feed you. You don't lift one finger."

Jane smiled. "Okay." She watched him spread caviar on a toast point with a delicate little silver spoon before lifting it to her lips. She opened her mouth and he placed it on her tongue.

"Good?" he murmured.

She swallowed. "Wonderful," she purred, holding his gaze.

"Here, try the pâté." He scooped some up on a cracker and fed it to her, his groin tightening at her breathy little moan of pleasure.

He fed her cheese and sausage, the fresh grapes, and more of the caviar and pâté. She was sighing and moaning with every bite, watching him out of heavy-lidded eyes and flicking his skin with her tongue every chance she got. He responded with little nibbly kisses to her neck, smiling when he felt her shudder under his mouth.

He had a bit of a smirk left on his face when he pulled back to pick up another grape, and her eyes narrowed. With a calculating gleam, she took the proffered fruit into her mouth, catching his fingers between her lips as she did so.

"Hmmmmm…" she moaned, flicking her tongue over his fingertips as she swallowed the grape. "So firm and juicy." She released his fingers with a pop. "Can I have another?"

The only warning that she got was the sudden flare in his eyes and a low growl, and she found herself flat on her back with a big pile of predatory male looming over her. She bit back a grin and blinked at him innocently. "Is something wrong?"

"You're a little tease, you know that?" he growled, and she felt her nipples tighten in helpless response.

"So?"

"So, you know what happens to teases, don't you?" Ian gathered her wrists in his hands and brought them above her head. He pinned them so that she was stretched out, her breasts thrust forward and straining. She flexed her hands in his grip, feeling her fingers brush against the edge of her desk.

She lifted a brow. "What's that?"

He leaned down, swiped his tongue over the skin under her ear, and whispered. "I'm going to show you." She felt him shift both of her hands so he held them in one of his, felt him reach behind him with one hand. Then heard the rattle of metal.

"What the hell…?" Jane tried to lift up, out of his grip, but he held her fast, and she felt the cool touch of metal on her wrists. He sat up, and she craned her neck to look at her hands. He'd pulled them to the leg of her desk and handcuffed them, the chain of the cuffs around the desk leg. She gave the cuffs a testing tug and was met with the firm resistance of police-grade steel.

She turned back to find him leaning back on his haunches, arms crossed and surveying her with a look of intense satisfaction. "Well." She wriggled a little, adjusting her position so as not to put so much strain on her arms. "Now that you've got me here, what're you planning to do with me?"

"Oh, I've got a few ideas," he smirked.

"Well, do you think you could hurry it up a bit?" she asked, doing her best to sound bored. "I have other things I could be doing, you know."

He merely raised one eyebrow and turned to the picnic basket. He began rummaging around, and she tried to shift her position to see around him. Without turning around, he rumbled, "Stay still. You'll hurt your hands."

She stuck out her tongue at his back and subsided, putting on a suitably vague expression when he turned back around, sliding his hands behind his back. She forgot that she was supposed to be indifferent and scowled at him. "What's behind your back?"

"My hands?" he said, grinning at the frustrated look on her face. He reached for the waistband of her jeans.

"I'm going to get cold," she complained as he unfastened them and peeled them off. He tossed them across the room and slid his hands under her hips to peel down her panties.

Ian grinned at her as he shoved her underwear in his pocket. "Oh, I wouldn't worry about catching a chill. I think you'll be warm enough soon."

He tackled the buttons of her cotton blouse, leaving it to hang off her shoulders, then unhooked her front closure bra and shoved it aside. "There," he said, satisfaction evident in his tone. "That's better."

"What's better about it?" Jane grumbled, shooting him a mock glare. "I'm cold, handcuffed and I wasn't finished eating."

"Oh, are you still hungry, baby?" he queried. He reached behind him for the fondue pot, setting it down within easy reach, and dipped a finger into the warm pool of chocolate. "Here," he said, lifting it to her lips. "Have a snack."

She took his finger into her mouth, sucking it clean. "Hmmmm…" she murmured as he pulled his finger free. "Want more."

He chuckled. "Too bad, darling. Now it's my turn to tease."

Jane watched as he reached into his back pocket and pulled out a fine-tipped brush. She recognized it from the Japanese calligraphy display in the store. He stroked it once across her belly, and she caught her breath at the sensation.

He smiled. "Like that, do you?"

Jane swallowed, her throat gone suddenly dry. "It's okay," she managed.

"Uh-huh." The smile widened into a grin, and she knew he wasn't buying it. "Well, let's see how this works," he said, and dipped the brush into the fondue pot.

She held her breath as he swirled the brush in the chocolate, coating it with a thick layer of the sweet confection. He raised it dripping from the pot and held it suspended over her right breast. They both watched as a drop gathered on the pointed tip, clung to the bristles until it became too heavy and dropped.

She gasped as the warm syrup hit her breast, then moaned as he dipped the brush in it, swirling a pattern of chocolate around her breast and over her nipple with an artist's flair. He returned to the pot for another dip, repeating the process on her left breast before setting down the brush and admiring his handiwork.

"You just look good enough to eat," he rumbled, his eyes so dark with lust they were almost black.

Jane was panting, straining against the handcuffs as she writhed under his sensual gaze. "What's stopping you?" she gasped.

"Good point," he growled, and lowered his head.

She arched hard, as far as her restrained hands would allow, moaning as he swirled his talented tongue over her breasts. He took his time, catching every last smidge of chocolate, and by the time he lifted his head she was in agony.

"Please, Ian," she cried, and tried to lift her legs around his hips.

He caught her knees in his hands, holding them apart with easy strength despite her struggles to free herself. "Now, that's what I like to hear. You say please so sweetly, baby." He swiped her nipple with his tongue one last time. "But I don't really think you've learned your lesson about teasing quite yet."

Jane threw her head back on a desperate gasp. "I have, I have! I promise!"

"Well, why don't we just see?" he murmured, and picked up the brush again.

Jane tossed her head from side to side, mindless with pleasure as she felt him paint her dripping pussy with the brush. The warm sauce felt searing on her overly sensitive flesh, and without warning, she spun off into orgasm.

When she came back to earth, she opened her eyes to find Ian watching her with masculine satisfaction stamped on his features. "You okay?"

"Think so," she panted, struggling to catch her breath.

"Good." He grinned. "Because we're not done."

"Oh, God!" she screamed as his head dipped between her thighs and his tongue snaked out to flick her clit. He growled, shoved her thighs wider, and with the flat of his tongue covered her entire slit with one firm swipe. She screamed again as the orgasm bore down on her, and again as she realized he wasn't stopping.

By the time he finally lifted his head and began tearing at his slacks, she'd had four orgasms and felt like a quivering pile of Jell-O. She watched through hazy eyes as he shoved his pants down past his hips, freeing his erection. He gripped the backs of her knees, pulled her legs high and wide, and plunged to the heart of her in one firm stroke.

The sudden sensation of fullness where she'd been so achingly empty only moments before sent Jane hurtling back into orgasm. The rhythmic clenching of her sensitive sheath on his cock was too much for him to bear, and within moments, he tumbled after her into oblivion. She dimly heard his hoarse shout of satisfaction, felt him empty himself into her, and incredibly felt the spasms begin anew.

It was long moments before either of them could speak; the only sound in the room the ticking of the clock and their harsh breathing.

Jane finally attempted to speak. "So, that's what happens to teases."

Her only answer was a muffled rumble, as Ian didn't lift his face from where it was buried in her neck.

"So, what exactly is my incentive not to tease?"

He chuckled and raised his head. "That's a good point." He looked up to where her hands were still cuffed to the desk. "How're your hands doing?"

"They're a little sore," she admitted. "I was doing a lot of pulling."

Since his pants were still around his knees, he didn't have to move much to dig the key out of his pocket. He undid the cuffs, drawing her arms down and gently rubbing at the chafed skin of her wrists. He smiled down at her. "Better?"

"Much." She leaned up to kiss him, then shoved at his shoulders, hooking her legs around his waist and nudging him to his back. She settled over him, straddling his thighs, and picked up the calligraphy brush.

"My turn," she grinned.

He laughed and folded his hands behind his head. "Have at it, darlin'," he rumbled.

She took her time, swirling and painting, and cleaning up after the brush with her lips and tongue. Before long, he was groaning, arching up into her every touch and tangling his hands in her hair. When he couldn't take it any longer he pulled her up his body and drove deep in a hard piecing thrust that seemed to go straight to her core. It was a fast, sweaty ride and when it was done, they collapsed in a limp, sweaty heap on the floor.

"I still have to look for the packing slip," she murmured drowsily, snuggling firmly into the curve of his shoulder.

His arm came up around her, tugging her close. He rumbled, "Nap now. Packing slip later."

"'Kay," she sighed, and drifted off to sleep.

When they awoke a couple of hours later, he stayed true to his word and hunted packing slips with her in his underwear. Then he fucked her brains out on a pallet of dictionaries in the loading area.

* * * * *

They were having a great time, talking and laughing, and learning about each other. He learned that she loved Chinese food and the Beatles, but hated Thai and Cher. She learned that he thought Steven King was overrated, but loved Jonathan Kellerman. They discovered that they both liked action movies and slapstick comedy, especially the old vaudeville routines. A heated argument broke out one night over who was funnier, the Three Stooges or Abbott and Costello. Jane recited the entire dialogue from "Who's On First" while Ian ticked off Shemp's good points on his fingers. They finally settled the issue with a quick and sweaty grapple on the sofa, with both agreeing to call it a draw.

Ian felt he was making serious progress at showing her the merits of a relationship with him. He knew she was having a good time, knew she enjoyed being with him. But he still sensed her holding back, like she just couldn't figure out what he was up to.

* * * * *

What the hell was he up to, anyway? Jane muttered to herself as she perused the contents of her closet, trying to figure out what to pack. Ian wasn't exactly acting strange, but he sure wasn't acting like guy just out for fun, which is how he'd made this whole deal sound when he'd proposed it to her nearly three weeks ago. Fun and games for a month, he said, then if everyone's not happy we'll call it a day. Only he seemed to be making a campaign for keeping the thing going. And she wasn't sure what to do about that.

"Knock, knock. Anybody fucking in there?"

Jane snorted out a laugh, glancing at the doorway to see Lacey tentatively peeking her head around the frame.

"No, no fucking going on. It's just me, having a nervous breakdown." Jane turned back to her closet. "How did I not know that I have nothing to wear?"

"Um, yeah." Lacey stood at Jane's side and stared into the closet, the contents of which could likely stock Saks for a Labor Day sale. "There's nothing in there all right, for say, a trip to Mars. Everything else is covered, though." She looked at the bed, where garments were strewn about like confetti. "What's going on?"

Jane snatched a blue sweater off its hanger, regarded it thoughtfully, and tossed it over her shoulder. It landed amid its comrades at the foot of her bed. "I've got that Chamber of Commerce charity thing tonight."

Lacey held up a pair of leggings in a dark charcoal color. "Um, that's formal, right?"

"Yeah. I'm wearing that."

Lacey followed her nod to the black gown hanging on the bathroom door in its protective bag. "Why are you playing shopping spree if you already know what you're wearing?"

"Oh, this isn't for the dinner—it's for tomorrow and Sunday. I'm spending the weekend at Ian's." She sat down heavily on the floor, narrowly missing one of last season's Jimmy Choo slingbacks. "I think I'm having a nervous breakdown."

"Why?" Lacey slipped off the bed to sit on the floor across from Jane. "You've spent the night over there before."

"Yeah, but that was always spontaneous, you know? Sort of like, 'hey, its late, I'm tired from all the great sex—I'll just head home in the morning.' This is different—we're spending the *weekend* together."

Lacey stared. "I'm still not seeing the problem here, Janey."

Jane pulled a Kate Spade bag out from under her hip and tossed in the closet. "It's like, planned. A couple thing. People who are just experimenting with sex for a month don't spend weekends together, for Christ's sake. Couples do that."

"So, you're a couple. What's wrong with that?"

"I didn't sign up for couple!" Jane plowed her hands through her hair in frustration. "I signed on for a month of fun, to explore the whole submission thing."

"How's that part of it going, by the way?"

She shrugged. "It's great, actually. Really hot. There's—I don't know—this sense of freedom about giving up control. I don't have to make any moves, no decisions. I just get to go with the flow."

"What if he tries something you don't like?"

"Oh, he's only done that once. He started talking about trying anal sex. I had to nip that in the bud."

"You've done that before, haven't you?"

"Yeah." Jane mused. "But it wasn't very good, and it felt weird. I think in order to do that with someone, you have to really trust them."

"And you don't trust Ian."

"Oh, sure I trust him. I mean, I trust him to not do anything that'll hurt me physically, and I trust him to remember that I'm allergic to carrots. That he'll pick me up when he said he would. That kind of thing."

Lacey held up a finger. "But you don't trust him emotionally, do you?"

"What do you mean?"

"You just said you trust him not to hurt you physically. But you don't trust him not to break your heart. That's why no anal sex."

"What does *that* mean?"

"Well, think about it. You said that the one time you did the butt thing it felt weird. Possibly, because you weren't in love with the guy you were doing it with. At least, you couldn't trust him. Which makes it kind of hard to relax and enjoy the experience."

Jane frowned. "So you're saying that you have to be in love with someone to let them fuck your ass?"

Lacey rolled her eyes. "No, I'm saying that that particular act is for you a very intimate one. And in order to have that level of trust in another person, *you* probably have to be in love with him."

"So, not everybody has to be in love, just me?"

"In a nutshell, yeah."

Jane considered that for a moment. "I think you're full of shit."

"I think you're in love with this guy and you're afraid."

Lacey arched one delicately arched brow when Jane remained silent. "Nothing to say?"

Jane shook her head. "No. Because I'm afraid you might be right." She turned pleading eyes on Lacey. "I think about him all the time. I can barely get through the day without remembering something he did, or said, and I get this huge sappy smile on my face. Sometimes I ache—physically ache, because I just want to be touching him, or sitting next to him. What if I am falling in love with him? What the hell am I supposed to do about it?"

"Why do you have to do anything about it, except enjoy?"

Jane sighed at the confusion in her friend's voice. "I've never been in love before."

"So? It's about time, right?"

"I'm really scared, Lace." Jane bit her lip. "I mean, what if I let myself fall totally head over heels in love with him, and it turns out he's just out for fun and games?"

"Sweetie, you just got through saying you think he wants more than that."

"Yeah, but what if I'm wrong?" Jane flung a pair of opera-length gloves at the bed, watched them drift to the floor.

"What if I trust him, and believe in him, and he lets me down?"

"Listen, dollface," Lacey scooted through the pile of pashmina and denim between them to grasp Jane's hand. "You're never going to find out what's possible with him unless you go for it. And I mean all the way, no holds barred. You've got to trust him, and believe in him, or it won't matter how much he wants you and cares about you. It won't work if you're always holding on to that one little piece of yourself because you're afraid you'll get hurt."

Jane nodded. "I know. I know you're right. It's just hard, you know? Letting someone else in like that."

"I know." She gave Jane's cold fingers a squeeze. "But honey, let's talk seriously for a second here. This is a great guy. He's gainfully employed, he's amazingly cute, from what I could see he's dynamite in the sack and he really, really likes you. Didn't he listen to you go on and on about the evil being perpetuated by the books on tape industry last week? Without once checking to see if you were running a fever or asking if you were on any medication?"

Jane gave a watery chuckle. "Yeah."

"Well, there you go. That's not the behavior of a man who's just in it for the hot sex. If that were the case, he'd have given you something else to do with your mouth!"

Jane laughed. "Okay, okay. You're right. I just have to go for it. I'm still scared, though. Really scared."

"Baby." Lacey held her hand tighter. "Everybody gets scared when it comes to this stuff. That's how you know it's real."

"Well, then I guess it's real. 'Cause even the *thought* of him breaking my heart makes me wanna puke."

"Well, then it's real. Like there was ever a doubt."

"Okay." Jane drew in a deep breath, letting it out in a whoosh. "I'm going to do it."

"Do what?"

"Fall in love with him!" Jane stared at Lacey exasperated.

Lacey giggled. "Baby, you're already in love with him. You just decided to start believing it."

"Well, it's the same thing."

"Uh-huh, right." Lacey pushed herself to her feet.

"Lace?"

"Yeah?"

"You ever been in love like that? Where you feel like puking and singing at the same time?"

"Once, I thought I was." Lacey's eyes took on a faraway look. "A long time ago."

Jane frowned when she just stood there, her usually expressive features still and solemn. "Lace, you okay?" she said quietly.

Lacey gave a faint smile. "Sure, sweetie. Just old ghosts creeping up on me."

"You wanna talk about it?"

"No." Her smile grew bigger. "That's a story for another time. I'll leave you to pack for your couples weekend." She turned for the door.

"Lace?" Jane waited until she turned around. "Thanks, hon."

"Anytime, pal. Call me if you need me, okay?" Lacey waited for Jane's nod, and with one last smile, was out the door.

Jane sat on the floor and looked at the disarray of her closet. So, she was in love. It didn't change the fact that she still didn't have anything to wear.

Chapter Twelve

At 6:45 p.m. Jane hauled her enormous duffel and garment bag out of the back seat of the cab and started up the walk to Ian's townhome. She tossed her hair back over her shoulder and tried without much success to quell the nervous butterflies in her stomach. Even though she'd decided that Lacey was right, that she needed to try trusting Ian and her feelings for him, she was still nervous about the weekend.

She'd never felt so excited and sick to her stomach at the same time. She rang the bell, shifting the duffel over her shoulder to ease the weight. She tried taking a couple of calming breaths as she heard him disengage the locks to open the door. She opened her mouth to say hello, but the words got stuck in her throat as she looked at him.

He was already halfway dressed for the evening, the formal white dress shirt hanging open over his bare chest, cuffs still loose at the wrist. Jane took in the hard planes of his chest, the whorls of hair that tapered to his navel and disappeared in that glorious little happy trail into the waistband of the tuxedo pants. They hung low on his narrow hips, and his feet were bare. She tilted her head, looking at his bronzed feet peeking out from under the cuffs of his pants. Man, she was pretty far gone if his feet were turning her on.

"Hey, gorgeous." Ian leaned in to press a kiss to her lips, taking both bags from her hands as he did. He shifted them to one brawny hand and slipped an arm around her waist, leading her into the house. She felt a warm glow in the pit of her stomach at the casual gallantness of the gesture. He was always doing stuff like that, she thought as she watched him drape her garment bag over the back of a wing chair. He opened doors for her, put a guiding hand at the small of her back when they walked. He never left her clothes in a mangled heap on the floor—well, that one time he did, but the dress was in shreds. And he did surprise her the next day with a new one to replace it.

He turned and caught her staring at him, and he sent her a quizzical look. "What're you thinking so hard about over there?"

Jane smiled easily, relaxed for the first time since talking to Lacey amidst the ruin of her closet. Her friend was right—he was a great guy. And she was in love with him.

She crossed to him, sliding her arms under the open shirt to wrap around him. "I'm just thinking how fabulously sexy you are." She nuzzled her face into the musky heat of his throat, smile widening as she felt his pulse quicken under her lips.

"Hmmm..." he rumbled, sliding wide palms up and down her back and making her shiver in delight. "You're in a mood, aren't you? What brought this on?"

"I'm just happy." She slipped her tongue out to taste his collarbone. "Is that okay?"

"It's working for me," he rumbled. He grabbed a fistful of her hair, tugged her head back and took her mouth.

Jane moaned and opened her mouth wider, humming in delight as his tongue slid past her lips. He thrust in and out of her mouth in a slow, deliberate rhythm that she could feel all the way down to her toes, and she shivered and curled her own tongue up to meet his. He tugged her hair hard, forcing her head back even further as the kiss changed from a seduction to a conquest, his mouth taking hers without mercy.

She whimpered and began to suckle strongly, pulling his tongue deeper into her mouth, and he groaned at the exquisite sensation. He wrenched his lips from hers, breathing heavily, and she opened her eyes to find his glittering down at her.

"Whatever you did to put yourself in this mood, keep doing it," he rasped.

She laughed hoarsely, her blood beating a hammer pulse in her throat. "Kinda wish we didn't have to get ready for the benefit."

He groaned and dropped his head to her shoulder. "Do we really have to go?"

"Yes, we do. Remember, it's good for business?" Jane shivered as he began to nuzzle her neck. "Ian…"

He sighed, straightened with a last nibble of her neck. "I know, I know." He grimaced, reaching down to adjust himself. "I think I'll skip watching you get dressed, if you don't mind."

She tucked her tongue in her cheek. "I need a shower, too."

"Now you're just torturing me."

Jane laughed, suddenly so full of love for this man that she couldn't keep it in anymore. "You make me happy, Ian."

He stilled, the grin that had appeared at her laugh softening into a tender smile, his eyes glowing down at her. He rested his forehead on hers. "You make me happy too, Jane."

She closed her eyes and drew in a shuddering breath. His words washed over her like warm rain, easing the knots of tension that had tied up her stomach. She hadn't meant to blurt that out, and for one dizzying moment she'd been terrified that he would reject her somehow. But he hadn't, and she felt the protective wall around her heart crack just a little more.

Jane reached up, cupping his face in her hands and brushed a soft kiss across his lips. "If you'll let go of my hair," she whispered, "I'll go take a shower."

"Okay," he whispered back, and with a last tug, released her.

She reached over to scoop up the garment bag from the chair, but he beat her to it, and the duffel bag. He gestured for her to precede him up the stairs. "C'mon, you can shower while I finish getting dressed."

"Sure you can handle me showering in the next room?" She waggled her brows at him over her shoulder as she started up the stairs.

"No. That's why I'm dressing in the guest room."

Jane let out a peal of laughter and ran lightly up the stairs, Ian following at a pace more suitable to avoiding bodily injury in his aroused state. "Laugh it up, woman," he hollered. "You'll get yours."

"Promise?" she called back, then shrieked as he began taking the stairs two at a time, and scampered into the bath with him hot on her heels.

* * * * *

Jane managed, with extravagant promises of exotic sexual favors, to shoo him out of the bathroom. She showered hurriedly, thankful that she'd taken the time to shave her legs that morning and didn't have to worry about it. She scrubbed her skin until it gleamed, then smoothed a light body oil over her body while she was still damp from the shower.

She took extra care with her hair and makeup, slid into the brand new lingerie she'd stopped for on the way over. The thigh-high stockings, barely there thong panties and stiletto heels made her feel sexy and strong. The dress was backless, with a built-in bra so she didn't need to wear one, and she wondered with a wicked grin how long it would take Ian to figure that out.

She slipped the dress off the padded hanger and stepped gingerly into it, careful not to catch her heel in the hem. She tugged the bodice up over her breasts, slid her arms through the skinny straps and studied the effect in the mirror.

The black silk was a shimmering column that hugged her curves from breast to knee, falling in a straight line to the tops of her shoes. The slit up her left leg was the only thing that made it possible to walk. The bodice was square, with wide-set spaghetti straps that crossed beneath her collarbones, draped over her shoulders and attached to the dress at the small of her back to form a V that framed the bare skin of her back. It was modeled after a dress that Marilyn Monroe had worn in *The Seven Year Itch*, and it made her feel fabulously sexy.

She turned, eyeing the dress from every angle in the mirror. She grinned. He was going to swallow his tongue when he got a load of her. She picked up the small evening bag that she'd packed with the essentials, sent herself a wink in the mirror and sailed out of the bathroom.

Jane stopped in the bedroom to pull her dress coat out of the garment bag that was draped over the foot of the bed, then started out to look for Ian.

He was standing at the foot of the stairs, straightening his bowtie in the hall mirror. He hadn't heard her yet, so she took the opportunity to study him.

He was frowning faintly in the mirror as he fiddled with the tie. His big hands were tanned dark, the contrast to his snow-white dress shirt causing her to catch her breath. She loved to look at his hands on her skin, loved the differences between her pale complexion and his brawny, bronzed male skin when they were making love. Just thinking about it made her pulse speed up and her pussy grow damp with need.

He finished fiddling with the tie and began checking the studs on his shirt, running his fingers down the center of his chest to make sure they were all securely fastened. Jane drew in a breath as she pictured her tongue following the same path. The slight sound caught his ear, and he flicked his eyes to her image reflected in the mirror.

Jane smiled, slow and female, as she saw his eyes widen and his throat work in a swallow. As he turned she started down the stairs, letting her fingers trail down the satiny wood of the banister, and kept her eyes on his until she stood on the bottom step. They were standing eye to eye, the heels and step bringing her to his height.

"Baby." He settled his hands on her shoulders, slid them down the silky smooth skin of her arms to grasp her hands. He bent down to kiss her, lazily moving his lips over hers, with just a teasing hint of tongue. "You look delicious."

"Hmmm." She smiled against his mouth, curling her fingers into his. "You look pretty damn fine yourself, you know."

Ian dipped his head to her throat, inhaling the scent of warm woman and body oil. The combination threatened the fit of his trousers once again. "You sure we can't miss this shindig?"

"Yeah, I'm sure," she sighed, almost purring as he peppered her shoulder with soft kisses.

He placed one last lingering kiss on her shoulder, sighing as he pulled himself away from the siren song of her bare flesh. "Okay." He took her coat from where it was draped across her arm, held it open for her. She turned to slip her arms into the sleeves, grinning as she heard his indrawn breath at the first sight of her bare back.

He settled the coat on her shoulders, then gripped them in firm hands and turned her to face him. "Did you pick that dress to torture me?"

"No, I picked it because it was gorgeous, on sale and didn't need any tailoring." She tapped his bowtie and slanted him a look from under her lashes. "The torturing you part is just a side bennie."

"You do know you'll pay for it later, right?"

She nearly purred at the gravel in his voice. "Oh, I'm counting on it."

He growled. "Come on, woman, before you make me forget my gentlemanly upbringing." He put his hand on her back to guide her through the kitchen to the garage door as she laughed.

Jane stepped into the garage behind him, pulling on her gloves while he made sure the door was secure. When he finished and she turned to walk with him to the car, the sight that greeted her had her faltering. She stumbled to a stop on feet gone suddenly numb, and Ian grasped her arm to steady her. There, nestled in the dim light of the narrow garage, was one of her dearest fantasies come to life in gleaming chrome and steel. She drew in a gasping breath. "Is that yours?"

She could feel his gaze on her, hear the confusion in his voice. "Yes. Problem?"

She slowly stepped forward, drifting down the steps without feeling the cement beneath her feet. She let out a reverent breath. "I thought the Rover was your car."

He moved to stand beside her, and she tore her eyes away from the vision. He was looking at her with puzzlement. "I drive the Rover for work and for every day. Ronnie here is so valuable, I keep her garaged and only bring her out for special occasions, like tonight. What's going on, Jane?"

She ignored the question and started walking again, not stopping until she was standing close enough to touch. "Ronnie?" She looked over at him as he stopped beside her.

Ian grinned and ran a gloved palm over the curve of the hood. "She always reminded me of Veronica from the Archie comics. Gorgeous, mysterious, aloof. And thousands lust after her in vain. So," he gave the hood a gentle pat, "she was Veronica from the first moment I had her. Ronnie for short."

Jane grinned. "Veronica." She turned back to the car, lifting her hands as if to run them over the surface of the roof. She stopped and looked to him for permission. "Can I touch it?"

Her voice was soft, almost reverent, with a definite note of pleading in the tone. He grinned, amused. "Sure. I didn't know you knew about cars."

Jane raised her hands to the roof, and then impatiently tugged her gloves off so that she could touch it with bare skin. Letting the gloves drift to the floor, she rubbed her palms over the curve of the door. She shook her head in absent answer to his question. "I don't know squat about cars." She swallowed heavily. "But this one..." her voice trailed off on a soft moan. She slowly walked around to the rear of the compact machine, trailing her fingers along the line of it in awe. When she was standing in the back of the car, she stopped, hands resting on the trunk, and lifted eyes gone dark with lust to his.

"What year is it?"

The confusion on Ian's face was clearing, to be replaced by a slow, sensual smile. "1967." He moved around to stand behind her, the scent of him wrapping around her like a blanket. He snuggled his pelvis against the firm curve of her ass, placed his hands over hers to hold them in place on the trunk of the car. He leaned down to brush his lips over her cheek. "Do you like the car, Jane?" he whispered.

Jane caught her breath at the feel of him nestled against her ass. She swallowed, and managed a hissing "Yes."

He gave the sensitive shell of her ear a teasing lick. "Is it turning you on?"

Jane moaned and closed her eyes. "Oh, God, yes."

Ian blew a soft breath on the sensitive spot just behind her ear, and she shivered. "Do you want me to tell you about it?"

His voice had gone dark and low with excitement, and she felt her pussy clench in response. "Yes," she moaned.

He blew out another soft breath, and rumbled thickly, "Say please."

She arched into the hard curve of his body and ran her tongue over lips gone suddenly dry. She didn't hesitate, didn't even entertain the thought of doing so. "Please, tell me more."

She felt Ian smile against her neck, then the wet heat of his mouth and the bite of his teeth as he nipped lightly at the sensitive skin there. "A 1967 Shelby Mustang GT 500, with a 428 cubic inch, V8 engine. Seven liters." He drew his hands up her arms and slid his palms to her breasts, and the combination of his mouth on her neck and the sweet friction on her breasts had her nipples stabbing into his palms through her dress.

"Four speed manual transmission." He began to rotate his palms slowly, both soothing and exacerbating the ache in her breasts and causing her nipples to tighten almost painfully. She moaned and tried to bring her hands up to grasp his neck, but he quickly shifted his hands, clamping them over hers and pressing them into the smooth surface of the trunk. "Keep them there, no matter what." He nipped the back of her neck with enough force to sting. "Understood?"

Since she was breathing like a marathon runner on mile twenty-five, she merely nodded her head in response. It was apparently enough, because he slid his hands up her arms and continued.

"As I was saying." He brought one wide gloved palm back to her right breast and renewed the slow massage, while the other hand settled on her left thigh.

"Zero to sixty in six seconds," he bit gently into her earlobe and began to pluck at her nipple, pulling and twisting so that she whimpered out loud.

"355 horsepower, with a top speed," he dipped his tongue into the whorls of her ear and stroked his left hand up her thigh, gathering her skirt in his hand as he went, "of 132 miles per hour."

Ian moved his hand around to her ass, pushing her dress and coat to her waist so that he was stroking skin left bare by her skimpy thong. The rush of cool air on her exposed flesh had her cunt clenching in anticipation, and she could feel the flood of wet heat soaking through the thin barrier of silk. "The paint," he dipped his head and attached his mouth to her neck, applying a strong suction that seemed to arrow straight to her belly. He released her skin with a soft pop, "is Brittany Blue."

He abandoned her breast and cupped the smooth, cool cheeks of her rear in both leather-clad palms. "And it's original," he used his hands to pry her cheeks apart, and the cool air on the tender crevice between them sent a shiver up her spine, "to the car."

Jane groaned, unable to keep the sound back. His voice, his hands and mouth, the cool surface of the car beneath her palms, was all combining to bring her desire to a fever pitch. She pressed her hips back into his palms, and felt him shift his grip to her hips. The action brought her bare butt in direct contact with the silk fabric of his tux, and she could clearly feel the hard ridge of his cock pressing against her from the other side of his zipper. She moaned again, letting her head drop forward and pushing back even harder, eager to feel that delicious erection more firmly.

Ian clamped his hands firmly onto her hips, stilling her frantic undulations. He pressed his hips firmly into hers, pinning her to the car, and leaned over so that his mouth was once again pressed to her ear. "Tell me what you want, Jane."

Jane struggled to make her brain function, to get her lips to move and her voice to work so that she could answer him. Her breath was sawing in and out of her lungs, her heart thundering in her ears. The ache in her breasts, in her cunt, was unbearable. Her entire body, her whole being, was crying out to have him inside her. For him to fuck her hard and fast, to ease the incredible tension and send her flying.

He tugged sharply on her hips, bringing her splintered focus away from the furious clamoring in her body and back to him. She felt him dig his fingers more firmly into her flesh, and she knew she'd wear his mark by morning. He spoke directly into her ear—his voice rough with his own harsh breathing, and the knowledge that his control was hanging by a thread brought her a heady sense of power.

"Tell me. What do you want, Jane?" It was a demand this time, and he punctuated it with a sharp thrust of his hips. It drove her clit firmly into the edge of the trunk, and the sharp burst of pleasure at the contact loosened her vocal cords.

"I want you to fuck me," she sobbed, pressing her hips frantically into his. The urge to take her hands from the surface of the car nearly overwhelmed her. She wanted to grab his hips and press herself into him, but she knew if she moved her hands, if she ignored that command, that he'd only draw the torture out, perhaps over the whole night. The thought of sitting through that tedious dinner with this inferno raging inside her, unfulfilled, was enough to keep her hands exactly where they were.

Ian removed one hand from her hips, and she felt his knuckles brush against the aching flesh between her thighs. She realized he was opening his fly, and sent out a quick prayer that that meant he was going to put her out of her misery. Soon.

He hooked one finger in the thin string that ran between the cheeks of her ass, and with one sharp twist, snapped the delicate elastic in two. When he released it, the fabric fell to dangle between her legs, still attached in the front but no longer covering the bare, needy flesh of her cunt. She felt the air shift as his hand continued to work behind her, releasing his straining cock from the confines of his pants.

Jane went still as she felt him fit the flared head of his cock to her weeping pussy. He slid a scant inch inside her, stretching her tender opening and causing her breath to hitch in her throat. She could feel her moisture drench his cock. Her pussy was grasping and clenching in an effort to draw him further into her heated depths, but he remained stubbornly still, and she felt a sob of frustration welling up in her chest.

Ian leaned over her, forcing her to bend further over the trunk of the car, and his hands briefly left her hips. He brought them to her chest, reaching inside the bodice of her dress and scooping her breasts into his gloved hands. He shifted them so they spilled out of the low neckline, and pressed her even further forward, so that her nipples came into contact with the cold surface of the car. She reveled in the chill that provided sharp contrast to the heat of him pressed against her back, between her legs. It made her all the more desperate to have him fully inside her.

His hands slid back to her hips, and he set his mouth at the curve of her shoulder. "How do you want me to fuck you, Jane? Slow and easy," he trailed his tongue in a long slow lick from her neck to her ear, "or hard and fast?" He set his teeth in the curve of her shoulder and bit down.

Jane groaned, her head going light at the feel of his teeth on her. "Please," she sobbed, her chest heaving with the effort to speak, "fuck me hard! Please please please please please!"

She had barely uttered the last "please" when he growled, his teeth still set in her skin, and thrust, burying his full length in her wet, clinging depths with one stroke. The force of it drove her firmly into the car, and her breath exploded out of her lungs at the dual sensation of her clit pressing into the trunk and his thick cock firmly lodged inside her.

He didn't give her time to catch her breath, setting a hard, driving rhythm that pushed her clit firmly into the edge of the trunk and caused her bare breasts to slide over the Mustang's smooth surface on each stroke. Within moments, she was moaning with every thrust, and whimpering with every withdrawal. The lust that coiled in her belly wound tighter and tighter with every push of his hips.

Ian let out a rumbling growl and slid one arm around her pelvis to grind himself even more firmly inside her. His thrusts became more frantic, shorter and sharper as she felt him losing control. She threw back her head at the sensation, her own orgasm bearing down on her with hurricane force. She suddenly felt him expand even further inside of her and explode, and the sensation of his come pumping into her triggered her own orgasm.

Jane cried out hoarsely, the sound dwarfed by Ian's shout of satisfaction. She could feel the rippling contractions of her pussy tugging at his cock, milking him dry. He continued to thrust as he came, prolonging the spasms rocking her body, until he was drained. He slumped over her, breathing hard, as her pussy continued to ripple around his spent flesh.

Jane lay sprawled beneath him, pressed into the car, and concentrated on drawing breath. She shuddered as the occasional aftershock shimmered through her system. Every time her flesh would involuntarily clench down, his cock would twitch in response, and she concentrated on bringing her system back under control, knowing she wouldn't be able to take another round like that.

They lay there for long moments, their harsh breathing echoing in the small space. Finally, Ian lifted himself onto his palms, and dropped a tender kiss on her temple. "You can move your hands now, darling."

"Hmmmmm," Jane sighed. "Don't want to move at all."

Ian chuckled. "We have to move. We're going to be late for the benefit."

"Okay," Jane murmured. "You go first."

She felt him shift, gathering himself to move, and gave an involuntary gasp as she felt him pull free from her grasping cunt. The sweet friction set off another round of aftershocks, and she shivered deliciously. She could feel his come and her own fluids begin to leak from her pussy as she lay there.

She lifted her head slightly as he peeled the remnants of her thong down her legs, lifting first one foot then the other to aid him in its removal. She watched over her shoulder as he used what was left of it to wipe his cock clean, before tucking himself back into his trousers. He'd never even taken his pants down, just unzipped his fly, and the idea that he'd been so greedy to have her set off a warm glow in her chest.

She remained still as he went over to a workbench on the far side of the room and gathered a roll of paper towels He returned to her, tearing off a few sheets as he walked. He used the rough paper to clean her tenderly, gathering most of their combined juices from her swollen flesh and wiping the insides of her thighs dry.

He tossed the paper towels and her ruined underwear into a nearby trash can, then pulled her skirt and coat down to cover her backside. She pushed up with her hands, preparing to stand, and he gathered her under her arms and pulled her upright. She turned in his arms, brushing her hair back from her face and met his lips as they came down on hers in a lingering kiss.

"So, do you have any more cars?" she grinned.

Ian threw back his head on a shout of laughter and cuddled her even closer. "No, but I think we got good use out of this one." He dropped a kiss on the top of her head.

"That's an understatement." Jane clung to him as he began leading her around to the passenger door. "I don't think my legs are working right yet."

He was still chuckling as he helped her into the car. "We can skip the dancing portion of the evening."

Jane's grin turned into a light grimace as she settled herself into the car. She was shifting in her seat as he came around to the driver's side, pausing to scoop her gloves up from where she'd dropped them. As he settled himself behind the wheel, she sent him a look. "I need to go upstairs and get something out of my bag."

He frowned. "What?"

She raised a brow. "Panties." She grimaced and shifted again in the seat. "Plus, I'm still pretty gooey. I should clean up a little more thoroughly."

Ian grinned. "I don't think so."

Jane blinked. "What do you mean, you don't think so? I *know* I'm not wearing any panties, and I'm pretty sure if you think about it real hard, you'll remember why. And I really do need to clean up a bit more."

"Oh, I remember." He winked. "But I don't think I'll let you get another pair. And I cleaned you up pretty good, so you don't have to worry about it soaking through your dress."

Jane frowned at him. "But why can't I have any panties and clean up just a little bit more?"

"Because," he said, reaching over to slide one hand across her hip, "I really like the idea of you walking around that ballroom, looking gorgeous and sophisticated and businesslike, with no panties on and my cum still wet on your pussy."

Despite the fact that she'd just come harder than she ever had in her life, Jane felt a little twinge of renewed desire at the look in his eye. She leaned over and kissed him, hard and brief, before settling back in her seat and reaching for the seatbelt.

"Well, okay." She held up a finger. "Just this once."

He turned the key in the ignition, bringing the engine to life with a roar, and grinned when her eyes nearly crossed at the sound. "We'll see."

Chapter Thirteen

Jane smiled politely and tried frantically to remember the name of the person she was talking to. She was pretty sure he was a city councilman. She was absolutely sure he was a pompous ass. He was currently on a tirade about the lack of morals frequently portrayed in today's popular fiction, and she figured she had about thirty more seconds of outward calm left before she lost her temper and verbally blasted him through the back wall.

She shifted on her skyscraper heels, sucking in a breath as the motion caused her thighs to slide together. The slickness between them was driving her crazy, reminding her of their encounter on the car and keeping her on the razor edge of arousal the whole night. It was very disconcerting to be thinking about her lover's cum dripping from her pussy while the mayor was talking about the diversity and ingenuity of the average Chicago small business owner.

The pompous ass was still talking, and suddenly jabbed her shoulder with his chubby finger to emphasize a point about the depravity of public libraries. Teeth on edge, she decided she'd heard just about enough. She opened her mouth to tell him what he could do with his narrow-minded views and possibly break his finger when she felt an arm come around her waist from behind.

"Excuse me, George." Jane looked up gratefully as Ian smiled genially at the councilman and gave her hip a squeeze. "But I need to steal this lovely lady from you for a moment; the mayor would like a word."

George, looking for all the world like a warthog with male pattern baldness, nodded briskly. "Of course, of course. I understand completely. Can't keep the mayor waiting, even if he is a Democrat, eh?" He laughed uproariously at his own joke, causing the trio of chins bulging out of his collar to jiggle madly.

Jane smiled faintly and turned with Ian, unable to resist one last glance at the chins. "I owe you one."

"And I plan to collect, just as soon as we say our goodbyes and get out of here."

She quirked a brow as he led her through the crowded ballroom, unable to keep the grin from her face. "What, you're not enjoying the food, the drink, the posturing of idiots?"

He snorted. "Not especially, no."

"Thank God. I'd hate to think I was in love with a man who liked this snoozefest."

Ian stopped walking so suddenly she would've tripped over his feet if he hadn't been quick enough to catch her. "Jeez, Ian. Give a girl some warning!"

She untangled her feet from her dress, looked up to find him staring at her with a frozen expression. "What's wrong? Oh, shit..." she whispered, and could've cheerfully bitten off her own tongue and choked on it when she realized what she'd said.

"You said you're in love with me."

"No, I didn't." Jane picked up her skirt and started walking towards the ladies' room as fast as she could in three-inch heels.

"Yes, you did." He caught up with her at the row of payphones outside the restrooms, dragging her to a halt with a hand at her elbow. "You said you'd hate to think you were in love with a man who liked this snoozefest."

"I know what I said!" She stared at her feet for a moment then peeked up at him through her lashes. "I didn't mean it?"

He shook his head green eyes bright and fixed on her. "Try again."

Jane chewed her lip. "It's the liquor talking."

"You had one glass of wine all night. Strike two." He waited, patience straining, while she chewed her lip and stared at the floor. "Dammit, Jane!"

"All right, I love you!" she shouted, folding her arms across her chest and scowling at him. "Happy now?"

"Well, it's fairly obvious that you're not. Care to tell me why being in love with me puts you in such a grumpy mood?"

"It doesn't. Not really." She shrugged.

"Jane, someone who's happy about being in love does not try to take it back the first time she says it." His voice lowered dangerously. "So tell me what's going on."

"Well, how should I know how a person in love is supposed to behave? I've never *been* a person in love before and it's scary and hard, and I don't know what the hell I'm doing!"

He frowned. "Being in love is hard?"

"Yes, it's hard!" She propped her hands on her hips and narrowed her eyes at him. "This emotional vulnerability crap is for the birds. It makes me nuts. I don't know what I'm supposed to say, or do, or expect. I mean, this was supposed to be just fun and games, a month of crazy sex. And now I'm in love with you, which screws all that up." She threw up her hands. "So yes, it's fucking hard, all right?"

Ian was quiet for a moment, his expression inscrutable, and Jane braced herself for whatever he was going to say. Then he started to chuckle. Her jaw dropped as the chuckles grew into guffaws, and the guffaws grew into belly laughs, until he was holding his sides and roaring, and half the people in the room were staring at them.

"You son of a bitch," she spat, and punched him square in the face.

"Ow!" He clamped a hand over his spurting nose and scowled at her. "What did you do that for?"

Jane watched with satisfaction as blood dripped between his fingers. "That was for laughing at me, you jackass. A woman tells you she loves you and she's scared, and you laugh at her? Count yourself lucky that this dress is too damn tight for me to kick you in the balls."

"Oh, I'm sure he'll be very appreciative of that fact, once he stops bleeding."

Jane glanced up as the man stepped forward through the small crowd that her punch had attracted, a look of sublime amusement on his hard, handsome face. He was as tall as Ian, with the same broad shoulders and tough build. His tawny hair was cut short, and had a slight curl to it that might've looked girly on a lesser man. His brown eyes were bracketed by laugh lines, and glowed with mirth.

He pulled a handkerchief out of his breast pocket and handed it to Ian. "Here, pal."

Ian mumbled a thank you and pressed the cloth to his face, still glaring at Jane. She stuck out her tongue at him, and then turned to the stranger when he laughed.

"You two know each other?" she snapped, thoroughly annoyed by the way he was grinning.

"Yes, ma'am." He held out a hand. "Devon Bannion, at your service. Ian and I knew each other in the military."

Jane automatically shook hands. "Nice to meet you, even if you do have questionable taste in friends."

Devon chuckled. "Oh no, the pleasure is all mine. Ian's told me all about you."

Jane slowly turned to look at Ian, narrowed her eyes. "Is that so?"

Ian rolled his eyes at her, a considerable feat considering that he'd tilted his head back to try and stop the bleeding.

"Yes, he mentioned your store. I meant to stop by a while ago, but I just got back into town. I made it in today for a coffee. You've got a clever little place there. Comfortable, relaxing. I enjoyed it."

"Oh. Well, thank you." Jane smiled at Devon, charmed in spite of herself by the mirth still in his eyes. "I'm sorry we had to meet under such appalling circumstances." She aimed a glower at Ian.

Ian gingerly took the handkerchief away from his face. When the bleeding didn't start again, he straightened slowly, glaring at Devon, who was still holding her hand.

"Do you mind," he said in a slightly nasal voice, "turning loose of my woman?"

"Don't you call me 'your woman' in that tone of voice!"

"Jesus, Janey! Would you just calm down and give me a chance to explain!"

"Fine." Jane turned toward him, tugging her hand from Devon's loose grip and folding her arms across her chest. One foot began to tap on the floor. "Explain."

Ian glared balefully at the small group of onlookers they'd attracted. "Fine. You want an explanation? You're getting one, baby." He grabbed her hands and yanked her to him. "I wasn't laughing because the thought of you being in love with me is funny. The thought of you being in love with me makes me the happiest man on earth, because I feel the same way about you."

Jane softened, her chest tightening with emotion. She ignored the collective sigh of their audience at his words to concentrate on his face. "Really?"

"Really."

"Oh, Ian." She reached up to kiss him, but drew back suddenly, bumping his nose in the process. "Wait a minute." She frowned, ignoring his curses at the jolt to his bruised face. "That doesn't explain why you were laughing at me."

He was pinching his nostrils shut with one hand to stem the renewed flow of blood, so he sounded a little funny when he said, "I was laughing because all the while you've been trying to keep from falling in love with me for fear of ruining the fun and games, I've been using the fun and games to try to get you to fall in love with me. Because, baby," he released his nose to wrap both arms around her, "I fell for you the second I saw you rolling around on your kitchen floor, laughing with Lacey."

"Oh God, that's so sweet," she sighed, wrapping both arms around his neck and going up on tiptoe to press a gentle kiss to his lips. "Ian?"

"Hmmm?"

"I might have a hard time saying it, and it might take me a while to get used to it, but I really do love you."

"I love you too, Jane. So much," he winced, feeling his nose with cautious fingers, "that it hurts."

She burst out laughing. "I'm not going to say I'm sorry for punching you. I wouldn't mean it."

He rolled his eyes. "Great."

"But I will take you home and get you some ice for it." She aimed a flirty look at him from beneath her lashes while she toyed with the hair at his nape. "And maybe I can come up with something to keep your mind off it for a while."

"It's a deal."

"Excuse me." They both turned to look at Devon, who was still standing nearby. "I just wanted to say goodbye." He held out a hand to Ian, who shifted Jane to his left side to take it.

"You're leaving?" Jane asked.

"No, just getting back to work. I'm working private security for this gig, and since the scuffle seems to be over," he sent Jane a quick wink, "I'd better get back to it."

"Well, it was nice meeting you," she said.

"Believe me, sugar, the pleasure was all mine. I wouldn't have missed seeing the boss here get sucker punched for all gold in Fort Knox."

Jane frowned. "The boss?"

"It's a long story, honey." Ian dropped a quick kiss on her forehead.

"Okay." She shrugged, and then held out a hand to Devon. "I hope we'll see each other again soon."

He flashed her a lightning grin as he took her hand. "Oh, count on it, darlin'." He raised her hand to his lips for a quick brush of his lips, and with a final wink, he was gone.

Jane watched him melt into the crowd of tuxedos and evening gowns and then turned to Ian. "Interesting friends you have, Ian."

He smiled as Devon disappeared from sight. "Yeah." He looked down at her. "Are you ready to go now? My nose is killing me."

"Aw, poor baby." She grinned at his murderous expression. "Let's get you some ice."

"Don't forget, you promised to take my mind off it," he reminded her as they headed for the coat check. "And you still owe me exotic sexual favors from earlier."

"Well, maybe we can combine the two." She sent him a slow wink as he helped her into her coat.

"Hot damn." He pulled her outside to the valet station, passed the freckle-faced boy in the red jacket a twenty along with his valet stub. "I'm in a hurry, kid. I'll double that if you can get my car here in two minutes."

* * * * *

"Hold still. This might hurt a little," Jane cautioned as she gently settled the ice pack on Ian's swollen nose. He winced a bit at the pressure, but reached up to hold it in place. "How does it feel?"

He shot her a look. "Like I got punched in the face."

"Well, you deserved it. I thought you were laughing at me during one of the most vulnerable moments of my life. If I'd had a weapon, I likely would've done more damage."

His eyes softened and he reached for her, pulling her down so that she lay next to him on the wide bed. "I'm sorry, baby. I didn't think. I hope you realize that I would never try to make you feel silly or embarrassed."

She nodded, the action rubbing her head against his hard shoulder. "I know." She looked up at him. "It's just that I have a hard time trusting sometimes, and you laughing just brought all that forward."

He frowned. "You mean you have a hard time trusting me?"

She shook her head. "Not really. I mean, I know you'd never hurt me, and that I could always count on you to be there if I was in trouble. In my head, I know that. But my heart is a little harder to convince." She shrugged. "I guess it's just that I don't trust all this is real. That I'll wake up one day and find that it was all in my imagination, that you don't love me or want me, and that would break my heart."

He shifted to his side to face her fully, putting the ice pack on the bed behind him. "Is this what you were talking about earlier? About trying to not fall in love with me, keep it all fun and games? So you wouldn't be hurt?"

She bit her lip, emotion clogging her throat at the tenderness in his gaze. "I really didn't want you to break my heart," she whispered, blinking madly to keep the tears at bay. "And if I didn't fall in love with you, then you couldn't."

"Oh, baby." He lowered his head, pressing his forehead to hers and staring deep into her eyes. "I promise you that I will never, ever let anyone hurt you. Even me. I'd cut out my own heart before I let that happen."

Jane's breath hitched on a watery sob. "That might be a little extreme. I'll settle for hearing that you love me again."

"I love you." He pressed a kiss to her left eyelid, then her right. "I love you." He settled his lips on hers with gentle sweetness that had fresh tears gathering in her eyes. "In my whole life, I've never loved anyone the way I love you. You're it for me, Janie."

"Oh," she sighed, burrowing her face into the warm curve of his neck, breathing in the scent of him. The tightness in her chest eased, replaced by a wonderful warmth as his arms tightened around her.

He simply held her for long minutes, stroking her back, and she felt an unbelievable calm settle over her. For the first time, her mind was settled and her heart was quiet, safe and secure with the knowledge that he'd always be there to hold her.

Long minutes passed before either of them moved, content to simply hold onto one another. Then Jane suddenly rememberd.

"Oh!" she picked her head up off his chest, swiping her hair out of her face with fumbling fingers. "I promised you I'd take your mind off your nose, didn't I?"

He smiled tenderly, cupping her face in his hand. "Believe me honey, you did." He dropped a tender kiss to her bare shoulder. "Are you comfortable enough in that dress?"

She frowned. "Yes, why?"

"Because I don't want either of us leaving this bed until morning." He reached down for the blanket folded at the end of the bed, pulling it over them and wrapping his arms tight around her. "I'm going to hold you all night, just like this."

She sighed and nestled closer. "Okay."

"But I'm taking a rain check on the exotic sexual favors."

Jane burst out laughing. "Oh, God, I love you!"

"I love you too," he whispered in her ear, and she drifted off to sleep believing it.

Chapter Fourteen

Jane was awakened in the morning by an urgent need for the bathroom. The thin gray light trickling into the room warned her that it was obscenely early, and she tried to go back to sleep. It was cozy under the blanket, and she didn't want to leave. But, now that she was awake, she was having a hard time ignoring the pressure in her bladder and soon it became more than she could stand.

She eased out of bed quietly, lifting Ian's arm from around her waist and placing it gently on the mattress. She knew he was a light sleeper—he usually woke immediately when she left the bed, so she was expecting it when he popped open his one eye that wasn't hidden in the pillow and rumbled, "Where do you think you're going?"

She grinned. "Unless you're a lot kinkier than you've let on, I figure I better hit the bathroom fairly quickly."

"Ugh." He made a face, and she laughed.

"Go back to sleep," she murmured. "I'm going to change and then make breakfast. I'll bring it to you."

The one visible eyebrow lifted in surprise. "You're going to cook?"

She snorted. "Listen pal, I love you, but let's be real. I'm going to pop a few frozen waffles in the toaster and open a can of fruit cocktail."

He closed his eye. "Thank God. I thought I was waking up with the wrong woman."

She chuckled, heading into the bathroom and making quick use of the facilities. The fuzzy taste in her mouth reminded her that she'd gone to bed the night before without brushing her teeth, so she took care of that little chore while she was in there. She peeled out of her evening gown with a sigh of relief, glad to be free of the garment. She hated sleeping in her clothes. She left the dress in a heap on the bathroom floor—it desperately needed dry cleaning. She tiptoed quietly through the bedroom, snagged one of Ian's dress shirts from the closet and headed for the kitchen.

She buttoned herself into the shirt while rummaging through the refrigerator. She knew he was expecting frozen waffles, and wouldn't have cared if she'd brought him sawdust, but she felt like celebrating. Since she didn't see any champagne chilling in the refrigerator, she supposed she'd have to break her long-standing vow against cooking from scratch and celebrate with a mushroom omelet.

She dug out the ingredients and went to work, chopping mushrooms and half a leftover ham steak with more enthusiasm than skill. She nicked herself twice, and thanked God aloud that the cheese was already shredded and she didn't have to experience the horror of doing it herself. She broke two eggshells into the bowl and spent a good ten minutes trying to extract them from the slippery mixture of egg and milk, cursing all the while. She finally managed to wrest the last little piece of shell from the bowl, and poured the mix into the skillet, where the mushrooms and ham were already sizzling.

She managed to flip the omelet without breaking it in half, added the cheese and flipped it closed. While that melted, she dug out two forks and a serving tray. She slid the omelet onto a plate, plunked the pop-top can of fruit cocktail next to the plate on the tray and grabbed a two liter bottle of grape soda from her stash in his vegetable drawer and added it to the tray. The perfect breakfast.

She had a little trouble balancing the bottle on the tray—it kept wanting to topple over. So, she wedged it under her arm and started up the stairs. She'd gotten halfway there when the phone in Ian's office started to ring, and she cursed, quickening her step. When she hit the top of the stairs, she very carefully set down her burden and ran lightly into the office, hoping to muffle the phone before the ringing woke him.

She snatched the old-fashioned desk phone off the workstation and quickly flipped the switch on the bottom to shut off the ring. She knew his machine would pick up the call without a problem; he told her that he almost always let the machine screen the calls to his business line. She held still for a moment, listening for any movement coming from the next room, but didn't hear anything. Jane sighed with relief that the phone hadn't wakened him—she really did want to surprise him with the omelet.

She'd set the phone on the desk and turned back to the door when a splash of yellow her eye. Jane chuckled and picked up the plastic figurine of Sponge Bob Squarpants. She grinned, thinking about him looking at the cartoon character while he was doing background searches or talking with clients. His sense of the ridiculous was just one of the things that she adored about him.

She set the figure back down on top of the files that it had been perched on, and then the label on the top file seemed to jump out at her. "Denning, Jane".

She moved like lightning, snatching it from the rack and staring at her name on the label. He had a file on her. She struggled to make sense of that, tried to come up with a reasonable explanation for what could be in it, but her brain was frozen in shock, and for long moments, she could only stare at it.

Her first instinct was to open the file and read it. Following close on the heels of that was the urge to run into the bedroom and smack him in the face with it, demanding an explanation. Dammit, she *trusted* him, and he repaid her by sneaking around behind her back, gathering information on her. That was what he did, after all. That's what all that fancy black equipment in this room was for, gathering information that normal people couldn't find. What had he found on her?

She fumed, crushing the edges of the folder in her hands as she fought to bring her temper under control. How could he betray her trust like that? How could he?

She was halfway to the door, planning a black eye to go with his swollen nose, when she stopped dead in her tracks. She stared down at the folder, thinking hard. She was not going to go flying in there, accusing him of betraying her, when she didn't know what he'd done, exactly. All she had was a file with her name on it, a file that could contain any number of things. She swallowed the lump in her throat. She couldn't do that, couldn't accuse blindly. She began to open the file, to see for herself its contents, but then stopped. She did trust him. Trusted that he wouldn't hurt her, trusted that he loved her. She headed for the door, the folder still in her hands, unopened. She would trust him in this.

* * * * *

Ian rolled over at the sound at the door, smiling when he saw Jane clad in one of his dress shirts and carrying a tray into the room. He grinned as he saw the giant bottle of grape soda lying sideways on the tray, shaking his head. "Grape soda for breakfast?"

"It's the nectar of the gods."

He frowned at the sick smile on her face, the odd stiffness in her tone. "What's wrong, honey?"

She stopped beside the bed, still holding the tray, and took a deep breath. "I need to ask you something."

"Anything. Baby, you're shaking." He reached out to take the tray from her, set it on the bed before taking her hands in his. "Tell me what's wrong."

She simply pointed. "I need you to tell me why you have that."

He glanced to the tray and froze. Lying flat on top of the tray, hidden from view from the front by the giant bottle of soda, was the file.

"Baby, I can explain."

She nodded blue eyes steady on his. "I know you can. I know that. I trust that." She drew in a shuddering breath. "But I'm kind of new at this trust thing, so maybe you could hurry up and explain before my ass-kicking instinct clicks in and punches you again?"

"Okay." He drew her down to sit on the bed beside him, keeping a firm hold on her hands. The last thing he needed was a black eye.

"Remember the morning after we met? In your apartment?"

She nodded. "Yes."

"When I left that morning, I got the definite sense that you were planning to do a fast fade on me, keep me at arm's length and boot me out of your life fairly quickly. Am I wrong about that?"

She shook her head, eyes on their joined hands. "No, you're not wrong."

"Okay." He drew a deep breath. "Well, I decided that I needed to find out a little more about you. I knew that you were special, that I wanted to get to know you better. But I wasn't sure you'd let me. So when I came home that day, I did a run on you."

She blinked. "A run?"

"A standard background search. It's usually comprised of financial information, criminal history and some personal information, depending on how deep a search is run."

"Okay." She drew in a breath, and let it out slowly. "How deep did you run?"

"I just did a surface search, Jane. I wanted to get a better idea of what was important to you, what made you tick. I wasn't trying to invade your privacy, and honestly, I only gave the information a quick once-over."

"What did it tell you about me?"

He nudged her chin up with one finger, waiting for her eyes to meet his before he spoke. "It told me you love your store, that you're dedicated to making a success of it. It told me you have a big and generous heart, and that you take care of the people you love."

Jane peered up at him through her lashes. "Did it happen to include a little incident from my sophomore year in college?"

"I do seem to recall seeing something about skinny-dipping in the university president's pool." He grinned in relief when she laughed. "Does this mean you're not angry with me?"

She smiled at him. "No, I guess not. I mean, I can't blame you for wanting more information than I was willing to give. And I'd have done the same if I'd thought of it." She shrugged. "And had the resources for it. Which reminds me—can I use you for the employment checks I do at the store? This is probably a lot more thorough then I can get with the service I'm using now."

"Sure. And I won't even charge you."

Jane snorted. "No kidding, you won't charge me. I figure I've got a lifetime of free security work coming to me for this one."

Ian sighed. "Yeah, you probably do. I have to say, I'm relieved. I though you were going to blast me through the back wall for a second there."

"Oh, I thought about it. But I decided that it wouldn't be a very trusting thing to do. And when you love somebody, you trust them. Right?"

He wrapped his arms around her and squeezed. "I love you, Jane."

"I love you, too." She sighed. "Promise me no more secrets, okay?"

He hesitated a beat too long, and she pulled back to stare at him. "There's more?"

"Just one teeny tiny little thing."

She narrowed her eyes. "How teeny tiny?"

"So teeny tiny it hardly even matters."

"How 'bout you let me be the judge of that?"

"Okay. The thing is, I didn't just run into you by accident at the bar that first night. I knew you were going to be there."

She goggled. "How?"

"I was sitting in the café that afternoon when you and Lacey came up with your opposite plan."

Jane's mind raced, going over the layout of the café in her head, and her jaw dropped. "You were in one of the fireplace chairs!"

He nodded. "I watched you come into the café, saw where you sat down. I wasn't really paying attention until you got agitated and your voice rose. You were talking about finding someone to tie you up and fuck you. So," he shrugged, watching her carefully, "I started paying attention."

"So you overheard where we were going to be, and decided to show up for an easy piece of ass?"

"No." He gripped her hands tightly, his eyes fierce and intent on her face. "Believe me, Jane, it wasn't like that. I thought you were a beautiful, sensual, funny woman after that conversation, and I wanted to see you."

"So let me see if I get this. You overheard me talking with Lacey about the whole opposite experiment, you'd already noticed me and you thought you'd show up where I was going to be on the chance that I'd experiment with you."

Ian sighed. "That's a bit cruder than I'd put it, but essentially, yes."

"You didn't put on this dominant Alpha male personality just to get me into bed, did you?"

"Jane, please." He rolled his eyes. "I can't help being Alpha any more than you can help being a White Sox fan. It's part of who I am. I could probably fake it for a few hours, but not for a whole month. This is the real me."

Jane nodded slowly, watching his eyes. "Okay, just checking."

He waited a beat. "Is that it? That's all you're going to say?"

"Pretty much."

"You're not mad at me?"

"Nope."

"Well." He slumped back onto the bed. "That's a little anticlimactic."

"Oh, you're not off the hook yet, buddy boy. I'm still not really happy with you." She folded her arms across her chest and frowned as severely as she could with her lips twitching. She watched him fight a grin of his own and settle more firmly into the pillows.

"Oh, really?"

"Yes. I made this lovely breakfast for you." She flipped the file off the tray to reveal the now cold and congealed omelet. "And now it's ruined."

Ian bit back a grin at the blackened slab of egg on the plate, still runny in places. "And it looks like it was delicious, darling."

She narrowed her eyes on him. "Is that sarcasm I'm hearing? Sarcasm and derision at my lovingly prepared offering?"

He schooled his features into what he hoped was a sober expression. "Of course not, sweetie. I'm touched that you cooked for me, I really am." He waited a beat. "If I say I'm sorry will you promise never to do it again?"

Jane gamely swallowed the laugh that tickled her throat. "Insults will not get you those exotic sexual favors you've been waiting for."

"You know that I don't really have to ask for them, don't you? Under the terms of our agreement, which I believe is still in effect, I can just take them whenever I want."

"Oh yeah." She chewed her lip thoughtfully, eyes dancing with merriment. "Well, it is part of the agreement. And I wouldn't want to get a reputation as a welsher."

He nodded. "That's very wise." He watched her as she rose from the bed to slowly walk to the window.

"But," she turned, one finger pointed at him, "I do think that I've been a trifle easy for you. And I wouldn't want to get the reputation for being easy, either."

Ian placed his hand solemnly over his heart, but he couldn't do a thing about the grin on his face. God, he loved her like this. "I won't tell a soul, I promise."

She scoffed. "Oh please, I know how you men talk. You've probably already told all your pals at the gym how I just jump when you snap your fingers."

"Never!" he vowed.

"Well." She sniffed, looking down her nose at him and fighting to keep the grin off her face. "I guess I believe you this time. But I think you might be taking me for granted a little. So this time, you're gonna have to work for it."

She stuck out her tongue at him. "Catch me if you can," she chortled, and flew out the bedroom door.

Chapter Fifteen

Jane flew down the stairs to the first floor. By the time she hit the bottom stair he'd recovered from the shock and with a roar that echoed throughout the house, came thundering after her.

She took a quick left off the hallway, skidding to a halt on the far side of the butcher-block island. In a blink he was there, framed in the doorway, and she caught her breath at the sheer sexuality coming off him in waves.

He was still half in his tux from the night before, the shirt hanging open and framing that wonderful muscled chest. She felt herself starting to drool and snapped her eyes back to his face. If she didn't want this game to be over too soon, she was going to have to keep her eyes on his. He was clever, and fast, and used to being the hunter. He'd catch her eventually—that was the point, after all—but she didn't want to make it too easy for him.

"Woman," he rumbled. "You better get your fine ass up in that bed where it belongs before I teach you a lesson."

Jane made herself look him up and down, a disdainful look on her face, even though she wanted to trip him and beat him to the floor. "You think you can teach me a lesson?"

He narrowed his eyes and began to move, walking into the room with the slow stalking gate of a panther on the prowl, and Jane instinctively backed up. His eyes lit up with an unholy gleam, the warrior in him recognizing her abrupt movement for the retreat it was. "Oh, honey," he growled, his voice so low that it was almost unintelligible, "you have no idea the things I can teach you."

"Is that right?" Jane continued to walk slowly backwards, circling the butcher block until her back was to the open doorway, and their original positions were nearly reversed. "Well, that's an interesting idea, sugar, but I really don't find you all that appealing." She couldn't suppress a shiver at the snarl that curled his lip at that, but she forced her features to maintain their look of bored distain.

"Oh no?"

"You're just not my type." She shrugged, a nonchalant gesture that was at complete odds with the alert tension in her gaze. "So thanks for asking, but no thanks. Why don't you go find someone else who'll play caveman with you?"

"I think you misunderstand me."

Jane swallowed. The almost feral look on his face was turning her bones to mush and her muscles to putty. Not to mention the effect that it was having on her pussy. She had the urge to look down and see if she was dripping on the tile.

She had to swallow again before she could speak, and even then, all she could manage was, "Oh? How's that?"

Ian grinned. "I'm not asking," he growled, and leapt over the counter.

Jane shrieked, eyes wide with genuine fright as he came over the counter like a wild animal, all glittering eyes and bared teeth. Instinct kicked in, and she turned and fled with his breath hot on her neck.

She raced for the stairs, taking them two at a time with him close on her heels. She knew he'd let her get away in the kitchen. He was bigger, stronger and his legs were a heck of a lot longer than hers—he could've had her flat on the cold tile in about four seconds. Obviously, he was enjoying this little game as much as she was.

Her heart in her throat, she hit the top of the stairs and sprinted for the bedroom. She leapt on top of the bed, intent on using it as a short cut to the bathroom and its connecting hallway door, when she felt his hand close over her ankle.

With a howl, she found herself facedown on the bed with two hundred and sixty pounds of predatory male on her back.

She could feel his breath on the side of her face. He wasn't even breathing hard, reaffirming her suspicions that she'd only gotten as far as she had because he'd let her.

"Well, well," he rumbled, satisfaction clear in his tone. "Look at what we have here."

She bucked once underneath him, a movement that was quickly quelled by the simple act of him dropping his weight more fully onto her body. He was careful to allow her room to breathe, but that's about all she had room to do. He covered her completely, and with a moan, she went limp under him.

"That's it," he crooned, and swiped his tongue across her jaw. "Just relax, take your punishment like a good girl."

She started. "Punishment?"

"Hmmmm." He nipped her earlobe hard enough to make her yelp, but then soothed the sting with a sucking kiss. "You tried to back out of our deal."

"I wasn't trying to back out," she gasped, "I was renegotiating."

"Same thing." She felt him shift over her, and tried to find some wiggle room to get away, but he was still holding her too firmly for her to get anywhere. She managed to work her arms out from under her torso where he'd pinned them, and was reaching for the headboard for leverage when suddenly she saw a flash of white in the corner of her eye, and then he was snatching her wrists and dragging them behind her back.

"Hey!" she cried.

"You just keep misbehaving, Jane." She felt him begin to bind her hands at the small of her back, and she realized the flash of white was the sash of her robe. "Trying to renegotiate the deal. Trying to get away." He finished tying her hands, giving the knots an experimental yank to make sure they wouldn't come undone. "You keep it up, and you'll be getting the longest spanking on record."

Jane froze. "Spanking?"

"Seems a suitable punishment for a naughty girl, don't you think?"

She felt him shift off her, giving her time and room to wiggle away, but her brain was stuck on the word "spanking". Despite all the experimenting they'd done with bondage and submission in bed, they'd never crossed the line into physical punishment. She knew he wouldn't hurt her, that it was all part of the game, but she still felt a knot of fear curl in her belly.

"Jane." She started, his voice was right at her ear, and she was surprised to find that while she'd been trying to wrap her mind around the fact that she was thirty-one years old and about to get a spanking, he'd shifted so that he was seated on the edge of the bed with her draped face down over his lap.

"What?" she gasped, her breathing coming quick and harsh.

"Remember, all you have to do is say stop. Okay?"

She swallowed. "Okay."

"Good girl." He brushed a kiss across the nape of her neck. "Say it if you need to, okay?"

She nodded, and felt him straighten and flip the tails of her borrowed shirt up over her hips, exposing her backside. He rubbed one broad palm over her bare ass while keeping the other hand firmly across her back to keep her still.

"Such a pale, pretty ass," he murmured. "I can't wait to see it turn bright pink under my hand."

Jane felt him raise his hand and braced herself. She couldn't believe how wet she was, how stiff her nipples were, just anticipating his hand meeting her flesh. She was focused on the throb in her pussy, so when the first blow landed it startled her. She let out a whimper at the sensation of heat that spread out from the smack, then groaned when he repeated the blow on the other cheek.

He rained blows on her butt with a steady rhythm, letting the sting settle into heat before landing the next, and within moments she was writhing across his lap, moaning and pulling at her bonds, thrusting her hips high for each blow. When he stopped, she was panting and uttering soft little cries, hips rolling in search of relief.

"There." Satisfaction was ripe in his tone as he rubbed both callused palms over her ass. He'd stopped holding her down when it became clear that she wasn't going to try to go anywhere. "That's just the shade of pink I was going for."

He leaned down to whisper in her ear. "Did you learn your lesson, Janey?"

"That depends," she panted. "If I say yes, will you stop?"

"Well, I think we'll move on from the spanking, but I'm sure not done with you yet."

"Then yes, I've learned my lesson."

He chuckled. "I'm so glad. But just to be sure…"

Jane squeaked as he suddenly flipped her upright to stand between his spread knees, steadying her until she had her feet firmly under her. He grabbed a pillow from the bed and tossed it at her feet, then placed his hands on her shoulders and pushed gently. "On your knees, baby." He steadied her as she wobbled, her bound hands making it difficult for her to balance as she lowered herself to the pillow, then unzipped his pants and drew out his already hard cock. "Now suck."

Jane licked her lips and flicked her gaze from the lust burning in his gaze to his hard cock. The tip was already drooling pre-cum, proof that he was enjoying their little punishment game as much as she was. She leaned forward, careful of her balance with her hands tied, and gently swirled her tongue around the head, savoring the salty taste of him. He growled in response, releasing himself and sliding his fingers into her hair on either side of her head, and she began to suck.

Over and over, she took him to the back of her throat, drawing firmly on his pulsing flesh and moaning as he clenched his hands tighter in her hair on every down stroke. She could feel the gathering storm in her cunt spinning out of control, and it occurred to her that if she got any more turned on she'd likely come just from blowing him. The thought distracted her enough so that on the next stroke he slid past her gag reflex and into her throat. He groaned at the sensation of her throat rippling around his throbbing length, and she struggled to breathe through her nose even as she reveled in the knowledge that she'd taken all of him. She suddenly pictured how she must look, hands tied behind her back, nose buried in his belly, ass pink from his hand, and almost came from the image alone.

"That's it." Ian tugged her head up pulling free of her with a groan, and in one move reached down, lifted her from her knees and tossed her facedown on the bed. He made quick work of his own clothes, tearing the shirt from his shoulders and shucking his slacks with lightning speed. He slid one arm under her pelvis and lifted her high enough to slide two pillows under her, then arranged her on them so that they canted her hips high, her pussy open and ready. He reached forward with one hand and grasped a fistful of her hair, pulled her head slightly back and plowed into her with one firm thrust.

Jane screamed when he slammed into her, the walls of her cunt pulsing frantically in an effort to adjust to his girth. He began fucking her hard, rubbing her clit against the pillows with every thrust, the hand that was tangled in her hair yanking her back at the same time that his pounding pushed her forward, his hips slapping her tender ass. The combination of push and pull, pleasure and pain, was the most potent thing she'd ever experienced. She could feel her orgasm bearing down on her like a freight train, braced herself for the impact, when he suddenly pulled out.

"No!" she wailed, swiveling around to see him. "Why did you stop?"

His face was a tight mask of lust. "Because I'm not done yet."

"What…?" She started to ask what the hell that meant when she saw him reach in the bedside drawer and pull out a tube of lubricant and a condom.

She craned her neck to watch him as he popped the cap on the tube and squeezed a thick line of the shiny stuff onto his fingers. He moved slowly and deliberately, giving her plenty of time to say no, to stop him. But she simply watched as he brought his fingers to her upturned ass, and she stiffened as she felt him touch the delicate skin of her asshole.

"Relax," he murmured, and began working one slick finger into her. She gasped at the tight pinching sensation, instinctively clamping down on the invader, and felt her pussy pulse in response. Moaning at the sensation, she forced herself to relax, and felt him add a second finger to the first.

He worked his fingers in and out of her ass for long moments, stopping frequently to add more lubricant, until she was panting and pushing her hips back against him.

"I'm going to fuck your ass, Jane."

She groaned at the dark promise in his voice and pushed her hips back on his fingers. "Oh, God, yes," she hissed, whimpering when he pulled free, twisting his wrist and wringing a cry from her.

"I'm going to fuck it hard, for as long as I want to. Do you know why, Jane?" She heard the tear of foil, the snap of latex, and then he was bent over her, covering her back. She could feel his condom-covered cock firm against her hip.

"Why?" she moaned, arching into his body.

He bit her shoulder. "Because I can," he rumbled in her ear, and she felt him move his hand to fit the broad head of his cock to her waiting hole.

She went still at the first touch of his cock to her tender flesh, focusing all her concentration on relaxing to let him in. He slid in slow and steady, pausing briefly to give her a chance to adjust, then slid all the way home in one smooth motion.

Jane lay pinned beneath him, gasping at the astonishing sensation of fullness. He felt huge in her ass, much bigger than he'd ever felt in her pussy, and she could feel her delicate tissues shivering around him as they struggled to accustom themselves to this new invader. She felt her pussy dripping honey onto the pillows beneath her, and flexed her Kegel muscles experimentally.

"Oh Jesus," he moaned. "Do that again." She did, flexing her muscles and clamping down tight, and he groaned again, and then started to pull back.

Jane whimpered at the sensation, shivers of delight racing up and down her spine, as he pulled almost completely free before sliding forward again. He began a steady, even thrusting in and out of her ass, and soon she was pushing back to meet every single one.

"Oh please, Ian," she panted, chest heaving in an effort to get enough oxygen to her starved system. "Please, more."

"Do you want to come, Jane? Is that what you want?" He licked her ear, his breath heating her face, and he punctuated his words with a heavy thrust.

She cried out, the heavy push of his hips bringing her orgasm inexorably closer. She could feel it hovering just out of reach, and she moaned in frustration. The constant friction and delicious stretch of his cock in her ass was keeping her poised on the brink, each thrust bringing her closer and closer, but she couldn't go over, and nearly sobbed with frustration. "Please, Ian! I need to come!"

"Tell me how it feels first. I want to hear how it feels to have me deep in your ass." His voice was rough in her ear, his breath coming shallow and fast as he raced toward his own satisfaction.

"Oh, God!" she wailed, struggling to bring her splintered thoughts into focus. "It feels huge..."

"What else?" he panted, his thrusts coming harder, faster.

"I feel full," she groaned, "so full of you." She flexed her bound hands against his abdomen, raking her nails across his taut flesh. "Like I'll never be empty again. Oh, God, Ian, *please*!"

"Okay, baby." He moved his arms from where they were braced on either side of her, sliding one across her shoulders and lifting her so that they were pressed firmly together, front to back, and slid the other under her belly to find her clit.

He flicked it with the barest touch of his finger, once, twice, and she exploded.

Dimly she heard herself scream as everything in her body seemed to clamp down and pulse, clenching and unclenching until the edges of her consciousness began to dim at the force of it. She felt him stiffen above her, his arms clamping tight around her as he roared out his own orgasm, and in the snug grip of her ass, she could feel his cock pulse with each spurt. The sensation was darkly erotic, and sent her spiraling off into space again.

He collapsed over her, his chest heaving with the effort to draw breath as her body continued to ripple and shudder around his invading flesh. Little aftershocks tore through her, mini-orgasms that were nearly as strong as the real thing and kept her whimpering uncontrollably.

Ian roused himself to pull her tangled hair off her face. "You okay?" he gasped.

Jane could only moan in response, still caught in the maelstrom of sensation that lingered in her system. She licked her lips and fought to speak. "Jesus, that was amazing."

He groaned. "You're telling me. I thought I was going to have a heart attack."

"If you're going to have a heart attack when we do this," she panted, still fighting for breath, "then I get to be on top. No way am I calling the paramedics to come get you off me."

He chuckled weakly. "It's a deal." He slid one hand under her jaw, turning her head gently and settled his lips on hers for a lingering kiss.

"Marry me, Jane."

She blinked at him, astonished. "Marry you?"

"Yeah, you know—marriage. White dress, flowers, 'til death do us part? I love you, I don't want to even imagine spending my life without you."

She smiled. "I love you, too. And yes, I'll marry you. But only if you untie my hands now."

He grinned and levered himself off her just far enough to work on the knots. She lay there, blissfully happy, when a sudden thought occurred to her. "Oh, my God!"

"What? What's wrong? Are you hurt?"

"No," she sputtered, and started to laugh. "I just thought of something."

"What?" He managed to choke out as her laughter had her ass tightening rhythmically on his cock.

She was howling with laughter. "When people ask, I'm going to have to tell them that you proposed to me with your dick in my ass!"

He began to chuckle as he finished untying her hands. "Do you want me to pull out and ask again?"

She grinned at him over her shoulder. "I wouldn't go that far."

"That's my girl." He wrapped his arms around her and rolled them to their sides, still joined, and nuzzled his face into her neck.

She sighed. "Yes, I am."

Why an electronic book?

We live in the Information Age—an exciting time in the history of human civilization, in which technology rules supreme and continues to progress in leaps and bounds every minute of every day. For a multitude of reasons, more and more avid literary fans are opting to purchase e-books instead of paper books. The question from those not yet initiated into the world of electronic reading is simply: *Why?*

1. ***Price.*** An electronic title at Ellora's Cave Publishing and Cerridwen Press runs anywhere from 40% to 75% less than the cover price of the exact same title in paperback format. Why? Basic mathematics and cost. It is less expensive to publish an e-book (no paper and printing, no warehousing and shipping) than it is to publish a paperback, so the savings are passed along to the consumer.
2. ***Space.*** Running out of room in your house for your books? That is one worry you will never have with electronic books. For a low one-time cost, you can purchase a handheld device specifically designed for e-reading. Many e-readers have large, convenient screens for viewing. Better yet, hundreds of titles can be stored within your new library—on a single microchip. There are a variety of e-readers from different manufacturers. You can also read e-books on your PC or laptop computer. (Please note that Ellora's Cave does not endorse any specific brands.

You can check our websites at www.ellorascave.com or www.cerridwenpress.com for information we make available to new consumers.)

3. ***Mobility.*** Because your new e-library consists of only a microchip within a small, easily transportable e-reader, your entire cache of books can be taken with you wherever you go.
4. ***Personal Viewing Preferences.*** Are the words you are currently reading too small? Too large? Too... ANNOYING? Paperback books cannot be modified according to personal preferences, but e-books can.
5. ***Instant Gratification.*** Is it the middle of the night and all the bookstores near you are closed? Are you tired of waiting days, sometimes weeks, for bookstores to ship the novels you bought? Ellora's Cave Publishing sells instantaneous downloads twenty-four hours a day, seven days a week, every day of the year. Our webstore is never closed. Our e-book delivery system is 100% automated, meaning your order is filled as soon as you pay for it.

Those are a few of the top reasons why electronic books are replacing paperbacks for many avid readers.

As always, Ellora's Cave and Cerridwen Press welcome your questions and comments. We invite you to email us at Comments@ellorascave.com or write to us directly at Ellora's Cave Publishing Inc., 1056 Home Avenue, Akron, OH 44310-3502.

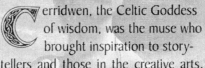

or anticipating certain notes; (c) paraphrasing melodic patterns; (d) breaking long notes into smaller rhythmic values; and (e) adding grace notes or embellishments to relatively long notes. To these elements could be added the technique of occasionally shifting from the middle register of an instrument, most often the violin, to another register an octave higher or lower" ("Musical," 286–87). See also M. Ḥāfiẓ, 195 and Racy, "Musical," 24–25.

101. Despite her much publicized announcement in 1926 that she had replaced her vocal accompanists with a *takht,* vocal accompaniment remained part of her performances and recordings sporadically for a surprisingly long time given the popularity of new instruments and growing ensembles. Whereas she invariably performed monologues alone as a solo, her *adwār* and *ṭaqāṭīq* included vocal responses (often provided by the instrumentalists) until about 1939. This practice may have marked her as a conservative; however her willingness to experiment showed in her brief use of a chorus of female accompanists during the late 1920s. They may be heard in "Tiraaʿi Gheerii," "Ṣaḥiiḥ Khiṣaamak," "Wi-l-Ḥadd Imta," and "Ma Trawwaq Dammak." This practice also had historic precedents in Egypt among *ʿawālim* but was a dramatic innovation for Umm Kulthūm who had worked primarily in the predominantly male realm of religious song and *qaṣāʾid.* Male and female vocalists singing together may be heard in "Ya Ruuḥi bila Kutri Asiyya," "Ibtisaam il-Zahr," "Miin illi Qaal," and "ʿAadit Layaali ʾl-Hanaʾ."

102. The term *takht* usually signified an ensemble of two to five instrumentalists; *firqa* denoted a larger ensemble. Instrumentalists frequently served as vocal accompanists as well. For a detailed discussion of the gradual enlargement of the *takht,* see El-Shawan, "al-Mūsīḳa," 142–221; also Racy, "Sound and Society."

103. The number of violins increased noticeably with al-Qaṣabjī's "Ya-lli Inta Ganbi" and "Feen il-ʿUyuun," most of the songs from the film *Nashīd al-Amal* and al-Sunbāṭī's new compositions "Salū Kuʾūs al-Ṭilā," "il-Noom Yidaaʿib ʿUyuun Ḥabiibi," and "Udhkurīnī."

Chapter Five

1. N. Ḥāfiẓ, 259.

2. Umm Kulthūm, quoted by Ḥasan ʿAbd al-Rasūl in "Umm Kulthūm tataḥaddath sāʿa maʿa ʾl-Sufarāʾ" (Umm Kulthūm speaks for an hour with the ambassadors), *al-Akhbār* (April 1969?), clipping from the archives of Dār al-Akhbār.

3. Maḥmūd Kāmil, public lecture, March 26, 1982.

4. Marsot, *Egypt's Liberal Experiment,* 205; see also Issawi, 123, 173, 230–31, and 269.

5. Issawi, 263.

6. Badawi, 204.

7. Fuʾād, 254. As early as 1926, Badīʿ Khayrī and lyricist Yūnis al-Qāḍī were favorably compared to Rāmī as being "closer to the spirit of the people" (*Rūz al-Yūsuf* no. 14 [January 25, 1926], 14).

8. Shūsha, 41.

9. Marilyn Booth's *Bayram al-Tunisi's Egypt* is an excellent and thorough study of this poet's work and his place in Egyptian society.

10. For another comparison see "al-Mar'a bayna Bayram al-Tūnisī wa-Mursī Jamīl ʿAzīz" (Women between Bayram al-Tūnisī and Mursī Jamīl ʿAzīz), *al-Aḥrār* (February 17, 1986), 10.

11. "Il-awwila fil-gharaam wil-ḥubb shabakuuni," then "il-awwila fil-gharaam wil-ḥubb shabakuuni bi-naẓrit ʿeen," and so on. Bayram used the same technique for a national song about Egypt's defeat of the Tripartite Aggression in 1956: *il-awwila* was Great Britain, *il-tanya* France, and *il-talta* Israel. These examples illustrate Bayram's use of a historic and familiar form for contemporary expression.

12. As well as religious songs, Zakariyyā authored some of the most popular bawdy songs in Cairo during the 1920s (*al-Tiyātrū* no. 6 [March 1925], 25; *al-Masraḥ* no. 38 [September 13, 1926], 22, and no. 25 [May 10, 1926], 23).

13. Ḥusayn, *Passage to France,* 2–3 and thereafter; Zakariyyā Aḥmad, "Min Dhikrayātī," *al-Rādyū 'l-Miṣrī* no. 232 (August 26, 1939), 6. See also Nazira Zain al-Din, "The Young Woman and the Shaikhs," quoted in Badran and Cooke, 278.

14. Ṣāliḥ Jūda, quoted in Fu'ād, 121. Also, Shūsha's characterization of his style as "al-ṭarab al-sharqī al-aṣīl allathī ḥāfaẓ fīhi ʿalá taqālīd al-ghinā' al-qadīm" (real eastern *ṭarab* that preserves the traditions of old singing), Shūsha, 28.

15. There is no single folk song style in Egypt, but rather a number of regional styles which are easily distinguishable to an Egyptian. Folk or *shaʿbī* songs are often described by Egyptians as "simple," a designation that places them within the larger conceptual framework used to discuss song while indicating difference: folk songs generally use smaller ranges of pitch and less modulation. As Shiloah wrote, these "simple songs have the color of a maqam, discernible to a well-trained ear" (Shiloah, 45).

16. I. Saḥḥāb, 95; "Dhikrayāt lam Tunshar ʿan Umm Kulthūm" (Unpublished memories of Umm Kulthūm), *Rūz al-Yūsuf* (February 2, 1976).

17. The job of nurse in Egypt was low in prestige and pay, undesirable work that only a very devoted or very needy person would normally undertake.

18. Most of this information about *ʿĀyida* was gleaned from a file of published criticism about the film in the private collection of Farīd al-Mizāwī of the Centre Catholique Égyptienne du Cinéma et de la Télévision, in Cairo; most clippings do not bear citations.

19. In the late 1940s, she gave the text for "Sahraan li-Waḥdi," and, later, that for "Lil-Ṣabr Ḥuduud" to al-Qaṣabjī, but was dissatisfied with his settings. In 1954, she turned down his "Yā Duʿāt al-Ḥaqq," commemorating the anniversary of the Egyptian Revolution, even though her rejection of it meant that she would have no new song for the occasion. "Yā Duʿāt al-Ḥaqq" was eventually performed by Fayda Kāmil. Umm Kulthūm also rejected al-Qaṣabjī's setting of the patriotic text "Nashīd al-Jalā'" in the 1950s (Kāmil, *Muḥammad al-Qaṣabjī,* 81–83; Shūsha, 44; personal communication, Ratība al-Ḥifnī, May 21, 1992).

20. Cachia, *Taha Husayn,* 86–87.

21. Ibid.

22. Smith, 398–99. "Haykal never sought . . . to restore faith among doubting Muslims," but he used religion for persuasive purposes (406).

23. Khouri, 26, 103; also 46.

24. Issawi, 266, 268.
25. Marsot, "Religion or Opposition," 552.
26. Khouri, 75.
27. Cachia, *Taha Husayn,* 29–30.
28. Jayyusi, *Modern Arabic Poetry,* 100; Badawi, 29.
29. Badawi, 32, 33. The ʿAbbāsid dynasty (750–1258) supported the efflorescence of Arabic poetry including the *qaṣīda;* the first half of the ʿAbbāsid period is often called the golden age of Arabic poetry.
30. Boolaky, 53.
31. *Al-wāḥida* is a quadruple pattern with a single accented beat.
32. On an occasion when Umm Kulthūm along with a number of literati were guests at Shawqī's home, he asked her to sing. The next day he sent her "Salū Kuʾūs al-Ṭilā" as a gift in tribute to her. According to Fuʾād, the original poem included lines addressed to the singer by name (Fuʾād, 189). These were altered when she decided to have the poem set to music, and the text appears without direct address to Umm Kulthūm in later editions of Shawqī's works. "Salū Kuʾūs al-Ṭilā" was premiered ca. 1938.
33. Shūsha, 59.
34. "Uḥibbuhā li-Qalbihā ʾl-Kabīr," *Rūz al-Yūsuf* no. 1431 (November 21, 1955), 27; transcript of a broadcast interview with Umm Kulthūm including discussion of this line in *al-Rādyū ʾl-Miṣrī* no. 576 (March 30, 1946), 6; al-Najmī, 63; *al-Idhāʿa al-Miṣrī* no. 922 (November 15, 1952), 4; Shūsha, 59.
35. *Al-Mūsīqá wa-ʾl-Masraḥ* no. 8 (September 1947), 298; "ʿUmdat al-Sammīʿa Yaqūl," *al-Kawākib* no. 1592 (February 2, 1982), 13.
36. Al-Sunbāṭī also taught at the Institute for Arab Music from 1933 and took as his student the soon-to-be star of film, Farīd al-Aṭrash. The diploma in music later became a sine qua non for Egyptian musicians aspiring to careers in Cairo (cf. El-Shawan, "al-Mūsīḳa," 109, 185). Umm Kulthūm had met Riyāḍ al-Sunbāṭī previously when both were children. Al-Sunbāṭī's father was a singer from al-Manṣūra, near Umm Kulthūm's home in the Delta. Like her father, al-Sunbāṭī's had trained his son to accompany him. The two fathers were acquainted and occasionally met while traveling (ʿAwaḍ, 146; Fuʾād, 93–94; Shūsha, 28).
37. Al-Sunbāṭī's neoclassical style was as evident in colloquial *ughniyāt* as in *qaṣāʾid.* "Jaddadt Ḥubbak Lee" began in *nahawānd* and proceeded through *bayātī nawā, rāst suznāk, rāst, suznāk, ḥijāz kār kurd, nawā athar, ḥijāz, bayātī nawā,* and *huzām* before closing. "Ḥasiibak lil-Zaman" and "Lissa Faakir" featured very few modulations but a great deal of variety within the two or three modes used: one musician observed that "only al-Sunbāṭī could manage so few changes of *maqām* without being boring."
38. "Al-ḍuluʿ" (the sides of the body, ribs or the breast in general) became "al-qulūb" (hearts or innermost core) in line 5 of the original, and "thawāban" (a reward for good deeds) became "ṣawāban" (something right, proper or correct) in line 25 (see Shawqī, 1:70–74).
39. *Rūz al-Yūsuf* no. 366 (February 25, 1935), 38.
40. *Rūz al-Yūsuf* no. 1234 (February 4, 1952), 31.

41. Najīb Maḥfūẓ, *Bidāya wa-Nihāya,* 149.

42. Personal communication, Jamāl Salāma, November 14, 1982.

43. Saʿid Ghabaris, "Umm Kulthūm kān maʿāhā ʾl-Jiḥāz al-Iʿlāmī" (Umm Kulthūm had the media on her side), *al-Usbūʿ* (September 1, 1975), 66; "al-Sunbāṭī wa-Rubāʿiyyāt Nājī" (al-Sunbāṭī and the Nājī quatrains), *al-Kawākib* (December 6, 1977); "Suʿād Muḥammad," *al-Kawākib* no. 1757 (April 2, 1985), 33.

44. Fuʾād, 259; Shūsha, 65; Ṣāliḥ, "15 ʿĀman maʿa Umm Kulthūm," *al-Kawākib* no. 1592 (February 2, 1982), 16. For more information about her involvement with the union, see Danielson, "Shaping Tradition," 306–7.

45. Inexpensive biographies frequently contain pages devoted to her jokes and witticisms, often at the expense of others.

46. Personal communication, Medhat Assem, January 28, 1986.

47. "Fī ḥāla min al-ṣūfiyya." Quoted in "Umm Kulthūm Tataḥaddath Sāʿa maʿa ʾl-Sufarāʾ" (Umm Kulthūm speaks for an hour with the ambassadors), clipping from *al-Akhbār,* 1969, in the archives of Dār al-Hilāl.

48. "Ṣawt min al-Janna: Min Shawqī ilá Umm Kulthūm" (A voice from paradise: from Shawqī to Umm Kulthūm), *al-Mūsīqá wa-ʾl-Masraḥ* no. 12 (January 12, 1948), 456–57. Al-Ḥifnī also wrote approvingly of the *qaṣāʾid* sung and composed by Nādira on texts by the poet ʿAbbās Maḥmūd al-ʿAqqād.

49. *Al-Rādyū ʾl-Miṣrī* no. 576–83 (March 30–May 16, 1946); *al-Mūsīqá wa-ʾl-Masraḥ* no. 1 (February 1947), 19; *al-Idhāʿa* (January–May 1955).

50. "Ṣawt min al-Janna: Min Shawqī ilá Umm Kulthūm" (A voice from paradise: from Shawqī to Umm Kulthūm), *al-Mūsīqá wa-ʾl-Masraḥ* no. 12 (January 12, 1948), 456–57. Similarly, "All the people are becoming poets," ʿAbd al-Wahhāb observed, "singing lines of Shawqī and [expressing] his great thought" (quoted in *Ākhir Sāʿa* no. 2102 [February 5, 1975], 30).

51. For instance, "Because of Umm Kulthūm and al-Sunbāṭī, literary Arabic has been disseminated on cassettes," Jalīl al-Bundārī, "Umm Kulthūm al-Layla" (Umm Kulthūm tonight), *al-Akhbār* (April 7, 1966).

52. Personal communication, Dr. ʿĀdil Abū Zahra, May 25, 1992; Dr. Abū Zahra was referring to the al-Sunbāṭī *qaṣāʾid* (such as "al-Thulāthiyya al-Muqaddisa") that Umm Kulthūm sang in the 1960s.

53. "Al-Sunbāṭī," proclaimed *Rūz al-Yūsuf* in 1952, "is a genius at *qaṣāʾid*" (*Rūz al-Yūsuf* no. 1239 [March 7, 1952], 27). Other critiques of al-Sunbāṭī appeared in Sāmī al-Laythī, "Inna Aḥsan Aṣwāt" (The best voices), *Rūz al-Yūsuf* no. 1387 (January 10, 1955), 40; Shūsha, 42; "Ākhir al-Umanāʾ ʿalá ʾl-Mūsīqá ʾl-Sharqiyya" (The last guardian of eastern music), *al-Idhāʿa wa-ʾl-Tilīfizyūn* no. 2478 (September 11, 1982).

54. Muḥammad al-Mahdī al-Majdhūb, quoted in al-Naqqāsh, "Umm Kulthūm wa-ʾl-Muthaqqafūn," 59.

55. Ḥasan ʿAbd al-Rasūl, "Umm Kulthūm tataḥaddath Sāʿa maʿa ʾl-Sufarāʾ" (Umm Kulthūm speaks for an hour with the ambassadors), clipping from *al-Akhbār,* 1969, in the archives of al-Akhbār, "Umm Kulthūm—Riḥlāt" file. Similarly, "I really like to sing in standard Arabic because it is near to the understanding in all the sister Arab countries" (Ṣafiyya Nāṣif, "Umm Kulthūm Tughannī 4

Alḥān Jadīda" [Umm Kulthūm will sing four new songs], *al-Muṣawwar* (May 3, 1968).

56. ʿAbd al-Wahhāb, interview in *Ākhir Sāʿa* no. 2102 (February 5, 1975), 30.

57. Al-Shawwā, quoted in al-Naqqāsh, "Lughz Umm Kulthūm," 31.

58. Hegland, "Conclusion," 236.

59. The term "Weststruckness" was coined by the Persian writer Jalāl Āl Aḥmad (see his *Gharbzadegi*).

60. Voll, 148; also 135.

61. Hegland, "Introduction" in *Religious Resurgence*, 7.

Chapter Six

1. Muṣṭafá Maḥmūd, "Limādhā Uḥibb Ṣawt Umm Kulthūm" (Why I love the voice of Umm Kulthūm), *Rūz al-Yūsuf* (June 27, 1966).

2. Personal communication, Jamāl Salāma, November 14, 1982.

3. Racy, "Creativity and Ambience," 11.

4. Al-Naqqāsh, "Liqāʾ maʿa Umm Kulthūm," 40; Ṣāfiyya Nāṣif, "Umm Kulthūm Tughannī 4 Alḥān Jadīda," *al-Muṣawwar* (May 3, 1968). On another occasion she remarked that innovation in music began with the song text, for without it, the composer would have nothing with which to work (*Umm Kulthūm: Qiṣṣat*, 53; see also Fu'ād, 446). This point was stressed by many of her colleagues including the composer Balīgh Ḥamdī (personal communication, November 2, 1982) and Muḥammad al-Disūqī (personal communication, November 14, 1982).

5. The song was in celebration of the evacuation of foreign troops from the Suez in 1956 ("Ṣoot il-Salaam," *al-Kawākib* no. 282 [December 25, 1956], 24).

6. All of the composers and poets with whom Umm Kulthūm worked were male. Few women composed music in the commercial domain. Umm Kulthūm was among those who did as were Nādira, Laure Daccache, and Bahīja Ḥāfiẓ, who complained about the difficulty she encountered in having her work taken seriously (see, e.g., Ceza Nabarāwī's interview of Bahīja Ḥāfiẓ in *L'Égyptienne* [September 1928]). Many women wrote poetry and some published it. Virtually none were song lyricists, possibly because women desiring that their command of language and poetic style be taken seriously dared not venture into the realm of song lyrics, generally cast in colloquial Arabic and considered to require less poetic skill than literary Arabic (see Booth, "Colloquial Arabic Poetry, Politics, and the Press in Modern Egypt," nn. 24 and 43).

7. Zakariyyā Aḥmad, quoted in *Umm Kulthūm: Qithārat*, 112.

8. Al-Sunbāṭī, quoted in ʿAwaḍ, 147.

9. From an interview with the poet reprinted in ʿAbd al-Fattāḥ Ghaban, "Bayram yataḥaddath ʿan Umm Kulthūm" (Bayram speaks about Umm Kulthūm), *Rūz al-Yūsuf* (March 24, 1975).

10. Umm Kulthūm, quoted in Jalāl al-Juwaylī, "Wa-ākhir Ḥadīth Maʿahā" (The last interview with her), *al-Jadīd* no. 75 (February 15, 1975), 51.

11. Personal communications, Dr. Ḥasan al-Ḥifnāwī (August 22, 1982), Dr. Ratība al-Ḥifnī and Dr. Maḥmūd Kāmil (May, 1992); similarly, Fu'ād, 193 and Shūsha, 43.

12. Fu'ād, 360; also, Aḥmad Rāmī's essay in *al-Idhā'a wa-'l-Tilīfizyūn* no. 2557 (February 15, 1986), 25, originally written in November 1947. She learned "al-Aṭlāl" from a tape made by al-Sunbāṭī, and Sayyid Makkāwī prepared cassette tapes of both his songs for her (personal communications from Sayyid Sālim (November 16, 1982) and 'Abd al-'Azīz al-'Anānī (February 1, 1986)).

13. Personal communication, 'Abd al-Mun'im al-Ḥarīrī, January 11, 1982; he was not suggesting that notes need not be properly tuned but rather that there existed an allowable range of variation and embellishment in their articulation.

14. Personal communication, Balīgh Ḥamdī, November 2, 1982. This practice brought difficulties for Balīgh: like many of his youthful contemporaries, he depended on notation. To work with Umm Kulthūm he had to notate his compositions and then memorize them. A few exceptions were made. Notation was used for national anthems that included European harmony. And during the 1960s and 1970s, when younger members of the *firqa* were expected to play older songs, they were occasionally given notated music in order to learn a song that the older members already knew well. In one such case a performance of "Wulid al-Hudá" was canceled because there were not enough notated copies for the young players ("al-Yawm ta'ūd Laylat Umm Kulthūm," *al-Jumhūriyya* [May 6, 1971]).

15. See El-Shawan's remarks on the changing backgrounds of instrumentalists in Cairo in "al-Mūsīḳa," 109, 181, 185. Notations of Arabic songs, often intended for performance on the piano, the parlor instrument of choice among upper-class Cairenes, had been in existence since at least 1920. Notated *adwār* were advertised for sale in *al-Kashkūl* (no. 92 [February 18, 1923], 10). Al-Qaṣabjī's "Yalli Shaghalt il-Baal" for Umm Kulthūm was offered for sale as piano sheet music, as were others of her songs (Racy, "Musical," 39). Some of Salāma Ḥijāzī's songs were notated for Jurj Abyaḍ's troupe during the 1920s (Fu'ād, 32).

16. Personal communications, 'Abd al-Mun'im al-Ḥarīrī (January 11, 1982), Sayyid Sālim (November 16, 1982), Sayyid Haykal (December 9, 1981), Sayyid al-Maṣrī (October 10, 1982), Muḥammad al-Disūqī (November 15, 1982). For her own similar description, see *Umm Kulthūm: Qiṣṣat,* 54–55.

17. Al-Naqqāsh, "Liqā' ma'a Umm Kulthūm," 39. For example, the text of "Wi-Daarit il-Ayyaam" was delivered to its composer, Muḥammad 'Abd al-Wahhāb, in August of 1969. He completed the composition that month, and rehearsals with Umm Kulthūm and the *firqa* were held through December. The recording was made and the song premiered in January of 1970. During this process, she sought opinions and advice from her circle of friends, but final decisions were usually her own (clipping from *Akhbār al-Yawm* [January 11, 1970] in the archives of al-Akhbār—"Ḥafalāt" file; personal communications from Muḥammad al-Disūqī, Dr. Ḥasan al-Ḥifnāwī, and Balīgh Ḥamdī in 1982).

18. Rāmī as quoted in Fu'ād, 443; also his November 1947 essay, reprinted in *al-Idhā'a wa-'l-Tilīfizyūn* no. 2557 (February 15, 1986), 25; Maḥmūd al-Sa'adnī in *Umm Kulthūm: Qithārat,* 9; cf. Fahmī's account of her work in cinema, *Widā'an,* 53.

19. *Al-Kawākib* no. 1592 (February 2, 1982), 18; personal communication, Ni'mat Aḥmad Fu'ād. Radio officials recounted an instance when she made a spe-

cial trip to the radio building to select the background music for an interview to be broadcast during Ramadan. To the protestations of the interviewer that she should not trouble herself with such a minor matter Umm Kulthūm replied, "You might choose inappropriate light music or music with instruments not compatible with the program. I'll be there tomorrow." The following day, they said, she spent three hours choosing the music (ʿAbd al-ʿAzīz Kāmil in *Widāʿan,* 35).

20. Personal communication, Sayyid al-Maṣrī; Aḥmad ʿAbd al-Ḥamīd, "al-Layla . . . Tashar al-Malāyīn maʿa Umm Kulthūm," *al-Jumhūriyya* (February 2, 1965); "Kayfa tamma 'l-Liqā' al-Sādis?" (How was the sixth meeting achieved?), *al-Jumhūriyya* (July 22, 1968), 60.

21. "Sirr al-Muhandis alladhī Rāfaq Ṣawt Umm Kulthūm" (The secret of the engineer who accompanied the voice of Umm Kulthūm), *Ākhir Sāʿa* (March 12, 1975).

22. Personal communication, May, 1992; Ṣāliḥ, "15 ʿĀman maʿa Umm Kulthūm" (Fifteen years with Umm Kulthūm), *al-Kawākib* no. 1592 (February 2, 1982), 10–13.

23. ʿAbd al-ʿAzīz Kāmil in *Widāʿan,* 35; Ḥamdī quoted in al-Khaṭīb, 49.

24. Racy, "Creativity and Ambience," 11.

25. Al-Naqqāsh, "Lughz Umm Kulthūm," 19; *al-Kawākib* no. 1592 (February 2, 1982), 15.

26. Personal communication, Dr. Ḥasan al-Ḥifnāwī, August 22, 1982. "Umm Kulthūm felt that a woman's hairdo is part of her personality and so she remained conservative in her hairdo as a kind of accentuation of her private personality" (*al-Ahrām* [February 4, 1975], 4).

27. Personal communication, Mansī Amīn Fahmī, February 15, 1982.

28. Egypt Air and Middle East Airlines each scheduled two extra flights from Beirut to Cairo especially for her concert in April, 1972 (Abū Naẓẓāra, "Ṣawt Umm Kulthūm bi-Alḥān Sayyid Makkāwī," *al-Akhbār* (April 6, 1972), 8.

29. Umm Kulthūm, "Jumhūrī" (My audience), *al-Kawākib* no. 50 (July 15, 1952); repr. in *al-Kawākib* (October 18, 1977).

30. These estimates are based on edited commercial recordings of live performances (Ṣawt al-Qāhira cassettes no. 009, 76012, 001 and 76041). The lengths undoubtedly varied from one performance to another as Umm Kulthūm encouraged the repetition of popular instrumental sections, especially those that featured solos. However, all of the introductions compared included some extemporaneous repetition, and the examples represent a version of performances that much of the listening public heard repeatedly and understood as the song.

31. Slawek, "Ravi Shankar as Mediator between a Traditional Music and Modernity," 178, also 169–70. Compare Kaufman, quoted in Waterman, *Jùjú,* 5; Waterman argues that technology actually "facilitated the application of deep Yoruba musical techniques. In short, Westernization of musical means enabled indigenization of musical expression" (*Jùjú,* 84).

32. Adapted from Fu'ād, 324.

33. Durriyya ʿAwānī, "Yahūd Sharqiyyūn jā'ū li-Samāʿ Umm Kulthūm" (Oriental Jews came to hear Umm Kulthūm), *al-Muṣawwar* (November 24, 1967).

34. Al-Najmī, 66–68.

35. *Al-Ahrām* (December 7, 1968); *al-Akhbār* (January 5, 1973); Muḥammad Tabarak [?], "Ghannat Umm Kulthūm wa-tabarraʿat al-Iskandariyya bi-100 Alf Junayh" (Umm Kulthūm sang and Alexandria contributed one hundred thousand pounds), *Akhbār al-Yawm* (September 2, 1972). From beginning to end with no repetitions, any of these songs would last about thirty minutes or slightly more.

36. Racy, "Creativity and Ambience," 26.

37. *Rūz al-Yūsuf* no. 195 (November 9, 1931), 21. Influential artists who associated themselves explicitly with authentic (*aṣīl*) Egyptian music and culture such as Zakariyyā Aḥmad, and later Sayyid Makkāwī and ʿUmar Fatḥī, sang with *ghunna* to great acclaim. Good examples are Zakariyyā's recordings of his own setting of Bayram al-Tūnisī's colloquial poetry such as "Ahl il-Hawa" and "Ḥatgannin ya reet ya Ikhwanna ma Ruḥtish Lundun wala Bariis," and Sayyid Makkāwī's "il-Arḍ Bititkallim il-ʿArabi."

38. Racy observed that, "In the earlier recordings the vocal production was generally nasal in quality. Although it must have been the norm in the pre–World War I musical culture, nasality as such was attributed by some informants to the religiously trained performers. . . . In the later recordings, although nasality did not disappear altogether, it diminished considerably. This change in tone-color was undoubtedly a result of westernization" (Racy, "Musical," 290).

39. In this example she used her strongest voice and chest resonance throughout the song, adding *baḥḥa* in her cadence for the phrase "You designed me," as she surged upward into the higher range of the song.

40. "Illi Ḥabbik ya Hanaah" exemplified her typical use of brief falsetto trills that here drew attention to the significant words "light of your eyes" in the first line, while in the second line they functioned as coloristic devices, less directly connected to the meaning of the text. Other examples are "Amānan Ayyuhā ʾl-Qamar al-Muṭill" (on the word *saqām*) and "Fii Nuur Muḥayyaak."

41. *Umm Kulthūm: Qiṣṣat,* 53.

42. Umm Kulthūm, quoted in al-Naqqāsh, "Liqāʾ maʿa Umm Kulthūm," 44.

43. "Al-Ḥadīth al-Ākhir," Ṣawt al-Qāhira cassette tape no. SC76015.

44. Fuʾād, 393; ʿAbd al-Fattāḥ Ghaban "Bayram Yataḥaddath ʿan Umm Kulthūm," *Rūz al-Yūsuf* (March 24, 1975); Ṭāhā Ḥusayn quoted in "Innahā Ajmal Ṣawt" (The most beautiful voice), *al-Idhāʿa wa-ʾl-Tilīfizyūn* (February 8, 1975). ʿAbd al-Wahhāb, among many others, repeatedly stressed Umm Kulthūm's treatment of text and expanded on the point in many ways: "She never once risked singing what she did not understand" (Fuʾād, 393); also *Umm Kulthūm: Qiṣṣat,* 20; *al-Idhāʿa wa-ʾl-Tilīfizyūn* no. 2603 (February 2, 1985), 12, and no. 2447 (February 6, 1982), 28; ʿAwaḍ, 102; Nabīl Raghab, "Umm Kulthūm: Fann lā yaʿrifu ʾl-Tashannuj" (Umm Kulthūm: an art that does more than emote), *al-Jadīd* no. 75 (February 15, 1975), 48.

45. Aḥmad Zākī Pāshā, quoted in al-Shawwā, 141.

46. Ibn Surayj, quoted in K. Nelson, 37.

47. Boolaky, 52. "Sheer joy," he wrote, "in the beauty of words and their collocation used to be one of the dominant characteristics of the early Muslims when

Arabic was the common language of all Muslims during the first 500 years of Islam" (52); Racy, "Music" in *Genius of Arab Civilization*, 130. Similarly, K. Nelson wrote, "evidence for the close association of poetry and music lies in the anecdotes and verses that, in testifying to the magical skill of the early singers, praise their language and poetic skills" (36).

48. However, not all of the characteristics associated with the poetic genres were apparent in their musical settings. Although the listener expected a correctly accentuated rendition of the poetic text, the rhythmic setting, whether metrical or not, did not always correspond to the poetic meter in which the text was cast, and thus metrical characteristics of the poetry did not carry over into the composition. Cf. Cachia, "Egyptian," esp. 88. Lane, 364.

49. Al-Khulaʿī added that the singer had license to omit case endings or soften emphatic consonants in those instances where the sound would be hard on the ear of the listener. He gave as an example replacing the *qāf*, a pharyngeal plosive, with the *hamza*, a glottal stop, to soften the aural effect without obscuring the meaning. Understanding poetry, he wrote, also eased the burden of memorization (*Kitāb*, 88). The importance attached to clear articulation has been observed in other parts of the Arab world as well. In the annotations to their transcription of the text of a popular *qaṣīda* from Algeria in 1886, Delphin and Guin remarked that "the singer articulates the words very well, the syllables are strongly accentuated and all the words detached from each other with rare neatness" (99).

50. Racy, "Musical," 262. Later in the century, critic Kamāl al-Najmī called for "musical grammar" suited to the Arabic language and its rhythms (51).

51. Similar repertories might include German *lieder*, for example, or American country-western song, in which the words must be clearly understood for the song to have its effect, and the sound of the language or dialect is usually essential to the style. To these one might contrast popular songs of Michael Jackson, in which the meaning and sound of the words seem less important than the overall color generated by voice, instruments, and special effects, or other twentieth-century repertories that feature singing on nonsense syllables or electronic distortion of a sung text to achieve the effect of the piece, e.g., Luciano Berio's "Omaggio a Joyce."

52. Al-Ḥifnī, 1:78.

53. Boolaky, 52.

54. K. Nelson, 101. Nelson's book provides a detailed and thorough discussion of recitation in Egypt upon which my discussion is dependent.

55. Further discussion appears in Danielson, "The Qurʾān and the Qaṣīdah."

56. K. Nelson, 15.

57. Ibid., 64, 65. She found that *taṣwīr al-maʿná* involved the selection of a *maqām* suited to the meaning of the text. These associations of ethos with musical modes, part of Arab classical music, are not strong in modern Egyptian song.

58. Ibid., 13.

59. Muḥammad al-Gharīb, "al-Ughniyya al-Dīniyya Tastahdif al-Qalb" (Religious song aims at the heart), *al-Idhāʿa wa-ʾl-Tilīfizyūn* no. 2633 (August 31, 1985), 18–19.

60. Fuʾād, 348.

61. Personal communication, Kamāl Ḥusnī, May 2, 1982; see also Fu'ād, 51, 154; Shiloah; Al Faruqi, "Status of Music."

62. Touma discusses Mulla ʿUthmān al-Mawṣilī (1854–1923), an Iraqi singer who also recited the Qurʾān. The combination of the two occupations may have been widespread in the Arab world (Touma, 52).

63. Zakariyyā Aḥmad, quoted in ʿAwaḍ, 111.

64. Bourdieu, 601.

65. El-Hamamsy, 302.

66. Mitchell, 143; see also 132–33, 148–49, and 86–87. Compare Lila Abu-Lughod's discussion of the aesthetics of poetic rendition in *Veiled Sentiments:* "Improvisational talent and ability to play with linguistic forms are highly valued in Bedouin culture. . . . Bedouins are sensitive to the graces and evocative power of oral textual elements such as sound, alliteration, intonation and rhythm, elements that are highlighted in recitation. When sung, much of the effect of the **ghinnāwa** depends on the delivery (usually plaintive), the singer's skill, and the quality of his or her voice" (173).

67. As the Committee on Maqāmāt, Īqāʿāt, and Compositional Genres of the 1932 conference concluded, in answer to the question of whether it were possible to invent new vocal genres, "Bāb al-ijtihād maftūḥ." The committee borrowed this phrase from theology where it refers to systematic, original thought, through which a scholar or judge, in the absence of precedent, could formulate a correct position, usually calling upon analogy (*Kitāb Muʾtamar,* 88, 136).

68. Of the 94.6 percent of her repertory for which the melodic mode is known, only 4.1 percent lies outside the system of *maqāmāt.* This small percentage includes the experimental pieces of al-Qaṣabjī and national anthems (which often were expected to be cast in the mold of Western harmonized martial music).

69. "Kull ma Yizdaad" (1932) by Dāwūd Ḥusnī, for instance, began with a brief instrumental introduction reminiscent of a *dūlāb;* the voice entered at the lower end of the *maqām* and ascended in traditional stepwise fashion. The piece included the improvisatory *hank* essential to the genre since the days of ʿUthmān as well as choral responses performed by her male instrumental accompanists. Another good example of a *dawr* is Zakariyyā's "Imta 'l-Hawa" (1932). To these one might contrast ʿAbd al-Wahhāb's innovative setting of "Fil-Layl lamma Khilī" (1929).

70. Racy, "Waṣlah," esp. 401; Racy, "Musical," 55–56.

71. Upon his return from the Cairo Conference of 1932, Erich von Hornbostel wrote that "the most famous singer in Cairo, Umm Kulthūm . . . in one of her endlessly long songs" took the opportunity, when the melody resembled a European musical style, to adopt a bel canto style of singing for the pleasure of the European listeners. He remarked that "die 'Barbaren' wissen also, dass es das gibt, und könnens auch" (The "Barbarian," Hornbostel says, tongue-in-cheek, knows that [bel canto] exists and can also do it) (17). Although claims for her skill in varied repetition date from early in her career, the contemporary listener may only hear these in renditions dating from the 1940s and later, when live recordings of her perfor-

mances began to be made, collected, and released commercially. The best examples of her skills date from the 1940s and 1950s when her voice, musical skill, and sensitivity had fully matured and before age caused her voice to become less flexible. Good later examples include the lines "Ya ma badariiha" and "Kunt bashtaq lak" from Balīgh Ḥamdī's "Biʿiid ʿAnnak" (premiered in 1965, Ṣawt al-Qāhira cassette no. SC76009) and the line "Qalu ʾl-maḥabba qadar" from his "Ḥakam ʿAleena ʾl-Hawa" recorded in 1973.

72. El-Shawan, "al-Mūsīḳa," 32. Replication later became a goal for the Firqat al-Mūsīqá ʾl-ʿArabiyya of Cairo, a state-supported group whose mandate was to preserve the heritage of Arabic music. The history of this group is discussed thoroughly in El-Shawan.

73. Ibid., 265–66.

74. Lois al Faruqi lists numerous ornaments with their Arabic names and explanations in "Ornamentation in Arabian Improvisational Music"; see also her "Nature of the Musical Art of Islamic Culture" (esp. 187–88) and her *Annotated Glossary of Arabic Musical Terms.*

75. K. Nelson, 160. In the context of Qurʾanic recitation, she wrote that "the real test of the reciters' (and musicians') skill is the melodic cadential formula" (126); see also 127–30.

76. ʿAbd al-Wahhāb, quoted in *Umm Kulthūm: Qiṣṣat,* 19, 20, and in *Widāʿan,* 28.

77. Cf. Racy's transcription of cadences in *bayātī,* "Musical," 313.

78. Compare K. Nelson, 126.

79. This excerpt is also discussed in chap. 5, example 5.

80. Concert tape from the collection of ʿAbd al-ʿAzīz al-ʿAnānī; the lines begin "Qad saqaytu ʾl-ḥubba waddī."

81. Cf. Frith, quoting *Rolling Stone* editor Paul Nelson's description of a similar engagement of listeners with music and texts: "when I first heard [Jackson Browne's 'Farther On'], I was absolutely unable to put any space between myself and someone else's childhood" (Frith, "Why Do Songs Have Words," p. 94).

82. Sawa, "Oral Transmission," 256.

Chapter Seven

1. First line of "Wi-Daarit il-Ayyaam."

2. Doctors recommended treatment in one of the countries having mineral waters. The following summer she spent a month at Vichy and returned feeling better, "although," she said, "I am bound by the limitations of a strict diet prohibiting most kinds of food" (*Rūz al-Yūsuf* no. 268 [April 3, 1933], 37; no. 269 [April 10, 1933], 29; *Ākhir Sāʿa* no. 163 [August 22, 1937], 40; *al-Rādyū ʾl-Miṣrī* no. 183 [September 1938], repr. in *al-Idhāʿa wa-ʾl-Tilīfizyūn* no. 2665 [April 12, 1986], 40).

3. Samīra Abāẓa, quoted in "Ṣadīqat al-ʿUmr li-Umm Kulthūm" (The lifetime friend of Umm Kulthūm), *al-Idhāʿa wa-ʾl-Tilīfizyūn* (February 7, 1976); *al-Rādyū ʾl-Miṣrī* no. 601 (September 21, 1946), 5.

4. Shūsha, 82; "Hal Tushawwaḥ Tasjīlāt Umm Kulthūm?" (Will Umm Kul-

thūm's tapes be ruined?), *Uktūbir* (February 5, 1978), 73; ʿAbd al-Fattāḥ Ghaban, "Bayram yataḥaddath ʿan Umm Kulthūm" (Bayram speaks about Umm Kulthūm), *Rūz al-Yūsuf* (March 24, 1975).

5. Sharīf Abāẓa in *Umm Kulthūm: al-Nagham al-Khālid,* 42; Fuʾād, 277, 287–88; ʿAwaḍ, 124.

6. The recipient of her early affections was variously thought to be her cousin Ṣabr, another cousin (whom she was said to have married and who subsequently became seriously ill and was hospitalized), and a young *ʿūd* player who left her because he believed he could never keep pace with her career (*al-Ṣabāḥ* no. 96 [July 3, 1928], 11; *al-Kashkūl* no. 58 [June 25, 1922], 4; *Umm Kulthūm: Qithārat,* 34; *Rūz al-Yūsuf* no. 234 [August 8, 1932], 24–25; no. 185 [August 31, 1930], 18). Two other suitors mentioned were Ḥifnī Bey al-Darīnī and his former employer, Prince ʿUmar Ibrāhīm, whom there is no indication that she ever met (*Rūz al-Yūsuf* no. 80 [May 19, 1927], 12). One of the more bizarre reports involved a villager from Upper Egypt who filed a lawsuit against her claiming that he was her husband and demanding that she return to his house. Umm Kulthūm was compelled to appear in court to vindicate herself (Shūsha, 72; Fuʾād, 222).

7. In 1931, for instance, she was received by the family of the eminent politician Fatḥ Allāh Barakāt, not as a paid performer but as a family acquaintance, come to offer congratulations on the birth of a son (*Rūz al-Yūsuf* no. 194 [November 2, 1931], 18).

8. Personal communication from Dr. Buthayna Farīd, a member of Sharīf Ṣabrī's family, January 7, 1985.

9. Fuʾād, 272; in fact, judging by various reports over the long term, Maḥmūd Sharīf was a kind man and a musician of some considerable talent.

10. Personal communication, Dr. Muḥammad Ḥasan al-Ḥifnāwī, August 22, 1982; Dr. Ḥasan al-Ḥifnāwī in *Widāʿan,* 6; Shūsha, 75.

11. *Rūz al-Yūsuf* no. 1241 (March 24, 1952), 32.

12. Issawi, 272.

13. Jack Crabb discusses the relationship of the new government to expressive artists in "Politics, History, and Culture in Nasser's Egypt." The revolution brought with it a good deal of upheaval on administrative levels and, as a result, at one point Umm Kulthūm felt her position in broadcasting to be threatened. She apparently contacted Shafiq Abū ʿAwf, the liaison between the Revolutionary Council and the Musicians' Union, who intervened on her behalf. He claimed to have settled the matter personally with Ṣalāḥ Sālim, ʿAbd al-Nāṣir, and ʿAbd al-Ḥakīm ʿĀmir. According to Abū ʿAwf, a complaint was filed against Umm Kulthūm resulting, at least in part, from dissatisfaction with her victory over ʿAbd al-Wahhāb in an election for the presidency of the union ("Al-Mawt bi-dūn Alam" [Death without pain], *al-Idhāʿa wa-ʾl-Tilīfizyūn* [February 5, 1983], 48; for notices of various disputes within the union involving Umm Kulthūm, see *Rūz al-Yūsuf* no. 1245 [April 21, 1952], 33 and no. 1250 [May 26, 1952], 32; also Anwar Zaʿlūk, "Qiṣṣat Awwal Liqāʾ bayna ʿAbd al-Nāṣir wa-Umm Kulthūm" [The story of the first meeting between ʿAbd al-Nāṣir and Umm Kulthūm], *Ṣabāḥ al-Khayr* [January 29, 1976]; Kāmil, *Muḥammad al-Qaṣabjī,* 80).

14. *Ahl al-Fann* no. 48 (March 12, 1955), cover and 4; *Rūz al-Yūsuf* no. 1425 (October 3, 1955), 33.

15. Singers who grew up learning Umm Kulthūm's repertory included Najāt ʿAlī, Nādira, Layla Murād, Najāḥ Salām, Laure Daccache, Nūr al-Hudá, and Rajāʾ ʿAbduh. In 1947, the Egyptian Bureau of Writers had been established to insure that lyricists and composers received royalties for the broadcasting of their songs abroad (broadcasting within Egypt having been governed by individual contracts). As a result of the efforts expended by this office, over 60,000 £E ($172,200) in royalties were paid to Egyptian composers and poets in 1955, including, of course, many who worked with Umm Kulthūm. Riyāḍ al-Sunbāṭī received 1,500 £E ($4,305), Aḥmad Rāmī and Bayram al-Tūnisī, each 1,000 £E ($2,870), and ʿAbd al-Wahhāb, 7,000 £E ($20,090) ("Limādhā Tuqāḍī Umm Kulthūm Muṭribātinā?" [Why is Umm Kulthūm suing our singers?], *al-Ahrām* [June 2, 1955]).

16. *Rūz al-Yūsuf* no. 1238 (March 3, 1952), 33. Suʿād Muḥammad claimed that, in 1948, she was denied a visa to Egypt because Umm Kulthūm had complained to her powerful friends about Suʿād's "stealing" of her songs (Saʿīd Ghabaris, "Umm Kulthūm kān maʿahā ʾl-Jiḥāz al-Iʿlāmī" [Umm Kulthūm had the media on her side], *al-Usbūʿ* [September 1, 1975], 65).

17. Sāmī al-Laythī, "Qiṣṣat al-Mawsim" (The story of the season), *Rūz al-Yūsuf* no. 1241 (March 24, 1952), 34; Shūsha, 43; "Dhikrayāt lam tunshar ʿan Umm Kulthūm" (Unpublished memories of Umm Kulthūm), *Rūz al-Yūsuf* (February 2, 1976); Fuʾād, 313; Saḥḥāb, 95; personal communication from Sayyid al-Maṣrī.

18. *Rūz al-Yūsuf* no. 1255 (June 30, 1952), 34. For more information about accompanying musicians, see Danielson, "Shaping Tradition," 291–94.

19. The commemorative national song was not new to her. "Zahr al-Rabīʿ" (1945) by Zakariyyā Aḥmad and Muḥammad al-Asmar was composed for a concert celebrating the founding of the Arab League. The Shawqī texts she sang during the 1940s were often considered to be nationalistic in content. "Bayna ʿAhdayn" (Between two eras), first performed in 1949, was overtly patriotic in character. Some authors have called "Nashīd al-Jāmiʿa" (The university song) Umm Kulthūm's first patriotic song (*Umm Kulthūm: al-Nagham al-Khālid*, 17–18).

20. It remained the anthem until late 1977, when it was replaced by the less militant "Bilaadi, Bilaadi" (My country, my country) by Sayyid Darwīsh. President Sadat apparently made this change for the occasion of Menachim Begin's visit to Egypt and the beginning of the Camp David peace talks.

21. Upon being asked about sales figures for the national songs, one response was "Who'd buy those?"

22. The song was written at the time of the Tripartite Aggression. Bayram used the formulaic "il-awwila . . . , il-tanya . . . , il-talta" (see chap. 5, and chap. 5, n. 11) to describe the actions of the three foreign powers involved.

23. See the little-known 45 rpm disc entitled "Shaʿb al-ʿIrāq" listed as no. 18 in the Ṣawt al-Qāhira record catalog of 1969, p. 13. According to the engineer Sayyid al-Maṣrī, this recording was made before his tenure with the company began in 1959; the song probably celebrated the 1958 Iraqi Revolution.

24. She did not appear in the film but recorded the songs, which were dubbed for actress Nabīla Nūr in the leading role.

25. Smith, *Rabiʿa the Mystic,* excerpted in Fernea and Bezirgan, 39, 43.

26. "Uḥibbuhā li-Qalbihā 'l-Kabīr" (I love her for her great heart), *Rūz al-Yūsuf* no. 1431 (November 21, 1955), 27; ʿAwaḍ, 112, 114.

27. This was the foundation for later autobiographies, including ʿAwaḍ's.

28. "Kawkab al-Sharq" (The star of the east), *al-Jumhūriyya* (July 29, 1961).

29. "Qiṣṣat Awwal Liqāʾ bayna ʿAbd al-Nāṣir wa-Umm Kulthūm," *Ṣabāḥ al-Khayr* (January 29, 1976); Abāẓa in *Umm Kulthūm: al-Nagham al-Khālid,* 43. As Issawi wrote, "The Palestine War proved to be disastrous, and the disappointing performance of the Egyptian army was only partly redeemed by such gallant acts as the defence of Faluja" (263).

30. Personal communications, Niʿmāt Aḥmad Fu'ād (May 12, 1982) and Dr. Ḥasan al-Ḥifnāwī (August 22, 1982); Fu'ād, 294.

31. For more information, see Danielson, "Shaping Tradition," 312–13.

32. A common view expressed by, among many others, al-Najmī in *al-Ghināʾ al-Miṣrī,* 71.

33. She had worked with professional lyricists before, including Ḥusayn Ḥilmī al-Ministirlī and Ḥasan Ṣubḥī during the 1930s; however most of her songs were written by Bayram, Shawqī, and Rāmi, who were poets first and song writers only incidentally.

34. The choice was not entirely her own, of course. While poets such as Bayram found writing song lyrics for a popular singer a good way to generate income, Bayram also found her editing of his work hard to bear, and some poets may have seen insufficient reason to tolerate the demands of such a difficult person.

35. Kāmil, *Muḥammad al-Qaṣabjī,* 83–84.

36. "Every time Umm Kulthūm argues with her composers, she thinks of singing something by Amīn Ṣidqī" (*Rūz al-Yūsuf* no. 1239 [March 7, 1952], 27; also no. 1425 [October 3, 1955], 33; I. Saḥḥāb, 29–30; N. Ḥāfiẓ, 296; personal communication, Balīgh Ḥamdī, November 2, 1982, who said that before they began work together Umm Kulthūm had learned virtually every one of his recorded compositions.

37. Personal communication, Sayyid al-Maṣrī (October 6, 1982); also Ṣalāḥ Darwīsh, "Umm Kulthūm fī Liqā'ihā maʿa 'l-Ṣiḥāfa" (Umm Kulthūm in her meeting with the press), *al-Jumhūriyya* (January 6, 1970) and Shūsha, 48.

38. According to her principal violinist, Aḥmad al-Ḥifnāwī, it was in a fit of pique with Riyāḍ al-Sunbāṭī that she sought the very young Balīgh Ḥamdī, to demonstrate to al-Sunbāṭī that her songs would succeed even when composed by a twenty-one-year-old boy (personal communication, July 1980; see also Sāmī al-Laythī, "Lil-Fann Faqaṭ" [For art alone], *Rūz al-Yūsuf* no. 1251 [June 1, 1952], 34).

39. Personal communications, Balīgh Ḥamdī (November 2, 1982) and Sayyid al-Maṣrī (October 10, 1982).

40. For instance, violinist ʿAbd al-Munʿim al-Ḥarīrī, referring to Balīgh's "Ansaak, ya Salaam" and "Ḥubb Eeh" (*al-Kawākib* no. 1592 [February 2, 1982], 16).

Balīgh claimed to have been influenced by Sayyid Darwīsh, Dāwūd Ḥusnī, Muḥammad al-Qaṣabjī, and Muḥammad Fawzī. Indeed, as the century progressed, it became fashionable for composers to associate themselves with composers whose works had become accepted as *turāth* such as Darwīsh, Ḥusnī, and Zakariyyā Aḥmad; few, if any, composers failed to claim indebtedness to Sayyid Darwīsh in particular.

41. Fu'ād, 325; *al-Kawākib* no. 588 (November 6, 1962), 17–18.

42. Personal communication, Balīgh Ḥamdī, November 2, 1982; al-Mawjī, "Qiṣṣat Alḥānī li-Umm Kulthūm" (The story of my songs for Umm Kulthūm), *al-Kawākib* (February 24, 1976).

43. Maḥmūd Khayrat was the father of the Egyptian composer Abū Bakr Khayrat; Darwīsh's well-known song is from the play *Al-ʿAshara al-Ṭayyiba,* first performed by Najīb al-Rīḥānī's troupe on March 15, 1920. ʿAbd al-Wahhāb placed this meeting in about 1923 (Aḥmad ʿAbd al-Ḥamīd, "al-Layla Tashar al-Malāyīn maʿa Umm Kulthūm" [Tonight the millions sit up with Umm Kulthūm], *al-Jumhūriyya* [March 17, 1965]); ʿAwaḍ dated the meeting in 1927 (132; Fu'ād, 125).

44. ʿAbd al-Ḥamīd, "Al-Layla Tashar al-Malāyīn maʿa Umm Kulthūm," *al-Jumhūriyya* (February 2, 1965); ʿAwaḍ, 134, 136. The memoirs of other musicians suggest that such appearances were not uncommon: they offered opportunities for cultivating patrons and supporters, doing business, remaining visible and, with luck, raising one's social status. Such gatherings formed important points of social articulation between performers and elites.

45. Racy noted these rhythmic juxtapositions in ʿAbd al-Wahhāb's early *qaṣā'id* as well as other features borrowed from European classical music ("Musical," 265–66).

46. Umm Kulthūm, quoted in Fu'ād, 258–59.

47. ʿAwaḍ, 135; personal communication, Maḥmūd Kāmil, March 19, 1982.

48. ʿAbd al-Ḥamīd, "Al-Layla Tashar al-Malāyīn maʿa Umm Kulthūm," *al-Jumhūriyya* (February 2, 1965).

49. Personal communication, Dr. Ḥasan al-Ḥifnāwī, August 22, 1982.

50. ʿAbd al-Wahhāb recalled the event in *Umm Kulthūm: Qiṣṣat,* 18; see also Shūsha, 46 and ʿAwaḍ, 136.

51. One of the by-products of Umm Kulthūm's role in Egyptian culture was the colloquial verb constructed from her name: *Takaltham,* to make [something] like [Umm] Kulthūm.

52. See ʿAbd al-Wahhāb's recollections in *Umm Kulthūm: Qiṣṣat,* 18 and in *Widāʿan,* 27; also personal communications, Aḥmad al-Ḥifnāwī in July 1980, and Dr. Ḥasan al-Ḥifnāwī in August, 1982.

53. "Indhār, min Umm Kulthūm ilá ʿAbd al-Wahhāb" (A warning from Umm Kulthūm to ʿAbd al-Wahhāb), *al-Jumhūriyya* (February 11, 1964).

54. The magazine *Ṣabāḥ al-Khayr* even published an article about the articles: it reported that, in the two weeks following the premier of "Inta ʿUmri," seventy-five notices and thirty full-length articles had been published in major Egyptian newspapers and news magazines, an average of more than one per periodical per

day. These numbers did not include pictures or photographic essays, broadcast interviews, television coverage, or articles published outside Egypt ("Fī Usbūʿayn Faqaṭ" [In only two weeks], *Ṣabāḥ al-Khayr* [February 27, 1964]).

55. Al-Najmī, "ʿInda mā yulaḥḥinūn li-Umm Kulthūm" (When they compose for Umm Kulthūm), *al-Kawākib* (February 24, 1968), 3; ʿAwaḍ, 136.

56. Al-Mawjī, "Limādhā najaḥat ughniyyat Inta ʿUmri??" (Why did Inta ʿUmri succeed?), *al-Jumhūriyya* (February 8, 1964).

57. Ḥamdī, ibid. Similarly, Medhat Assem remarked that neither Umm Kulthūm's performance nor ʿAbd al-Wahhāb's song was especially good. The song, he said, was more suitable to dance than singing, and so Umm Kulthūm adhered to the dancelike composition from beginning to end, forgoing her usual improvisatory excursions ("Ra'yuhum fī Ughniyyat al-ʿUmr" [Their opinions on the song of a lifetime], *al-Kawākib* [February 11, 1964]).

58. According to reports of the terms, 37.5 percent went to the poet and 62.5 percent to the composer. Umm Kulthūm got no part of these rights but took a percentage of recording sales ("Rubʿ Milyūn Junayh taksibuh Inta ʿUmri" [Inta ʿUmri earns a quarter of a million pounds], *al-Kawākib* [April 7, 1964]); Aḥmad al-Ḥifnāwī, personal communication, July 1980.

59. "Inta 'l-Ḥubb bilā Mujāmala" (Inta 'l-Ḥubb without flattery), *al-Jumhūriyya* (March 17, 1965); Fu'ād, 384–85.

60. Between 1956 and 1973 al-Sunbāṭī composed twenty-four patriotic songs, sixteen love songs, and five religious songs. Fifteen were *qaṣā'id.* His compositions constituted 60 percent of Umm Kulthūm's new repertory for this period.

61. Shūsha 42, 50, 51; ʿAwaḍ, 148; "al-Ḥadīth al-Ākhir ʿan al-Fann wa-'l-Ḥayāh maʿa Umm Kulthūm" (The last interview about art and life with Umm Kulthūm) Ṣawt al-Qāhira cassette tape no. 76015.

62. Nājī published "al-Aṭlāl" in segments in several issues of *al-Rādyū al-Miṣrī* in 1946 (no. 604 [October 12], 7; no. 605 [October 19], 7; no. 606 [October 26], 8; no. 607 [November 2], 9). The poem was probably new at this time; see also Bakr al-Sharqāwī in *Widāʿan,* 12. During his lifetime the romantic Nājī was criticized as escapist and sentimental, wanting a sense of reality and awareness of the age in which he lived. Describing Nājī's work, M. M. Badawi wrote, "There is remarkably little interest in wider issues, social or political in his work: to be exact there are four political poems" (Badawi, 130, 135, 204, 224).

63. Ṣāliḥ Jūda, "Mādhā ṣanaʿat Umm Kulthūm bi-Shiʿr Nājī?" (What did Umm Kulthūm do to Nāji's poem?), *al-Kawākib* (April 26, 1966).

64. While he was alive Nājī expressed his desire for Umm Kulthūm to sing one of his poems; and he had certainly been aware of her treatment of Shawqī's *qaṣā'id.* He may have realized that any poem she sang would be altered and felt no objection. ʿAbd al-Wahhāb also rearranged some of the Shawqī texts he sang (Jalīl al-Bundārī, "Umm Kulthūm al-Layla," *al-Akhbār* [April 7, 1966]; Fu'ād, 253; Ḥasan ʿAbd al-Rasūl, "Umm Kulthūm tataḥaddath Sāʿa maʿa 'l-Sufarā'," from the archives of *al-Akhbār* [1969], "Umm Kulthūm—Riḥlāt" file).

65. Muḥammad Tabarak, "ʿAṣr Umm Kulthūm" (The era of Umm Kulthūm), *al-Jadīd* (February 15, 1975), 39. On another, similar occasion, she had great fun

with her audience by varying the line "I drink with your hand." The second example was reported in *al-Rādyū 'l-Miṣrī* no. 585 (June 1, 1946), 2; the writer gave the title of the song as "il-Awwila fil-Gharaam," however the line was actually from "il-Ahaat": "I drink with your hand a cup that satisfies me, I drink with your hand a cup that burns me." In "Nahj al-Burda" she added artificial reverberation to accompany the word "chaos" (*fawḍá*), apparently to reinforce the concept of endless emptiness and total disorder associated with hell.

66. Good examples of the results are "Aqbal al-Layl," "al-Aṭlāl," "Laa ya Ḥabiibi," "il-Ḥubb Kida," "Lissa Faakir," "Ṭalamā tajrī," and also Balīgh's "Sīrat al-Ḥubb," and "Biʿiid ʿAnnak."

67. A good example is "Ana Fi-ʾntiẓaarak."

68. "Kullu raqṣa!" was a frequent complaint.

69. Personal communication, Muḥammad Sayyid Haykal, December 9, 1981; untitled clipping from *Rūz al-Yūsuf* (February 17, 1964), archives of *al-Akhbār*, "Umm Kulthūm—Firqa" file; *al-Akhbār* (March 8, 1965); "al-Layla Tashar al-Malāyīn maʿa Umm Kulthūm," *al-Jumhūriyya* (February 2, 1976); Ḥusayn ʿUthmān, "Alladhīna Yajlisūn warāʾ Umm Kulthūm" (Those who sit behind Umm Kulthūm), *al-Kawākib* (February 25, 1969); Abū Naẓẓāra, "Ṣawt Umm Kulthūm bi-Alḥān Sayyid Makkāwī," *al-Akhbār* (April 6, 1972), 8.

70. Personal communication, Aḥmad al-Ḥifnāwī, July 1980.

71. For instance, in a live recording of "Ḥayyart Qalbī," Ṣawt al-Qāhira cassette tape no. 019. The song was premiered in 1961. At other times she manifested surprising lightness and agility for her age, for instance in recordings of "Alf Leela wi-Leela" (premiered in 1969) and in her performance of "al-Aṭlāl" in Paris (1967). Writers recalled a remarkably high range mustered for her performances of "Huwwa Ṣaḥiiḥ il-Hawa Ghallaab," premiered in 1960 (al-Najmī in *Widāʿan*, 21; *Umm Kulthūm: al-Nagham al-Khālid*, 16). She managed a wide array of vocal colors in "Biʿiid ʿAnnak" (1965) and "Akādu Ashukku" (1960) (Ṣawt al-Qāhira cassette nos. 76009, 77212, 75161, 012).

72. The opening of "Hagartak" features a similar sobbing breathiness.

73. Boyd, *Egyptian Radio,* 1; see also his chart of transmission power, p. 10. For dates of the establishment of new stations, their wavelengths and transmission power, see the yearbooks published by the Egyptian government.

74. Umm Kulthūm, quoted in al-Naqqāsh, "Liqāʾ maʿa Umm Kulthūm," 41.

75. Fu'ād, 311; "Sirr al-Muhandis alladhī Rāfaq Ṣawt Umm Kulthūm," *Ākhir Sāʿa* (March 12, 1975); "Kawkab al-Sharq Hiya 'l-Waḥīda allatī lam Tara Nafsahā fī al-Tilīfizyūn" (The star of the east is the only one who did not see herself on television), *al-Jumhūriyya* (July 29, 1961).

76. Further details of this contract appear in Danielson, "Shaping Tradition," 260–61. Another way of gaining control was to form one's own company, an option taken by Muḥammad ʿAbd al-Wahhāb, ʿAbd al-Ḥalīm Ḥāfiẓ, and several actors. I am grateful to Sayyid al-Maṣrī, artistic director of Ṣawt al-Qāhira, ʿAbd al-Ḥamīd Ḥamdī, formerly general manager, and Muḥammad Jumʿa, formerly financial manager of the company, for information and explanations of Umm Kulthūm's and other recording contracts.

77. Appreciation of Umm Kulthūm was not merely a matter of large fees. In 1963 listeners in Kuwait sent her a new silver Cadillac equipped with a radio, a television, and a refrigerator. She requested a white telephone for her new car, making it the tenth auto in Egypt to have a phone. In 1965, out of delight with "Amal Ḥayaati," a listener from the Delta town of Damanhūr sent her a young cow and a seven-month-old water buffalo (*al-Jumhūriyya* [December 6, 1963] and Fu'ād, 334). These were substantial gifts, accepted with the grace befitting a landowning daughter of the Egyptian countryside. Further information appears in Danielson, "Shaping Tradition," 287.

78. Davis, "Religion against the State," 157–58. Ansari's *Stalled Society* provides a lucid analysis of the gap between the goals of ʿAbd al-Nāṣir's government and their realization by the mid-1960s, taking as its point of departure the defeat of a group of *fallaḥiin* by the interests of big landowners.

79. See, e.g., Chelbi, p. 304.

80. *Umm Kulthūm: Qithārat,* 134.

81. "Ghannat lil-Ḥubb . . . fa-jamaʿat 76,000 Junayh lil-Ḥarb," *Akhbār al-Yawm* (June 19, 1967); Muḥammad Tabarak, "Ghannat Umm Kulthūm wa-tabarraʿat al-Iskandariyya bi-100 Alf Junayh," *Akhbār al-Yawm* (September 2, 1972). Women often carried their wealth in the form of gold, or, less commonly, silver jewelry which they would sell, or in this case donate, if necessary.

82. She planned to sing in Moscow and Tashkent in late September of 1970. However, three days after her arrival there, President ʿAbd al-Nāṣir died and she returned to Egypt without performing ("Umm Kulthūm allātī Tanqul Nabḍ Miṣr ilá Mūskū" [Umm Kulthūm, who carries a little of Egypt to Moscow], *al-Kawākib* [September 14, 1970]).

83. "Riḥlātuhā . . . min Ajl al-Majhūd al-Ḥarbī baʿd al-Naksa" (Her trips . . . for the sake of the war effort after the defeat), *Akhbār al-Yawm* (February 1, 1970); "Umm Kulthūm Tughannī fī Bārīs," *al-Ahrām* (September 29, 1966); Īrīs Naẓmī, "Kayfa ʿĀshat Baʿlabakk Layāliya Umm Kulthūm?" (How did Baalbak enjoy Umm Kulthūm nights?), *Ākhir Sāʿa* (July 17, 1968); "Bi-Tilīfūn maʿa Umm Kulthūm (On the telephone with Umm Kulthūm), *al-Taʿawwun* (November 30, 1969); Shūsha, 62; clippings from the archives of *al-Akhbār,* "Umm Kulthūm—Riḥlāt" file, including *al-Akhbār* (June 27, 1967; August 13, 1969), *al-Ahrām* (August 1, 1968; January 17, 1969), and *al-Jumhūriyya* (April 25, 1969); ʿAwaḍ put the total at 2,000,000 £E ($4,600,000) (ʿAwaḍ, 150).

84. She also sang two *qaṣāʾid* by the Saudi Prince ʿAbd Allāh Fayṣal, but these texts were not deliberately intended to represent Saudi Arabia in her repertory.

85. "Ghannat lil-ḥubb . . . fa-jamaʿat 76,000 Junayh lil-Ḥarb" (She sang of love . . . and collected 76,000 £E for war), *Akhbār al-Yawm* (June 19, 1967).

86. Al-Naqqāsh, "Liqāʾ maʿa Umm Kulthūm," 48–49.

87. Umm Kulthūm, quoted in Muṣṭafá, 63–64.

88. Paraphrased from *al-Sharq al-Adnā,* as quoted by Fu'ād, 240–41.

89. Muḥammad ʿAlī Ḥammād in *Ākhir Sāʿa* no. 178 (November 28, 1937), 7. The writer's explanation of Umm Kulthūm's unusual behavior adopts the concept

of the "self-made woman," drawn from the Western ideas about individualism popular among certain groups of Egyptian intellectuals and familiar to the literate Egyptian public as a way to explain the pride and self-confidence that were also part of the persona of the *fallāḥa.*

90. "Umm Kulthūm tataḥaddath ilá 'l-Ta'awwun" (Umm Kulthūm speaks to *al-Ta'awwun*), *al-Ta'awwun* (February 9, 1969).

91. 'Awaḍ, 72; "Umm Kulthūm tataḥaddath ilá 'l-Ta'awwun" *al-Ta'awwun* (February 9, 1969).

92. "Al-Ḥadīth al-Ākhir" Ṣawt al-Qāhira cassette tape no. SC76015.

93. Umm Kulthūm, quoted in "Hal Tushawwaḥ Tasjīlāt Umm Kulthūm?" *Uktūbir* (February 5, 1978), 73. *Gada'* denotes a strong and competent man.

94. El-Hamamsy, 298.

95. Ibid., 299.

96. "Al-Ḥadīth al-Ākhir," Ṣawt al-Qāhira cassette tape no. SC76015; *Ākhir Sā'a* no. 137 (February 21, 1937), 20–21; al-Naqqāsh, "Liqā' ma'a Umm Kulthūm," 44.

97. This discovery gave her great pleasure despite the notorious difficulty of ascertaining descent through Ḥasan.

98. Ḥusayn, quoted in Hopwood, 172; Marsot, *Egypt's Liberal Experiment,* 21.

99. Abū Naẓẓāra, "Ṣawt Umm Kulthūm bi-Alḥān Sayyid Makkāwī" (The voice of Umm Kulthūm in a song by Sayyid Makkāwī), *al-Akhbār* (April 6, 1972), 8.

100. Muḥammad Wajdī Qandīl, "Riḥlāt al-Baḥth 'an al-Amal" (Trips in search of hope), *Ākhir Sā'a* no. 2102 (February 5, 1975), 25; Wajdī Riyāḍ, "Riḥlāt al-Maraḍ Kāmila ma'a Umm Kulthūm" (The journey of illness is over for Umm Kulthūm), *al-Ahrām* (February 4, 1975), 4; Shūsha, 82–83.

101. *Umm Kulthūm: Qithārat,* 69; Sayyid Makkāwī's recording of his song for Umm Kulthūm's use, from the library of 'Abd al-'Azīz 'Anānī; *al-Kawākib* no. 1592 (February 2, 1982), 17. "Awqaati Btiḥlaww Ma'aak" was eventually recorded by Warda.

102. *Widā'an,* 40, 42.

103. Shūsha, 58; *al-Kawākib* no. 1592 (February 2, 1982), 19.

104. Ṣāfiyya Nāṣif, "Umm Kulthūm tughannī 4 Alḥān Jadīda," *al-Muṣawwar* (May 3, 1968); *al-Jadīd* no. 75 (February 15, 1975), 51; "Dhikrayāt lam tunshar 'an Umm Kulthūm," *Rūz al-Yūsuf* (February 2, 1976); *Widā'an,* 33; and "'Indamā ṭālabatnī Umm Kulthūm . . ." *al-Kawākib* no. 1592 (February 2, 1982), 17; "Hal Tushawwaḥ Tasjīlāt Umm Kulthūm?" *Uktūbir* (February 5, 1978), 72.

105. Fu'ād claimed that this was the first time in the history of the newspaper that it had published such news about anyone (477, 479).

106. This plan was common for it allowed the traditional procession without compelling mourners to walk the entire distance to the cemetery.

107. According to Goldschmidt, four million mourners followed Nasser's funeral procession (291).

Legacies of a Performer

1. El-Hamamsy, 278–79.

2. Blum, "Conclusion: Music in an Age of Cultural Confrontation," 252.

3. Geertz, "Deep Play," in his *Interpretation of Cultures,* 451; Waterman, *Jùjú,* 218.

4. "Music," as Laing writes, quoting J. H. Prynne, "is truly the sound of our time, since it is how we most deeply recognise the home we may not have" ([iii]).

5. This conflict, of course, resonates with Adorno's idea that "sentimental songs can allow expression of deep frustration and disappointment, while at the same time neutralising them as possible occasions for action to change one's situation" (Laing, 22; see also 59).

6. ʿAlī ʿAbd al-Hādī, "Al-Ṣaʿāyda Waṣalū" (The Upper Egyptians arrived). Sharikat al-Nujūm al-Khams cassette tape (unnumbered).

7. Blum, "Conclusion: Music in an Age of Cultural Confrontation," 260; El-Shawan.

8. Personal communication, July 27, 1992.

References

ʿAbd al-Wahhāb, Muḥammad. *Mudhakkirāt Muḥammad ʿAbd al-Wahhāb* (The memoirs of Muḥammad ʿAbd al-Wahhāb), Muḥammad Rifʿat al-Muḥāmī, ed. Beirut: Dār al-Thaqāfa, n.d.

Abu-Lughod, Ibrahim. "The Mass Media and Egyptian Village Life," *Social Forces* 42 (1963): 97–104.

Abu-Lughod, Janet. "Migrant Adjustment to City Life: The Egyptian Case," *American Journal of Sociology* 47 (1961): 22–32.

Abu-Lughod, Lila. "Bedouins, Cassettes and Technologies of Public Culture," *Middle East Report* 159 (1989): 7–11, 47.

———. *Veiled Sentiments: Honor and Poetry in a Bedouin Society.* Berkeley: University of California Press, 1986.

Abū ʾl-Majd, Ṣabrī. *Zakariyyā Aḥmad.* Cairo: al-Muʾasassa al-Miṣriyya al-ʿĀmma lil-Taʾlīf wa-ʾl-Tarjama wa-ʾl-Ṭibāʿa wa-ʾl-Nashr, 1963.

Āl Aḥmad, Jalāl. *Gharbzadagi: Weststruckness,* trans. John Green and Ahmad Alizadeh. Lexington, Ky.: Mazda Publishers, 1982.

Altorki, Soraya. *Women in Saudi Arabia: Ideology and Behavior among the Elite.* New York: Columbia University Press, 1986.

Ansari, Hamied. *Egypt, the Stalled Society.* Albany: State University of New York Press, 1986.

ʿArafa, ʿAbd al-Munʿim. *Tārīkh Aʿlām al-Mūsīqá ʾl-Sharqiyya* (The history of the stars of oriental music). Cairo: Maṭbaʿat ʿAnānī, 1947.

ʿAwaḍ, Maḥmūd. *Umm Kulthūm allātī lā Yaʿrifuhā Aḥad* (The Umm Kulthūm nobody knows). Cairo: Muʾassasat Akhbār al-Yawm, 1971.

Azzam, Nabil. "Muḥammad ʿAbd al-Wahhāb in modern Egyptian Music," Ph.D. diss., University of California, Los Angeles, 1990.

Badawi, M. M. *A Critical Introduction to Modern Arabic Poetry.* Cambridge: Cambridge University Press, 1975.

Badran, Margot and Miriam Cooke, eds. *Opening the Gates: a Century of Arab Feminist Writing.* Bloomington: Indiana University Press, 1990.

Barbour, Neville. "The Arabic Theatre in Egypt," *Bulletin of the School of Oriental Studies* 8 (1935–37): 173–87, 991–1012.

Beck, Lois and Nikki Keddie, eds. *Women in the Muslim World.* Cambridge, Mass.: Harvard University Press, 1978.

Behrens-Abouseif, Doris. *Azbakiyya and Its Environs from Azbak to Ismāʿīl, 1476–1879.* Cairo: Institut Français d'Archéologie Orientale, 1985.

Berque, Jacques. *Egypt: Imperialism and Revolution,* trans. Jean Stewart. London: Faber and Faber, 1972.

Blum, Stephen. "Conclusion: Music in an Age of Cultural Confrontation," in *Musical Cultures in Contact: Collisions and Convergences,* ed. Margaret Kartomi and Stephen Blum. Sydney: Currency Press and Gordon & Breach, 1993.

———. "In Defense of Close Reading and Close Listening," *Current Musicology* 53 (1993): 41–54.

———. "Musics in Contact: The Cultivation of Oral Repertories in Meshed, Iran," Ph.D. diss., University of Illinois, 1972.

———. "Prologue: Ethnomusicologists and Modern Music History," in *Ethnomusicology and Modern Music History,* ed. Stephen Blum, Philip V. Bohlman and Daniel M. Neuman. Urbana: University of Illinois Press, 1991.

———. "Towards a Social History of Musicological Technique," *Ethnomusicology* 19 (1975): 207–31.

———, Philip V. Bohlman, and Daniel M. Neuman, eds. *Ethnomusicology and Modern Music History.* Urbana: University of Illinois Press, 1991.

Boolaky, Ibrahim. "Traditional Muslim Vocal Art," *Arts and the Islamic World* 1 (Winter 1983–84): 52–55.

Booth, Marilyn. *Bayram al-Tunisi's Egypt: Social Criticism and Narrative Strategies.* Exeter: Ithaca Press, 1990.

———. "Colloquial Arabic Poetry, Politics, and the Press in Modern Egypt," *International Journal of Middle East Studies* 24 (1992): 419–40.

Bourdieu, Pierre. "Outline of a Sociological Theory of Art Perception," *International Social Science Journal* 20/4 (1968): 589–612.

Boyd, Douglas A. *Broadcasting in the Arab World: A Survey of Radio and Television in the Middle East.* Philadelphia: Temple University Press, 1982.

———. *Egyptian Radio: Tool of Political and National Development.* Journalism Monographs no. 48. Lexington, Ky.: Association for Education in Journalism, 1977.

Braune, Gabriele. *Die Qasida im Gesang von Umm Kultum: Die arabische Poesie im Repertoire der grossten ägyptischen Sängerin unserer Zeit.* Beiträge zur Ethnomusicologie 16, 2 vols. Hamburg: Karl Dieter Wagner, 1987.

Brown, Nathan J. *Peasant Politics in Modern Egypt: The Struggle against the State.* New Haven, Conn.: Yale University Press, 1990.

Buṭrus, Fikrī. *Aʿlām al-Mūsīqá wa-ʾl Ghināʾ ʾl-ʿArabī, 1867–1967* (Stars of Arabic music and song, 1867–1967). Cairo: al-Hayʾa al-Miṣriyya al-ʿĀmma lil-Kitāb, 1976.

Cachia, Pierre. "The Egyptian Mawwal: Its Ancestry, its Development, and its Present Forms," *Journal of Arabic Literature* 8 (1977): 77–103.

———. *Taha Husayn: His Place in the Egyptian Literary Renaissance.* London: Luzac, 1956.

Chabrier, Jean-Claude. "Music in the Fertile Crescent," *Cultures* 1 (1974): 35–58.

Chelbi, Moustapha. "Um Kalthoum, la Voix d'Or de la Conscience Arabe," in

Les Africans, ed. Charles-André Julien et al. Vol. 3. [Paris]: Éditions J.A., 1977.

Clifford, James. "Introduction: Partial Truths," in *Writing Culture: The Poetics and Politics of Ethnography,* ed. James Clifford and George E. Marcus. Berkeley: University of California Press, 1986.

———. *The Predicament of Culture: Twentieth-Century Ethnography, Literature, and Art.* Cambridge, Mass.: Harvard University Press, 1988.

Connelly, Bridget. *Arab Folk Epic and Identity.* Berkeley: University of California Press, 1986.

Crabbs, Jack. "Politics, History, and Culture in Nasser's Egypt," *International Journal of Middle East Studies* 6 (1975): 386–420.

Crapanzano, Vincent. *Tuhami: Portrait of a Moroccan.* Chicago: University of Chicago Press, 1980.

Danielson, Virginia. "Artists and Entrepreneurs: Female Singers in Cairo during the 1920s," in *Women in Middle Eastern History: Shifting Boundaries in Sex and Gender,* ed. Nikki R. Keddie and Beth Baron. New Haven, Conn.: Yale University Press, 1991.

———. "The Qur'ān and the Qaṣīdah: Aspects of the Popularity of the Repertory Sung by Umm Kulthūm," *Asian Music* 19/1 (1987): 26–45.

———. "Shaping Tradition in Arabic Song: The Career and Repertory of Umm Kulthūm," Ph.D. diss., University of Illinois, 1991.

Davis, Eric. *Challenging Colonialism: Bank Misr and Egyptian Industrialization, 1920–1941.* Princeton, N.J.: Princeton University Press, 1983.

———. "Religion against the State," in *Religious Resurgence: Contemporary Cases in Islam, Christianity, and Judaism,* ed. Richard T. Antoun and Mary Elaine Hegland. Syracuse, N.Y.: Syracuse University Press, 1987.

Delphin, G. and L. Guin. *Notes sur la Poésie et la Musique Arabes dans le Maghreb Algérien.* Paris: Leroux, 1886.

Dreyfus, Hubert L. and Paul Rabinow. *Michel Foucault: Beyond Structuralism and Hermeneutics.* Chicago: University of Chicago Press, 1982.

Dwyer, Kevin. *Moroccan Dialogues.* Baltimore: Johns Hopkins University Press, 1982.

Egypt. Ministry of Finance. *The Census of Egypt Taken in 1907.* Cairo: National Printing Department, 1909.

———. *The Census of Egypt Taken in 1917.* Cairo: Government Press, 1920.

Elsner, Jürgen. "Ferment nationalen Bewüsstseins: die Musikkultur Algeriens," *Musik und Gesellschaft* 33/8 (1983): 456–63.

Erlmann, Veit. *African Stars: Studies in Black South African Performance.* Chicago: University of Chicago Press, 1991.

———. "Conversation with Joseph Shabalala of Ladysmith Black Mambazo: Aspects of African Performers' Lifestories," *World of Music* 31/1 (1989): 31–58.

Fakhouri, Hani. *Kafr el-Elow: An Egyptian Village in Transition.* New York: Holt, Rinehart & Winston, 1972.

Al Faruqi, Lois Ibsen. *An Annotated Glossary of Arabic Musical Terms.* Westport, Conn.: Greenwood Press, 1981.

———. "Music, Musicians and Muslim Law," *Asian Music* 17 (1985): 3–36.

———. "The Nature of the Musical Art of Islamic Culture: A Theoretical and Empirical Study of Arabian Music," Ph.D. diss., Syracuse University, N.Y., 1974.

———. "Ornamentation in Arabian Improvisational Music: A Study in Interrelatedness in the Arts," *World of Music* 20 (1978): 17–32.

———. "The Status of Music in Muslim Nations: Evidence from the Arab World," *Asian Music* 12 (1979): 56–84.

Feld, Steven. "Communication, Music, and Speech about Music," *Yearbook for Traditional Music* 16 (1984): 1–18.

———. *Sound and Sentiment.* 2d ed. Philadelphia: University of Pennsylvania Press, 1990.

Fernea, Elizabeth Warock and Basima Qattan Bezirgan, eds. *Middle Eastern Muslim Women Speak.* Austin: University of Texas Press, 1977.

Foucault, Michel. *The History of Sexuality.* Vol. 1: *An Introduction,* trans. Robert Hurley. New York: Vintage Books, 1978.

Frith, Simon. "Essay review: Rock biography," *Popular Music* 3 (1983): 276–77.

———. "Why Do Songs Have Words?" in *Lost in Music: Culture, Style, and the Musical Event,* ed. A. L. White. London: Routledge & Kegan Paul, 1987.

Fu'ād, Niʿmāt Aḥmad. *Umm Kulthūm wa-ʿAṣr min al-Fann* (Umm Kulthūm and an era of art). Cairo: al-Hay'a al-Miṣriyya 'l-ʿĀmma lil-Kitāb, 1976.

Geertz, Clifford. *The Interpretation of Cultures: Selected Essays.* New York: Basic Books, 1973.

Giddens, Anthony. *The Constitution of Society: Outline of the Theory of Structuration.* Berkeley: University of California Press, 1984.

———. *Profiles and Critiques in Social Theory.* Berkeley: University of California Press, 1982.

Goffmann, Erving. *Frame Analysis: An Essay on the Organization of Experience.* Boston: Northeastern University Press, 1986.

Goldberg, Ellis. "Leadership and Ideology in the 1919 Revolution." Paper presented at the Twenty-first annual meeting of the Middle East Studies Association of North America, Baltimore, 1987.

Goldschmidt, Arthur. *A Concise History of the Middle East.* 2d ed. Cairo: American University in Cairo Press, 1983.

Gronow, Pekka. "The Record Industry Comes to the Orient," *Ethnomusicology* 25 (1981): 251–82.

Ḥāfiẓ, Muḥammad Maḥmūd Sāmī. *Tārīkh al-Mūsīqá wa-'l-Ghinā' al-ʿArabī* (History of Arabic music and song). Cairo: Maktabat al-Anjlū 'l-Miṣriyya, 1971.

Ḥāfiẓ, Nāhid Aḥmad. "Al-Ughniyya al-Miṣriyya wa-Taṭawwuruhā khilāl al-Qarnayn al-Tāsiʿ ʿAshar wa-'l-ʿIshrīn" (Egyptian song and its development through the nineteenth and twentieth centuries). Ph.D. diss., Ḥilwān University, 1977.

El-Hamamsy, Laila Shukry. "The Assertion of Egyptian Identity," in *Ethnic Identity: Cultural Continuities and Change,* ed. George DeVos and Lola Ranucci-Ross. Palo Alto, Calif.: Mayfield, 1975.

Hassan, Scheherazade Qassim. "Survey of Written Sources on the Irāqī Maqām," in *Regionale Maqām-Traditionen in Geschichte und Gegenwart,* ed. Jürgen Elsner and Gisa Jähnichen. Berlin, 1992.

Hegland, Mary. "Introduction," in *Religious Resurgence: Contemporary Cases in Islam, Christianity, and Judaism,* ed. Richard T. Antoun and Mary Elaine Hegland. Syracuse, N.Y.: Syracuse University Press, 1987.

———. "Conclusion," in *Religious Resurgence: Contemporary Cases in Islam, Christianity, and Judaism,* ed. Richard T. Antoun and Mary Elaine Hegland. Syracuse, N.Y.: Syracuse University Press, 1987.

Heyworth-Dunne, J. *An Introduction to the History of Education in Modern Egypt.* 1939. Reprint, London: Frank Cass & Co., 1968.

Al-Ḥifnī, Maḥmūd Aḥmad, et al., eds. *Turāthunā ʾl-Mūsīqī min al-Adwār wa-ʾl Muwashshaḥāt* (Our musical heritage of Adwār and Muwashshaḥāt). 4 vols. Cairo: al-Lajna al-Mūsīqiyya al-ʿUlyá, 1969.

Hopwood, Derek. *Egypt: Politics and Society, 1945–1981.* London: Allen & Unwin, 1982.

Hornbostel, Erich M. von. "Zum Kongress für arabische Musik—Kairo 1932," *Zeitschrift für Vergleichende Musikwissenschaft* 1 (1933): 16–17.

Ḥusayn, Ṭāhā. *An Egyptian Childhood,* trans. E. H. Paxton. London: Heinemann, 1981.

———. *A Passage to France,* trans. Kenneth Cragg. Arabic Translation Series of the Journal of Arabic Literature 4. Leiden: Brill, 1976.

———. *The Stream of Days: A student at the Azhar,* trans. Hilary Wayment. Cairo: al-Maaref, n.d.

Issawi, Charles. *Egypt at Mid-Century.* London: Oxford University Press, 1954.

Jayyusi, Salma Khadra. *Modern Arabic Poetry: An Anthology.* New York: Columbia University Press, 1987.

———. *Trends and Movements in Modern Arabic Poetry,* 2 vols. Leiden: E. J. Brill, 1977.

Kāmil, Maḥmūd. *al-Masraḥ al-Ghināʾī ʾl-ʿArabī* (Arabic musical theater). Cairo: Dār al-Maʿārif, 1977.

———. *Muḥammad al-Qaṣabjī.* Cairo: al-Hayʾa al-Miṣriyya al-ʿĀmma lil-Kitāb, 1971.

———. *Tadhawwuq al-Mūsīqá ʾl-ʿArabiyya* (Savoring Arabic music). Cairo: Muḥammad al-Amīn, n.d.

Keddie, Nikki R. "Introduction: Deciphering Middle Eastern Women's History," in *Women in Middle Eastern History: Shifting Boundaries in Sex and Gender,* ed. Nikki R. Keddie and Beth Baron. New Haven, Conn.: Yale University Press, 1991.

Keddie, Nikki R. and Beth Baron, eds. *Women in Middle Eastern History: Shifting*

Boundaries in Sex and Gender. New Haven, Conn.: Yale University Press, 1991.

Al-Khaṭīb, ʿAdnān, ed. *Umm Kulthūm: Muʿjizat al-Ghināʾ al-ʿArabī.* Damascus: Maṭbaʿat al-ʿIlm, 1975.

Khayrī, Badīʿ. *Mudhakkirāt Badīʿ Khayrī: 45 Sana taḥt aḍwāʾ al-Masraḥ* (The memoirs of Badīʿ Khayrī: Forty-five years under the lights of the theater), ed. Maḥmūd Rifʿat al-Muḥāmī. Beirut: Dār al-Thaqāfa, n.d.

El-Kholy, Samha Amin. "The Function of Music in Islamic Culture (Up to 1100 A.D.)," Ph.D. diss., University of Edinburgh, 1953–54.

Khouri, Mounah. *Poetry and the Making of Modern Egypt (1882–1922).* Leiden: E. J. Brill, 1971.

Al-Khulaʿī, Kamāl. *Al-Aghānī ʾl-ʿAṣriyya* (Contemporary songs). Cairo: Ṭabʿat al-Sighāda, 1921; 2d ed., Cairo: al-Maktaba al-Miṣriyya, 1923.

———. *Kitāb al-Mūsīqá ʾl-Sharqī* (Book of oriental music). Cairo: Maṭbaʿat al-Taqaddum, ca. 1904–5.

Kitāb Muʾtamar al-Mūsīqá ʾl-ʿArabiyya (Book of the conference of Arab music). *Cairo:* al-Maṭbaʿa al-Amīriyya, 1933.

Lacouture, Jean, and Simonne Lacouture. *Egypt in Transition,* trans. Francis Scarfe. London: Methuen, 1958.

Laing, Dave. *The Sound of Our Time.* Chicago: Quadrangle Books, 1970.

Landau, Jacob M. *Studies in the Arab Theater and Cinema.* Philadelphia: University of Pennsylvania Press, 1958.

Landes, David S. *Bankers and Pashas: International Finance and Economic Imperialism in Egypt.* Cambridge, Mass.: Harvard University Press, 1958.

Lane, Edward William. *An Account of the Manners and Customs of the Modern Egyptians, Written in Egypt during the Years 1833–1835.* 1836. Reprint, The Hague and London: East-West Publications, 1978.

MacDonald, Duncan B. *Aspects of Islam.* 1911. Reprint, New York: Books for Libraries Press, 1971.

Maḥfūẓ, Najīb. *Bidāya wa-Nihāya.* Cairo: Dār Miṣr lil-Ṭibāʿa, 1949.

———. Cairo Trilogy. New York: Doubleday, 1991–93.

Mandelbaum, David. "The Study of Life History: Gandhi," *Current Anthropology* 14/3 (1973): 177–206.

Mansī, Aḥmad Abū ʾl-Khidr. *Al-Aghānī wa-ʾl-Mūsīqá ʾl-Sharqiyya bayn al-Qadīm wa-ʾl-Jadīd* (Oriental songs and music between the old and the new). Cairo: Dār al-ʿArab li-l-Bustānī, 1966.

Manuel, Peter. "Popular Music and Media Culture in South Asia: Prefatory Considerations," *Asian Music* 24/1 (1992–93): 91–99.

Marcus, Scott. "Arab Music Theory in the Modern Period," Ph.D. diss., University of California, Los Angeles, 1989.

Marsot, Afaf Lutfi al-Sayyid. *Egypt in the Reign of Muhammad Ali.* Cambridge: Cambridge University Press, 1984.

———. *Egypt's Liberal Experiment, 1922–1936.* Berkeley: University of California Press, 1977.

———. "Religion or Opposition? Urban Protest Movements in Egypt," *International Journal of Middle East Studies* 16 (1984): 541–522.

———. *A Short History of Modern Egypt.* Cambridge: Cambridge University Press, 1985.

———. "The Ulama of Cairo in the Eighteenth and Nineteenth Centuries," in *Scholars, Saints and Sufis: Muslim Religious Institutions in the Middle East since 1500,* ed. Nikki Keddie. Berkeley: University of Califoria Press, 1972.

Maṣabnī, Badīʿa. *Mudhakkirāt Badīʿa Maṣabnī* (The memoirs of Badīʿa Maṣabnī), ed. Nāzik Bāsīla. Beirut: Dār Maktabat al-Ḥayāh, n.d.

Al-Maṣrī, Khalīl and Maḥmūd Kāmil. *Al-Nuṣūṣ al-Kāmila li-Jamīʿ Aghānī Kawkab al-Sharq Umm Kulthūm* (The complete texts for all of the songs of the star of the east, Umm Kulthūm). Cairo: Dār al-Ṭibāʿa al-Ḥadīth, 1979.

Mernissi, Fatima. *Beyond the Veil: Male-Female Dynamics in Modern Muslim Society.* Bloomington: Indiana University Press, 1987.

Middleton, Richard. "Articulating musical meaning/Reconstructing musical history/Locating the 'popular,'" *Popular Music* 5 (1986): 5–43.

———. *Studying Popular Music.* Milton Keynes: Open University Press, 1990.

Mitchell, Timothy. *Colonising Egypt.* Cambridge: Cambridge University Press, 1988.

Musique Arabe: Le Congrès du Caire de 1932, ed. Philippe Vigreux. Le Caire: CEDEJ, 1992.

Muṣṭafá, Zākī. *Umm Kulthūm: Maʿbad al-Ḥubb* (Umm Kulthūm: temple of love). Cairo: Dār al-Ṭibāʿa al-Ḥadītha, [1975].

Al-Najmī, Kamāl. *Al-Ghinā' al-Miṣrī* (Egyptian song). Cairo: Dār al-Hilāl, 1966.

Al-Naqqāsh, Rajā'. "Aṣwāt aṭrabat Ajdādanā" (Voices that charmed our grandparents), *Al-Kawākib* (1965). Reprinted in *Lughz Umm Kulthūm.* Cairo: Dār al-Hilāl, 1978.

———. "Liqā' maʿa Umm Kulthūm" (A meeting with Umm Kulthūm), *al-Kawākib* (1965). Reprinted in *Lughz Umm Kulthūm.* Cairo: Dār al-Hilāl, 1978.

———. "Lughz Umm Kulthūm" (The secret of Umm Kulṭhūm). In *Lughz Umm Kulthūm.* Cairo: Dār al-Hilāl, 1978.

———. "Al-Mashāyikh wa-'l-Fann" (The *mashāyikh* and art), *al-Kawākib* (1965). Reprinted in *Lughz Umm Kulthūm.* Cairo: Dār al-Hilāl, 1978.

———. "Shawqī wa-Ḥayāt ʿAbd al-Wahhāb" (Shawqī and the life of ʿAbd al-Wahhāb), *al-Kawākib* (1969). Reprinted in *Lughz Umm Kulthūm.* Cairo: Dār al-Hilāl, 1978.

———. "Umm Kulthūm wa-'l-Muthaqqafūn" (Umm Kulthūm and the intellectuals), *al-Muṣawwar* (1968). Reprinted in *Lughz Umm Kulthūm.* Cairo: Dār al-Hilāl, 1978.

Nelson, Cynthia. "Biography and Women's History: On Interpreting Doria

Shafik," in *Women in Middle Eastern History: Shifting Boundaries in Sex and Gender,* ed. Nikkie R. Keddie and Beth Baron. New Haven, Conn.: Yale University Press, 1991.

Nelson, Kristina. *The Art of Reciting the Qur'an.* Austin, Texas: University of Texas Press, 1985.

Nettl, Bruno. *The Study of Ethnomusicology: Twenty-nine Issues and Concepts.* Urbana: University of Illinois Press, 1983.

Ortner, Sherry B. "Theory in Anthropology Since the Sixties," *Comparative Studies in Society and History* 26/1 (1984): 126–66.

Qureshi, Regula. *Sufi Music of India and Pakistan: Sound, Context and Meaning in Qawwali.* Cambridge: Cambridge University Press, 1986.

Racy, Ali Jihad. "Arabian Music and the Effects of Commercial Recording," *World of Music* 20 (1975): 47–58.

———. "Creativity and Ambience: An Ecstatic Feedback Model from Arab Music," *World of Music* 33/3 (1991): 7–28.

———. "Music," in *The Genius of Arab Civilization: Source of Renaissance,* ed. John R. Hayes. 2d ed. Cambridge, Mass.: MIT Press, 1983.

———. "Music in Contemporary Cairo," *Asian Music* 12/1 (1981): 4–26.

———. "Musical Change and Commercial Recording in Egypt, 1904–1932," Ph.D. diss., University of Illinois, 1977.

———. Review of Waṣlah Ghinā'iyyah (Nefertiti), Līh Yā Banafsaj (Sono Cairo), Cinera-phone Presents Mary Gibran (Cineraphone), Cheikh Sayed Darwiche (Baidaphon). *Ethnomusicology* 24 (1980): 603–7.

———. "Sound and Society: The *Takht* Music of Early Twentieth Century Cairo," *Selected Reports in Ethnomusicology* 7 (1988): 139–70.

———. "The Waṣlah: A Compound-Form Principle in Egyptian Music," *Arab Studies Quarterly* 5 (1983): 396–403.

———. "Words and Music in Beirut: A Study of Attitudes" *Ethnomusicology* 30 (1986): 413–27.

Rahman, Fazlur. *Islam.* 2d ed. Chicago: University of Chicago Press, 1979.

Reyes Schramm, Adelaida. "Music and the Refugee Experience," *The World of Music* 32/3 (1990): 3–21.

Reynolds, Dwight. "Heroic Poets, Poet Heroes," Ph.D. diss., University of California, Los Angeles, 1991.

Rice, Timothy. *May It Fill Your Soul: Experiencing Bulgarian Music.* Chicago: University of Chicago Press, 1994.

Ricoeur, Paul. "The Model of the Text: Meaningful Action Considered as a Text" in *Interpretive Social Science: A Reader,* ed. Paul Rabinow and William M. Sullivan. Berkeley: University of California Press, 1979.

Rizq, Qisṭandī. *Al-Mūsīqá 'l-Sharqiyya wa-'l-Ghinā' al-ʿArabī* (Oriental music and Arabic song), 4 vols. Cairo: al-Maṭbaʿa al-ʿAṣriyya, ca. 1936.

Roseman, Marina. "The New Rican Village: Artists in Control of the Image-Making Machinery," *Latin American Music Review* 4 (1983): 132–67.

Rouanet, Jules. "La musique arabe," in *Encyclopédie de la Musique et Dictionnaire du Conservatoire,* ed. A. Lavignac. Paris: Librairie Delagrave, 1922.

Ṣabrī, Muḥammad, ed. *Al-Shawqiyyāt al-Majhūla,* 2 vols. Cairo: Maṭbaʿat Dār al-Kutub, 1961–62.

Saïah, Ysabel. *Oum Kalsoum: l'Étoile de l'Orient.* Paris: Denoël, 1985.

Saḥḥāb, Ilyās. *Difāʿan ʿan al-Ughniyya al-ʿArabiyya* (A defense of Arabic song). Beirut: al-Muʾassasa al-ʿArabiyya lil-Dirāsāt wa-ʾl-Nashr, 1980.

Saḥḥāb, Victor. *Al-Sabʿa al-Kibār fī ʾl-Mūsīqá ʾl-ʿArabiyya al-Muʿāṣira* (The seven great ones in contemporary Arab music). Beirut: Dār al-ʿIlm lil-Malāyīn, 1987.

Sawa, George Dimitri. *Music Performance Practice in the Early ʿAbbasid Era 132–320 AH/750–932 AD.* Studies and Texts 92. Toronto: Pontifical Institute of Mediaeval Studies, 1989.

———. "Oral Transmission in Arabic Music, Past and Present," *Oral Tradition* 4/1–2 (1989): 254–65.

Seeger, Anthony. *Why Suyá Sing: A Musical Anthropology of an Amazonian People.* Cambridge: Cambridge University Press, 1987.

Seeger, Charles. *Studies in Musicology, 1935–1975.* Berkeley: University of California Press, 1977.

El-Shawan, Salwa. "Al-Mūsīḳa al-ʿArabiyyah: A Category of Urban Music in Cairo, Egypt, 1927–77," Ph.D. diss., Columbia University, 1980.

El-Shawan Castelo Branco, Salwa. "Some Aspects of the Cassette Industry in Egypt," *World of Music* 29 (1987): 3–45.

Shawqī, Aḥmad. *Al-Shawqiyyāt* (The works of Shawqī), 4 vols. Cairo: Maṭbaʿat al-Istiqāma, 1950.

Al-Shawwā, Sāmī. *Mudhakkirāt Sāmī al-Shawwā* (The memoirs of Sāmī al-Shawwā), ed. Fuʾād Qaṣṣāṣ. Cairo: Maṭābiʿ al-Sharq al-Awsaṭ, 1966.

———. *Al-Qawāʾid al-Fanniyya fī ʾl-Mūsīqá ʾl-Sharqiyya wa-ʾl-Gharbiyya* (The artistic foundations of oriental and western music). Cairo: Jibrāʾīl Fatḥ Allāh Jabrī wa-Walādihi, 1946.

Shelemay, Kay Kaufman. "Response to Rice," *Ethnomusicology* 31 (1987): 489–90.

Shiloah, Amnon. "The Status of Art Music in Muslim Nations," *Asian Music* 12 (1979): 40–55.

Shūsha, Muḥammad al-Sayyid. *Umm Kulthūm: Ḥayāt Nagham* (Umm Kulthūm: The life of a melody). Cairo: Maktabat Rūz al-Yūsuf, 1976.

Slawek, Stephen. "Ravi Shankar as Mediator between a Traditional Music and Modernity," in *Ethnomusicology and Modern Music History,* ed. Stephen Blum, Philip V. Bohlman and Daniel M. Neuman. Urbana: University of Illinois Press, 1991.

Slyomovics, Susan. *The Merchant of Art: An Egyptian Hilali Oral Epic Poet in Performance.* Berkeley: University of California Press, 1987.

Smith, Charles D. "The 'Crisis of Orientation': The Shift of Egyptian Intellectuals to Islamic Subjects in the 1930's," *International Journal of Middle East Studies* 4 (1973): 382–410.

Stewart, Kathleen. "Backtalking the Wilderness: 'Appalachian' En-genderings," in *Uncertain Terms: Negotiating Gender in American Culture,* ed. Faye Ginsburg and Anna Lowenhaupt Tsing. Boston: Beacon Press, 1990.

Sugarman, Jane. "The Nightingale and the Partridge: Singing and Gender among Prespa Albanians," *Ethnomusicology* 33 (1989): 191–215.

Al-Tābiʿī, Muḥammad. *Asmahān tarwi Qiṣṣatahā* (Asmahān tells her story). Cairo: Muʾassasat Rūz al-Yūsuf, 1965.

Tapper, Nancy and Richard Tapper. "The Birth of the Prophet: Ritual and Gender in Turkish Islam," *Man,* n.s. 22 (1987): 69–92.

Touma, Habib Hassan. "Die Musik der Araber im 19. Jahrhundert," in *Musikkulturen Asiens, Afrikas und Ozeaniens im 19. Jahrhundert,* ed. Robert Günther. Studien zur Musikgeschichte des 19. Jahrhunderts, Band 31. Regensburg: Gustav Bosse, 1973.

Turino, Thomas. "The Coherence of Social Style and Musical Creation among the Aymara in southern Peru," *Ethnomusicology* 33/1 (1989): 1–30.

———. "The History of a Peruvian Panpipe Style and the Politics of Interpretation," in *Ethnomusicology and Modern Music History,* ed. Stephen Blum, Philip V. Bohlman and Daniel M. Neuman. Urbana: University of Illinois Press, 1991.

———. "Structure, Context, and Strategy in Musical Ethnography," *Ethnomusicology* 34 (1990): 399–412.

Umm Kulthūm: al-Nagham al-Khālid (Umm Kulthūm: the eternal melody). Alexandria: Hayʾat al-Funūn wa-ʾl-Adab wa-ʾl-ʿUlūm al-Ijtimāʿiyya bil-Iskandriyya, 1976.

Umm Kulthūm: Qiṣṣat Ḥayātihā, Majmūʿat Aghānīhā wa-baʿḍ Nukātihā wa-Wafātuhā (Umm Kulthūm: the story of her life, collection of her songs and some of her jokes, and her death). Beirut: Maktabat al-Ḥadīth, ca. 1975.

Umm Kulthūm: Qithārat al-ʿArab (Umm Kulthūm: lyre of the Arabs). Beirut: Maktabat al-Jamāhīr, 1975.

Van Nieuwkerk, Karin. *Female Entertainment in Nineteenth and Twentieth-Century Egypt.* MERA Occasional Paper No. 6, June 1990.

Voll, John, "Islamic Renewal and the 'Failure of the West,'" in *Religious Resurgence: Contemporary Cases in Islam, Christianity, and Judaism,* ed. Richard T. Antoun and Mary Elaine Hegland. Syracuse, N.Y.: Syracuse University Press, 1987.

Wachsmann, Klaus. "The Changeability of Musical Experience," *Ethnomusicology* 26 (1982): 197–216.

Wahba, Magdi. "Cultural Planning in the Arab World," *Journal of World History* 14 (1972): 800–813.

Waterman, Christopher Alan. *Jùjú: A Social History and Ethnography of an African Popular Music.* Chicago: University of Chicago Press, 1990.

———. "Jùjú History: Toward a Theory of Sociomusical Practice," In *Ethnomusi-*

cology and Modern Music History, ed. Stephen Blum, Philip V. Bohlman and Daniel M. Neuman. Urbana: University of Illinois Press, 1991.

Widāʿan ʿan Umm Kulthūm (Farewell to Umm Kulthūm), ed. Muḥammad ʿUmar Shaṭabī. Cairo: al-Markaz al-Miṣrī lil-Thaqāfa wa-ʾl-Iʿlām, 1975.

Williams, Raymond. *Culture and Society, 1780–1950.* Garden City: Anchor Books, 1960.

———. *Marxism and Literature.* Oxford: University Press, 1977.

Witmer, Robert. "Stability in Blackfoot Songs, 1909–1968," in *Ethnomusicology and Modern Music History,* ed. Stephen Blum, Philip V. Bohlman and Daniel M. Neuman. Urbana: University of Illinois Press, 1991.

Al-Yūsuf, Faṭma. *Dhikrayātī* (My memories). Cairo: Rūz al-Yūsuf, 1953.

Zakī, ʿAbd al-Ḥamīd Tawfīq. *Aʿlām al-Mūsīqá ʾl-Miṣriyya ʿabra 150 Sana.* Cairo: al-Hayʾa al-Miṣriyya al-ʿĀmma lil-Kitāb, 1990.

Zayid, Mahmud. "The Origins of the Liberal Constitutionalist Party in Egypt," in *Political and Social Change in Modern Egypt: Historical Studies from the Ottoman Conquest to the United Arab Republic,* ed. P. M. Holt. London: Oxford University Press, 1968.

Zemp, Hugo. "ʾAreʾare Classification of Musical Types and Instruments," *Ethnomusicology* 22 (1978): 37–67.

———. "Aspects of ʾAreʾare Musical Theory," *Ethnomusicology* 23 (1979): 5–39.

Sources for the Illustrations

Musical Examples

1: Sono Cairo cassette tape 81277.
2: Les Artistes Arabes Associés compact disc AAA 024.
3: Sono Cairo cassette tape 85071.
5: Sono Cairo compact disc SONO 142-E.
6: Sono Cairo cassette tape 81001.
7: Sono Cairo cassette tape 80002.
8: Sono Cairo compact disc SONO 146-E.
9: Broadcast performance from the archive of Egyptian Radio.
10: Sono Cairo compact disc SONO 142-E.
11: Sono Cairo compact disc SONO 117-E.
12: Sono Cairo compact disc SONO 101.

Photographs

2: Cover photo, *al-Masraḥ* no. 16 (1 March 1926).

3: *Rūz al-Yūsuf* no. 74 (31 March 1927), p. 13. Reproduced courtesy of Dār al-Hilāl.

4, 6: *Al-Masraḥ* no. 14 (15 February 1926), pp. 14 and 7, respectively.

5: Cover, *al-Masraḥ* no. 1 (9 November 1925).

7, 24, 25: Farūq Ibrāhīm, *Umm Kulthūm* (Cairo: Salīm Abū Khayr, ca. 1973).

8: Ḥabīb Zaydan, *Majmū ʿat al-Aghānī ʾl-Sharqiyya ʾl-Qadīma wa-ʾl-Ḥadītha* (Cairo, 1935?).

9: *Al-Masraḥ* no. 3 (23 November 1925), p. 22.

10–13: Maḥmūd Ḥamdī al-Bulāqī, *al-Mughanni ʾl-Miṣrī,* 7th ed. (Cairo: Maṭba ʿat wa-Maktabat al-Shabāb, 1927).

14: *Al-Idhāʿa wa-ʾl-Tilīfizyūn* no. 2675 (21 June 1986), p. 57. Reproduced courtesy of Dār al-Hilāl.

15–16: *Al-Radyū ʾl-Miṣrī* no. 217 (13 May 1939), p. 3; and no. 536 (23 June 1945), cover. Reproduced courtesy of Dār al-Hilāl.

23: *Al-Ahrām,* 6 February 1975, p. 1. Reproduced courtesy of *Al-Ahram.*

Index

listeners (*continued*)
239n.40; fieldwork with, vii; heritage of, 46, 200; at home, 135–36, 158; in Kuwait, 248n.77; interest in a song, 2, 75, 105, 168, 180, 199, 217n.37; old, 126; radio and, 85, 89; relationship of to performers, 4, 71, 143, 206n.20; requests of, 84; responses of, 16, 135, 185, 229n.84; supportive, 79, 121, 133–34, 184; talk of, 4, 7; Western, 198, 240n.71; young, 137. *See also* audience
listening, 6–10; concept of, 132–33; with friends, 226n.52; and meaning of a text, 139; as participatory, 9; as performance, 206n.13; in small groups, 199–200; and speech, 205n.4

"Maa lak ya Qalbi" (song title), 76
al-Maghrabī, Ibrāhīm, 23
al-Mahdī, Amīn, 58, 64
al-Mahdī, Rūḥiyya, 58
al-Mahdiyya, Munīra, 13, 46–47, 49–50, 59–68, 87, 91, 172, 220n.68, 221n.86, 222nn. 87, 93, 97, 224n.20
Maḥfūẓ, Najīb, 39, 120
Māhir, ʿAlī, 34, 213n.60
Maḥmūd, ʿAlī, 26, 34, 103, 201
Maḥmūd, Muḥammad, 39
al-Majdhūb, Muḥammad al-Mahdī, 122
"Majnūn Laylá" (song title), 171–72
Makkāwī, Sayyid, 124, 169, 170, 192, 236n.12, 238n.37, 249n.101
"Mā lī Futint" (song title), 54, 96–97
al-Malījī, Faṭma (Umm Kulthūm's mother), 21, 53–54, 159, 209n.10
al-Manfalūṭī, Muṣṭafá Luftī, 76
al-Manyalāwī, Yūsuf, 24, 55, 218n.52
maqāmāt: changes in, 233n.37; command of the, 94, 116, 145, 228nn. 74, 75; and compositional practice, 71, 75, 77, 99, 115, 239n.57; establishment of the, 96, 147, 179; system of, 196, 240n.68; variety of, 12–13, 104, 150–51, 182
Marsot, Afaf Lutfi al-Sayyid, 24–25, 38, 111–12, 191, 214n.73, 220n.66, 227n.60
Maṣabnī, Badīʿa, 13, 48, 63, 67, 81, 87, 224n.22, 225nn. 31, 32, 230n.91. *See also* Ṣālat Badīʿa
mashāyikh, 21, 25–26, 28, 32, 41, 51–52, 56–57, 92, 103, 121, 141–44, 187, 190–91, 197, 201, 221n.82
al-Maslūb, al-Shaykh, 70
al-Masraḥ (magazine), 60, 64, 83, 222n.87
al-Maṣrī, Khalīl, 120, 226n.43
al-Maṣrī, Sayyid, 132, 170, 236n.16, 237n.20, 243nn. 17, 23, 244nn. 37, 39
al-Maṣriyya, Naʿīma, 54, 220n.68, 228n.71
"Ma Trawwaq Dammak" (song title), 231n.101
al-Mawjī, Muḥammad, 164, 170, 176–77
"Mawlāya Katabta Raḥmat al-Nās ʿAlayk" (song title) 217n.37, 220n.72
mawwāl, 10, 26–27, 67, 103, 107, 139–40, 146, 164, 210n.28, 216n.19, 220n.69
al-Māzinī, Ibrāhīm, 45, 187
Mechian, Setrak, 13, 17
Middleton, Richard, 6, 10, 15, 206nn. 10, 13, 207n.31
"Miin illi Qaal" (song title), 231n.101
"Miṣr allatī fī Khāṭirī wa-fī Damī" (song title), 161
"Miṣr Tataḥaddath ʿan Nafsihā" (song title), 164
Mitchell, Timothy, 19, 144
monologue: audience and, 75; as compared to operatic aria, 71; innovations in, 75, 78, 135, 223n.9; performance of the, 73, 76, 231n.101; virtuosity of, 72
Muḥammad, ʿAbd al-Wahhāb, 167–68
Muḥammad, Malak, 48, 66
Muḥammad, Suʿād, 120, 132, 162, 169, 191–92, 243n.16
Munīr, Muḥammad, 124
Murād, Layla, 48, 67, 92, 120, 216n.18, 243n.15
music: Arab classical, 239n.57; closeness of to poetry, 140, 238n.47; composition of, 48–49, 57; European classical, 77–78, 138, 164, 201, 245n.45; folk, 124, 197; government ministries on, 166–67; Egyptian heritage and, 77, 164, 238n.37, 241n.72; innovations in, 76, 132, 235n.4; military, 27, 164; new genres of, 145, 240n.67; popular, 14–16, 167; religious, 14, 182, 201; speech about, 4–7,

Qadrī, Faṭma, 48, 228n.71
qafla, 117, 149–51, 157
"Qamar lu Layaali" (song title), 124
al-Qaṣabjī, 'Alī, 34
al-Qaṣabjī, Muḥammad, 51–52, 54, 56, 59, 61, 71, 75–76, 78, 92, 102, 109, 117, 129–30, 134, 145, 163–64, 167, 169, 170–71, 177, 198, 218n.47, 223n.9, 230n.97, 231n.103, 232n.19, 236n.15, 240n.68, 244n.40
qaṣīda, 11, 23–24, 26, 28, 45, 47–48, 52–61, 67, 72, 79, 81, 88, 97, 100, 110–13, 115, 117, 121–26, 144–46, 162, 165, 171, 176–82, 192, 197, 199, 228n.74, 230nn. 91, 100, 231n.101, 233n.29, 234nn. 48, 52, 239n.49, 245n.45, 246nn. 60, 64, 248n.84
"Qaṣīdat al-Nīl" (song title), 182
al-Qiṣṣa al-Nabawiyya, 192
Qur'ān: learning the, 35, 57, 97, 103, 144; memorization of, 22, 70, 107; reading of the, 24, 26, 126, 141–44, 190; recitation of the, 4, 8, 10, 11, 14, 23–26, 29, 94, 96, 116, 122, 127, 141–44, 148, 158, 192, 197, 200, 209nn. 9, 13, 210nn. 18, 20, 229n.84, 230n.95, 239n.54, 241n.75; relationship of to music, 142–43

Rābi'a al-'Adawiyya (film), 164–67
Racy, Ali Jihad, 14, 43–45, 92, 132–33, 137–38, 211n.33, 215n.14, 216n.19, 218n.52, 220n.67, 228n.75, 229n.86, 230n.100, 238n.38, 245n.45
radio: accessibility of, 206n.19; broadcasting on the, 5, 85–89, 99, 109, 137–38, 162, 166; contracts with, 184; control of, 120, 185; development of, 1, 19, 50, 67, 117; dubbing from, 226n.43; impact on listeners of, 6; in the 1990s, 200; officials, 236n.19; ownership of, 226n.43; popularity of, 85, 183, 206n.18; production companies, 45; and recordings, 84; sharing of, 101; stars of, 91; transistor, 8, 9, 183; use of, 8, 173
radio stations: financial arrangements with, 86; local, 85, 162; national, 77, 85; new, 84, 247n.73; private, 85; Syrian national, 193; the Umm Kulthūm, 9, 199
al-Rādyū al-Miṣrī (magazine), 246nn. 62, 65
Raḥmī, Maḥmūd, 56, 61
Rāmī, Aḥmad, 56, 59, 71, 73, 76, 88, 92, 102, 110, 113, 122, 128, 131, 134, 149, 160–61, 168–69, 172–73, 218n.47, 219n.56, 223n.6, 226nn. 36, 50, 231n.7, 236n.18, 243n.15, 244n.33
"Raqq il-Ḥabiib" (song title), 109, 151–52, 163
record companies, 3, 13, 42, 67–68, 85, 105, 130, 184, 220n.67; Baidaphon, 65; Cairophon, 85, 105, 163, 226n.43; Gramophone, 27, 55, 66, 84, 210n.31, 218n.51, 219n.53, 225n.29; Misrophon, 170, 184; Odeon, 54–56, 63, 84, 86, 120, 218n.51, 219n.56; Ṣawt al-Qāhira, 184, 247n.76
recordings: broadcast, 163; commercial, 9, 27, 46, 50, 52, 54, 65, 84, 88, 96, 229n.77, 237n.30; contract, 184, 247n.76; editing of, 132; instrumental, 200; live, 138, 240n.71, 247n.71; narrative, 178; process of, 91, 131–32, 236n.17; quality of, 98; and radio, 84; sales of, 67, 73, 99, 163, 195, 218n.51, 221n.86, 246n.58; studio, 117, 131–32, 134; use of, 10; vocal accompaniment on, 231n.101
record player. *See* phonograph
religious song, 10, 14, 22–24, 26, 32, 34, 42, 46, 48, 51–56, 60–62, 103, 126–27, 142–43, 177, 197, 211n.41, 231n.101, 232n.12
repertory: broadcast, 114; creativity in, 72, 114, 125, 145; developing new, 52, 55, 63, 110, 121, 171; folk, 78, 143; innovations in, 63, 71, 125, 174; listeners' knowledge of, 133; mainstays of Umm Kulthūm's, 70, 115, 170; monologues in, 78; neoclassical, 199; political environment of Umm Kulthūm's, 197–98; populist, 109, 199; romantic, 88; of songs heard as excellent, 129; sound of Umm Kulthūm's, 158; Umm Kulthūm's control over, 47; Umm Kulthūm's development of, 2–4, 12, 14, 23, 42, 76, 109, 126, 139, 190, 219n.53, 224n.12; Umm Kul-

songs (*continued*)
181–82, 246n.60; national, 47, 49, 161, 164–67, 170, 173, 177, 184, 232n.11, 243nn. 19, 21, 246n.60; new, 46, 52, 129–31, 136, 182, 184; political meanings of, 199; popular, 28, 136, 164, 173, 239n.51; populist, 110, 121–25; production of, 129, 131; recordings of, 85, 174; and recitation, 141; religious, 94, 246n.60; renditions of, 139, 143, 146, 149, 158, 173, 196, 200; riddle, 107; *ṭaqāṭīq,* 11, 52–54, 56, 78, 92; texts of, 70, 73, 92, 95, 107, 122, 127–28, 131, 140, 147–49, 151, 158, 167–69, 178, 186, 235n.4, 243n.19; torch, 73; through-composed, 71, 75, 113, 223n.3; variations in, 146; writing of, 244nn. 33, 34. *See also* singers; *zajal*
"Ṣoot il-Salaam" (song title), 164
star performer(s), 15–16, 20, 29, 31, 42, 48, 55, 59, 66–67, 84, 87, 91, 109, 133, 170–71, 188, 195, 200, 202, 206n.35, 218n.52
style: of accompaniment, 153, 230n.100; Arab, 148, 172; changes in, 59, 177; of cinematography, 88; compositional, 74–75; determinants of, 135; direction in, 70–78; of dress, 133; folk, 174, 232n.15; improvisatory, 246n.57; innovations in, 71, 75, 123, 172, 196, 223n.4; juxtaposition of, 176; neoclassical, 233n.37; poetic, 53, 235n.6; of rendition, 127–28, 137, 141, 177; romantic, 70, 92; shift in, 61–62; Turkish, 10, 63, 93, 99; Umm Kulthūm's characteristic, 153, 158, 182; virtuosic, 92; Western musical, 172, 198
"Subḥān Man arsalahu Raḥma li-Kull man Yasmaʿ aw yubṣir" (song title), 217n.37
"al-Sūdān" (song title) 113–14, 121
Sufism, 24, 126, 127, 133, 210n.22
al-Ṣughayyara, Najāt, 170
Sukkar, Ismāʿīl, 23, 32, 103, 201
Sulṭān, ʿUmar, 38
al-Sunbāṭī, Riyāḍ, 76, 109, 113–17, 122–23, 129, 135, 161, 163–64, 167, 169–73, 177–82, 186, 192–93, 198, 231n.103, 233nn. 36, 37, 234nn. 51, 52, 236n.12, 243n.15, 244n.38, 246n.60

al-Tābiʿī, Muḥammad, 90
tajwīd, rules of, 141–42, 148
takht. See accompaniment
"Ṭalaʿ 'l-fajr" (song title), 98
"Ṭalamā tajrī" (song title), 247n.66
ṭarab, 11–12, 19, 132–33, 137–40, 198
taṣwīr al-maʿná, 57, 94, 139, 141, 142, 148, 239n.57
Tawḥīda, 46, 220n.68, 225n.27
al-Ṭawīl, Kamāl, 170
Taymūr, Muḥammad, 42, 45, 215n.1
Tharwat, ʿAbd al-Khāliq, 34, 213n.60
theater: audience, 133, 224n.14; closings of, 67; district, 42–43, 51, 82, 103; local movie, 101; matinees at the, 216n.16; musical, 43, 45–47, 50, 87, 89, 103, 171, 228n.71; owners, 68; as source of patronage, 42, 46; production, 3, 64, 81; rental of, 80, 91, 228n.70
"al-Thulāthiyya al-Muqaddisa" (song title), 234n.52
"Tiraaʿi Gheerii" (song title), 231n.101
al-Tūnisī, Bayram, 50, 102–3, 105, 107–8, 110, 123–24, 128, 139, 164, 167–69, 231n.9, 232n.11, 238n.37, 243nn. 15, 22, 244nn. 33, 34
turāth (heritage), 11, 14, 78, 123, 144–45, 150, 196, 199, 200, 244n.40
Turino, Thomas, 9, 16

ʿUbayd, Makram, 83
"Udhkurīnī" (song title), 148, 231n.103
ughniyya, 76, 88, 104, 107, 135, 145–46, 181–82, 223n.9
Unshūdat al-Fu'ād (film), 87
ʿUrābī, Aḥmad, 25
ʿUthmān, Muḥammad, 70, 145

Voll, John, 124

"Wa-Ḥaqqika Anta" (song title), 94
Wahbī, Yūsuf, 81, 227n.58
Wālī Pāshā, Jaʿfar, 117
"Wallaahi Zamaan Ya Silaaḥi" (song title), 164, 170
al-Ward al-Bayḍā' (film), 87
"il-Ward Jamiil" (song title), 109
"Wa-shakat li" (song title), 230n.97
waṣla, 47, 82, 136, 145–46, 196, 216n.15